PRAISE F

M000211731

"Fast-paced! Riveting! Emotional! Suspenseful! Compelling! Complex! This book brings it ALL!"

"It is also not the novel to start reading in the evening or the reader will find themselves losing sleep in your desire to learn what happens next."

"*The Girl They Took* by Leslie Wolfe is so good I can't find the words to describe how good it is. Definitely it is the best Tess Winnett book yet and maybe the best book Leslie Wolfe has written."

"The ending is so astonishing I truly believe no one can predict it."

"Plenty of twists and turns lead the reader to a satisfying conclusion."

"I've read most of this author's books and enjoyed each one, but this one ranks right up at the top, it's just that good." -- PWA Allen

PRAISE FOR LESLIE WOLFE

"The queen of suspense is back with another gripping installment in the Tess Winnett series."

"Leslie Wolfe has written another great mystery. Thank you for a great plot and outstanding characters."

Powerful! "Leslie Wolfe weaves a compelling story of an FBI agent who looks beyond the rule book in her quest to recover a kidnapped child."

THE
GIRL
THEY
TOOK

THE
GIRL
THEY
TOOK

LESLIE WOLFE

II **ITALICS**
ITALICS PUBLISHING

$\varPi$ ITALICS

Italics Publishing Inc.
ISBN: 978-1-945302-53-4
Edited by Joni Wilson.
Cover and interior design by Sam Roman.

ACKNOWLEDGMENT

A special thank you to Mark Freyberg, my New York City authority for all matters legal. Mark's command of the law and passion for deciphering its intricacies translates into zero unanswered questions for this author. He's a true legal oracle and a wonderful friend.

1

GONE

Seven minutes before curtain time, her daughter Paige had the worst case of the hiccups.

The small cast of the school play was gathered around her, waiting, and that only made things worse. Her brave girl seemed overwhelmed by the prospect of having to appear onstage, her initial excitement vanished the moment she'd set eyes on the auditorium brimming with chatty, restless people. She'd hidden her glittery face against Miriam's jeans and refused to leave the comfort of her mother's leg, leaving little else for her to do than talk to her in a low, soothing voice to build up the courage she'd lost.

"I'm so sorry," Miriam had whispered, looking at the teacher, Mrs. Langhorne. The woman smiled, feigning understanding and compassion, when her eyes glinted with impatient irritation as if it were Miriam's fault Paige had the hiccups. Or Paige's even. "I tried everything. I gave her water, the other teacher, Mr.—"

"Mowrey, yes," Mrs. Langhorne replied, shooting her wristwatch another concerned look.

"Yes, him. He tried to talk her out of it. It's not like we're not trying."

Mrs. Langhorne sighed, tapping her heel impatiently against the scratched, wooden floor of the theater backstage.

"This is not exactly a Broadway show, if you know what I mean," Miriam pleaded in a lower voice. "We can be a few minutes late if need be."

The woman rolled her eyes, a gesture she tried to hide under her long lashes and a quick turn of her head to the side. "This is the Universal Stage Theater." She sounded as if she was about to choke on her own indignation. "The school went through a lot of trouble to secure this venue on a Saturday evening, Mrs. Walsh. We might as well behave accordingly and start on time."

Miriam pressed her lips tightly together, gently caressing her daughter's curly, red hair and counting the seconds between hiccups. Seeing Paige so vulnerable tugged at her heart. For a moment, she thought of grabbing her little girl's hand and running out of there without looking back, just to give her daughter another second of safety and comfort. But she knew Paige would overcome her fears; she always did. Then she would shine on that stage, smiling like only she could smile, making sweet memories for the both of them.

That Langhorne should at least pretend to show some understanding.

Miriam wished she could tell that woman everything that was crossing her mind at the time but couldn't. Not if she wanted Paige to continue to attend the classes of the exclusive St. Moritz school. Even at the ridiculous tuition they were charging, the waiting lists were a mile long, and kids had their names on them since birth. That was, of course, if parents could make the commitment to pay fifty grand a year for their offspring's exclusive education.

Two other children, including the little boy who played Hansel, whispered something and giggled, shooting her daughter amused looks. Paige whimpered against her leg, the barely noticeable sound interrupted by a loud "hic."

"Let me try something, if I may?" a man asked in a low whisper, approaching from a dressing room. He was dressed for the stage and wore a mask and woodworker's coveralls with fake stains applied with stage makeup. Through the holes of the mask, his eyes seemed like anthracite.

Miriam looked at her watch and cringed. Two minutes until curtain. "Sure."

The man took Paige's hand gently and waited until the little girl look at him. "Wanna get rid of these hiccups so we can do the play and go home and watch TV?" He still whispered, no one else but the three of them privy to their conversation.

Paige nodded. "Hic."

The man held his hands in the air and looked at Miriam briefly as if asking permission again. "Hiccups are nothing but spasms of the diaphragm. Sometimes," he touched Paige's stomach right under her sternum with one expertly placed finger, "all you have to do is push the right button." He held his finger pressed against Paige's diaphragm for a few seconds, then took a step back. "Done." He grabbed both Paige's hands into his. "I'm willing to bet you one dollar you won't be hiccupping again today." There was laughter in his whispered voice.

Paige seemed disappointed. Maybe it was the thought of the dollar she wasn't going to earn, or perhaps she had stage fright like Miriam suspected and was looking for an excuse not to perform.

Crouching by her side, Miriam arranged her long, auburn curls and straightened her costume. She'd inherited Miriam's hair and complexion. She quickly wiped a fleck of glitter off her nose and put a swift kiss on her freckled cheek.

"Mom," Paige protested, shooting the other kids an embarrassed look.

So soon. She was only eight.

Mrs. Langhorne clapped her hands in typical kindergarten style, steering the kids toward their places for the curtain to raise.

Rushing to her seat and trying to step on the balls of her feet to keep the clicking of her high heels to a minimum, Miriam barely got there in time. She had an aisle seat, and the one next to her was still empty. Max, her husband, wasn't there yet. She checked her phone and saw a text message apologizing for a work-related delay that couldn't be avoided.

Across the aisle, another empty seat caught her attention. Paige's father, Darrel, hadn't arrived either. Miriam swallowed a bitter sigh. Tonight, Paige would learn how to act in front of a sizeable audience and how to deal with disappointment.

The theater was large, equipped with comfortable plush seats spaced to leave plenty of legroom. Miriam sunk into her seat, happy to be off her feet after what had seemed an endless day. She'd worked a few hours that morning, dealing with a staffing shortage at the pharmacy, then had rushed home to fix lunch and get Paige ready for the performance. They'd rehearsed lines together the entire week, to the point where Miriam had dreamed she was Gretel herself one night. She was beyond ready to be done with the school play, but it had been a wonderful opportunity for her to spend more time with her daughter. Thankfully, all she had to do after lunch and a quick nap for Paige was her hair, her nails with plenty of glitter, and another fitting of her costume, with last-minute sewing of hidden clasps required to keep the darn thing in place.

But Paige looked beautiful as Gretel, her long hair brought forward on her shoulders, her freckles picture-perfect, her starched white apron shining over her burgundy gathered skirt with ruffles, her smile beaming, full of confidence. Of course, that was at home, in the sanctity of her own bedroom. As soon as they'd reached the majestic theater, everything changed. She started trembling at first, then she needed the restroom three times in twenty-five minutes. Then the hiccups came.

But it was all sorted out now, and Miriam could rest for a few minutes. Thankfully, Paige's appearance on the stage was flawless, her first lines perfectly articulated, her voice strong, fearless. Whatever stage fright monsters had plagued her were gone as if they'd never existed.

Her little girl was a natural.

Mouthing the lines as Paige acted them, Miriam held back tears. Something tugged at her heart seeing her little girl there, vulnerable and brave in front of all those people, elbows locked with the boy who played Hansel, playfully jumping and walking in circles on her thin legs as if the whole world was hers. She was growing up so fast... too fast. Soon she'd be gone, a young woman with a life of her own, a house of her own, children of her own.

Among enthusiastic cheering from the gathering of parents, a gentle tap on her shoulder got her attention. "Excuse me, ma'am?"

She turned. A man leaned toward her to keep his voice down and still be heard while speaking with her. "Yes?"

"Do you have a red Subaru, with the tag number, um," he read from a note in his hand, "GHR-G-twelve?"

She frowned. She'd never been able to remember her tag, but she'd driven her burgundy Subaru Forester tonight. "Yes, what's wrong?"

The man straightened his back, but not completely, still hunched forward, his hands clasped together. "I'm so sorry, ma'am, but I'm afraid I caused it some damage when I pulled out of the lot." He threw a look over his shoulder. "The usher told me where to find you."

She sighed, screwing her eyes shut for a brief moment. One minute of peace, and it had to be shattered by this klutz who couldn't drive straight for the life of him. Son of a bitch. At least he'd had the sense to own up to his crap, instead of disappearing and leaving her with a dent or whatever to fix on her own. That much deserved some respect.

She threw Paige a regretful look, wishing she didn't have to leave the play to deal with the car nonsense. At least Paige wasn't paying attention to her, engulfed in her act, spreading confetti as breadcrumbs from her cute little brown satchel.

Miriam stood and followed the man who kept walking with his shoulders hunched forward and his head lowered as if begging forgiveness with every fiber of his body. It was rare to see someone acting like that these days when people didn't have decent morals anymore.

She turned toward the theater exit, but the man gently touched her elbow. "Follow me; it's shorter this way," he said, pointing toward a half-lit corridor that led to the now-closed coffee shop. Frowning, she tried to remember where she'd parked. By the time they arrived, the front parking lot was full, and she'd parked on the side, but which side? Torn between wanting to get back to her seat and some unnerving gut feeling, she hesitated but eventually gave in. The man, wearing a dark jacket zipped up to his chin, seemed kind, humble even, deeply embarrassed to find himself in that situation. He wore a ball cap that shaded his eyes in the dim light, but Miriam could tell he was smiling apologetically, showing two rows of teeth slightly stained by tobacco use. His beard was trim and dark, not a strand of gray in it. He must've been young, maybe even younger than her.

As they approached the door, her footsteps resounding loudly on the marble corridor, he fell behind a little as if getting ready to hold the door for her and let her exit first. "After you, ma'am," he'd said in a strangely excited voice.

That was the last thing she remembered before everything went dark. The half-baked question about that nuance in his voice. Why the excitement? What was he—

Then the blow to her head that had sent shards of light in her skull before darkness took hold of her mind.

When she came to, she was lying on the floor in what must've been the theater's janitorial closet, the smell of Pine-Sol and chlorine bleach unmistakable. Pitch dark except for a faint sliver of light coming in under the door, it was enough for Miriam to get grounded. Ignoring the thumping in her skull, she rose to her feet and tried the door handle, silently praying.

It opened without any resistance.

A thought zapped like lightning through her mind, leaving her breathless, her heart beating hard and fast against her rib cage.

Paige.

She ran all the way back through the corridor, noticing things were slightly different. Most lights were off now. There was an eerie silence, where before there used to be music coming from the stage, the high-pitched voices of the children, and the rhythmic clapping of the audience. Now the only rhythm she could hear was the frenetic beating of her own heart and the clacking of her high-heeled boots against the marble as she was rushing to find her little girl.

When she finally reached the auditorium entrance, she gasped. The doors were wide open, and the auditorium was shrouded in darkness.

Where her daughter had played Gretel in front of a cheering audience, only two faint stage lights remained. The theater was deserted and eerily silent; the only sound she could hear was her own heart, pounding in a frenzy against her chest.

"Paige," she called loudly, and the echo of her voice reverberated in the wide, empty space.

For a moment, she considered searching the backstage area where she'd last been with Paige before the play had started, but it made no sense. Those rooms were a mere curtain away, and not a sound came from there.

She rushed toward the main entrance and pushed the massive glass door. It opened after a brief resistance, and an alarm sounded. She stepped outside and stopped sharply at the top of the stairs, stunned, her blood turned to icicles. Darkness had fallen, thick and filled with ocean mist, lampposts like ghosts sprinkling yellow haloes against the sky.

The place where she'd parked her car was deserted, as was the entire parking lot. She was the only one there.

Paige was gone. They'd taken her little girl.

2

LATE

The tall and rather brawny district attorney for Broward County paced the floor while on the phone, every thirty seconds or so glaring at the digital clock affixed on the wall across from the window. Judge Pelaratti could talk forever; the old man loved to hear himself speak in that sanctimonious style most sitting judges develop with age and experience after spending way too much time as supreme gods of their courtrooms.

But Darrel Joyce was late for his daughter's play, and nothing his honor had to say was quite that urgent anyway. It was already after four, and he had to drive into downtown Miami, expecting the typical rush-hour gridlock to slow him to a crawl.

"Judge, if I may—" he started, but his honor overruled him as if he were in court. He swallowed a curse and shot the clock another look.

Two quick knocks on the door, and his assistant put her head in. She was smart, beautiful, and uncannily effective, a French Polynesian-born attorney by the name of Solange Jandreau or Sol for short. He'd learned to rely on her increasingly more, and she didn't seem to mind adding to her official duties the unofficial ones that kept Darrel Joyce afloat amid a flurry of obligations that never seemed to end. She'd pick up case documents from police precincts but also drop his car in for an oil change. She'd pick up his laundry, book air travel, keep track of his social agenda, while at the same time handle elegantly anything he threw at her from a professional perspective. If she weren't so perfect, he might've invited her out for drinks one night, but he didn't dare ruin their working relationship, although his wife had accused him many times of sleeping with her.

His ex-wife, who was going to crucify him if he was even one bloody minute late.

"Yes, I understand, but I was wondering if we couldn't continue this conversation on Monday—"

Now Pelaratti was downright shouting, claiming that his attempt to postpone their conversation was fueled by blatant disrespect for the issue he was trying to push. The judge had searing political ambitions as of late; he was lobbying for an initiative that was going to put his name out there, and he needed the DA on his side. The initiative, which had merit, had to do with the warrants needed to access the cell phones of suspected drug traffickers, but it could've definitely waited until Monday. But Pelaratti was a widower and hermit; weekends had little relevance for him, most probably spent in the absence of people he could pontificate to.

Shaking his head slowly and tugging at the knot of his tie to loosen it up, he looked at Sol with an unspoken question in his eyes.

Still standing in the doorway, she pointed at her wristwatch and mouthed, "You're late."

He pressed his lips in a thin line and gestured with the phone in his hand.

"Earbuds?" Sol mouthed, pointing with her fingers at her ears.

He nodded and lifted an enthusiastic thumb up in the air. She vanished, leaving the door open.

Hustling, he gathered the documents he wanted to work on over the weekend and his phone charger, crammed everything into his briefcase, then slammed it shut.

Still listening to the case his honor was making in favor of privacy rights of phone users regardless of race and legal status, he rushed out of the office and almost bumped into Sol, who was disentangling the white wire of a pair of earbuds. Impatient, yet finding time to smile and nod her way with gratitude, he yanked the earbuds from her hands and stormed out.

While connecting the earbuds, he waited for the elevator for a few seconds, then he realized the call would drop while he descended. All calls dropped in the elevator. His honor would not be sympathetic and would rush to assume he'd hung up on him on purpose. Darrel would never hear the end of it. Frustrated, he made his way toward the stairwell and started down the six flights of stairs to the parking lot, avoiding touching the dirty handrail as much as possible.

"I agree," Darrel said for the tenth time at least, rushing down the final flight of stairs, "The issue is much too critical to leave unaddressed. You have my full support." He grabbed the handle of the parking garage door, scrunching his nose in disgust. The place stunk of stale urine, and the door handle seemed greasy to the touch. "I'm sorry, you're breaking up," he added as he was entering the parking garage.

A few yards away from his car, he stopped, barely noticing what Pelaratti was saying, "So you couldn't have the decency to give me the time for this conversation in your office, like a professional of your stature is expected to? Fine, Mr. District Attorney, go ahead and run your damn errands." Three beeps signaled the call had been ended by the other party, but Darrel wasn't paying attention.

A large tow truck was taking up the width of the entire alley and completely blocking his car. The driver, wearing a yellow safety vest adorned with reflective strips, moved around the green Honda minivan he wanted to tow, scratching his head with meaty, grimy fingers.

"What's going on here?" Darrel asked, glaring at the man. "I need to leave. This is an emergency." His voice, famous in the entire district for intimidating countless witnesses on the stand, had no visible effect on the tow truck driver.

Just as slowly, he turned to the DA and replied, "I don't know if you'll be going anywhere soon. The chain broke. Maybe you should call a cab."

The Honda's front wheels were secured on the tow truck's fork, but one of the rusted chains was broken, and the Honda hung crookedly.

"What are you planning to do?" he asked, drilling into the man's eyes with his glare. "Spend the night here?"

"No, man, no need to get nasty," he replied, drawling his speech. It seemed everything about the man was happening in slow motion. "I'll call the head office. They'll send someone."

"Then do it already." He checked the time; it was almost five. He typed a quick text message to Miriam, blaming it on work; it was much faster than trying to explain what was going on. "How long until they come and—and fix this?" He gestured with his swirling hand in the air, impatient.

The man withdrew behind the Honda. "Um, two, maybe three hours."

He raised his hand in the air then let it fall in a gesture of frustrated powerlessness. Then he took out his phone and speed-dialed Sol's mobile number.

"Hey, can you get security down here in the parking lot? There's an issue."

It took almost an hour until the four security guards were able to remove the minivan from the tow truck's broken fork and set it back on the pavement, then drag it back into its parking spot to make room for the tow truck to pull out.

Darrel's white Lexus was right behind it. As soon as there was room, he floored it toward the interstate. It was almost six.

By the time he reached the theater, the sun was setting, and the parking lot was almost entirely deserted. A small group of parents he didn't recognize were still huddled next to a couple of vehicles. Three costumed kids were screaming and running around in circles on the neatly trimmed lawn.

Braking near them after having driven fast enough through the parking lot to earn himself some disapproving glances from the two overdressed mothers, he lowered the window and asked, "Is the play—"

Both mothers pursed their lips in almost identical gestures. "It's over; everyone's gone. You can go home." As he pulled off, he thought he heard a derisive comment naming him father of the year.

That, he deserved.

He called Miriam a few times, but her phone went straight to voicemail. Before hitting the traffic again on his way home, he stopped for a moment and breathed, running his fingers through his gray, crew-cut hair. It was one of those days when the entire universe seemed to rile up against him. No number of fists slammed against the steering wheel would fix that, but some ice cream for Paige and a bottle of wine for his ex and her new husband would probably smooth things over.

Tomorrow.

Not today, when emotions were raw and phones were turned off.

Resigned, he took Flagler to I-95 and spent the better part of an hour trying to leave the downtown Miami area. When Miriam called, it was dark, and he was almost at his house.

3

CALL

It was almost eight on a Friday night, and the Media Luna Bar and Grill was starting to fill up with rowdy customers. They filled the room with roars of laughter and hollering, some of their jokes making Tess laugh; those that didn't make her cringe or grind her teeth.

Spraying some more Windex on a fogged-up window, she tore off a new piece of paper towel and scrubbed it clean until all smears were gone and she could see her reflection clearly in the glass. Dark circles under her eyes, her shoulder-length hair tied unceremoniously in a ponytail, and just a touch of lipstick to bring color to an otherwise pale face, she barely recognized herself, but that was because the reflection in the window was laughing at a wino's dirty joke. She hadn't laughed in a while, her work casting a lasting shadow over everything in her life.

The front door opened, and a group of young people stumbled in, hollering louder than the patrons who'd been imbibing for a while, although they'd just pulled into the parking lot driving American muscle cars in bright colors and racing stripes. Glad to be finished with the self-imposed chore, she wrapped up her cleaning and threw everything under the counter. She would sort it out later.

Watching the newcomers with a critical eye, she washed her hands, then took off her cleaning apron and threw that under the counter too. Smiling, she asked, "What can I get you?"

"Grey Goose," a young man in ripped jeans and a plaid shirt ordered.

The girl wrapped around his neck like a vine licked her finger lasciviously and said, "Moscow Mule for me." Her eyes lingered on Tess's face, her lips, as if she were about to abandon her date and climb over the counter to make a pass at the bartender instead.

A bulky man elbowed his way closer to the counter. "Bud Light, cold as ice. Dyin' of thirst here."

She moved quickly and automatically, not thinking much about what she was doing, pouring drinks, mixing drinks, getting paid, giving change. Every few minutes, she looked at Cat, who sat on his chair a few feet toward the back, too tired to stand. His tall frame had dropped a few pounds lately, and she hadn't noticed that until his bones had started poking through the fabric of his worn Hawaiian shirts. His hair had thinned and turned almost entirely white, although it remained wavy and long like a rock star's, refusing to let go of the man's scalp. Knowing Cat like she did, he would've probably died of shame if he'd gone bald and, in his words, "Ended up looking like an accountant."

Her heart swelled seeing him smile at her. She wiped her hands on a paper towel and walked over, grabbing a bottle of Guinness on the way.

"Here you go," she said, then leaned against the counter, studying him closely.

He took a couple of thirsty gulps, then wiped the foam sticking to his upper lip with the back of his hand. "You didn't have to do the windows." He groaned. "You don't have to do any of it."

"I know I don't," she replied, smiling widely. She cared deeply for the man who had turned seventy-five recently. Only lately he had started showing his age, and that filled her heart with fear. Over the years, she'd grown closer to him than she'd been with her own father. Cat had nursed her back to health after she'd been injured, taken her in, put his entire life on hold, and risked his freedom to give her a new life and the possibility to live it her way. She willed away the saddening memories. "I just want to." At least this much she could do for him; keep his business afloat, help him on the busiest nights a little bit, although her bartending skills needed serious improvement.

He waved her off with a gesture of his bony hand. "You should be out there, dating or something, living your life. It's Friday night. Don't waste it on an old coot like me."

She laughed and squeezed his arm. "How many times do I have to tell you I'm happy to be here?" Her eyes brimmed with tears. Turning her head for a moment, she feigned interest in the hollering some of the patrons were escalating, as two of them had engaged in a drinking competition. They better not puke on the floor. "I get to tell everyone who cares enough to ask that I spent my entire weekend in a bar." She winked, and they laughed together, their voices harmoniously resonating.

"B—bartender?" a man called, stammering and rolling the Rs while slamming an empty bottle of beer against the counter. He wore denim coveralls and a loaded yellow toolbelt he should've left in his truck.

"I'll go," Cat said, grabbing the arms of his chair for support as he got up on shaky legs.

"No worries, I'll deal with him," Tess replied. "And after that, how would you like a burger? I'm starving."

"I'll fire up the grill," he offered, and she didn't say no.

"What can I get you?" she asked, already determined to cut him off.

"I want ano'er one of these," he said, seemingly barely able to stand and gripping the edge of the counter with both hands. He eventually landed his butt on a stool without falling.

"All you can get from me now is water or Coke. For anything else, please come back tomorrow."

He slid off his stool and propped his hands on the counter, leaning forward angrily. "So, you're gonna be like that, huh?"

"Yeah, I'm gonna be like that," she replied coldly, secretly hoping he'd call a cab. She'd made a promise to herself and part of it openly to Cat. She wasn't going to ruin his business by being the fed behind the counter, as some of the Palm Beach detectives jokingly called her. That would scatter Cat's patrons away faster than an October hurricane. But she wasn't going to sit idle and let drunks like that climb behind the wheel either.

"Okay, be a bitch," he hollered, then started faltering around the counter to serve himself. "I'll just serve myself." Cat dropped the steel turner on the griddle with a loud clack and approached.

Tess held her hand up with a smile. She had this.

Before she could grab the man's upper arm and escort him out, one of his buddies approached him and whispered something in his ear, shooting Tess fearful looks.

"I don't care about any of that," the man replied boastfully. "If Johnnie wants a drink, Johnnie gets a drink."

"Don't be an idiot, man," the other guy said. "You don't know who she is."

Tess pulled a small bottle of soda from the fridge and unscrewed the cap. She handed it to him. "On the house."

He took it scowling, then poured it on the floor defiantly, looking her straight in the eye.

Her phone rang, the ringtone a custom one she recognized. She threw Cat an apologetic glance, then took the call in a low voice. "Special Agent Winnett."

The drunk gawked at her, then clumped out of there double-time, careening dangerously toward his left. She rushed to the back room, where they kept the inventory. It smelled of stale booze and mildew.

"Winnett, this is Pearson," she heard her boss say after she closed the door, somewhat muting the barroom noise. "You have a case, and it's urgent."

She'd wanted to sit down for a moment, but she remained standing. "Should I come in?"

"No, you should go straight to the crime scene. It's the Universal Stage Theater downtown."

"Oh?" Murders rarely happened in venues with hundreds of witnesses. But she didn't ask; she knew her boss well enough to anticipate he'd give her all the details.

"It's a child abduction case," he said, the hesitation in his voice clear, unmistakable.

"Then why us? Why not CARD?" she asked, referencing the Child Abduction Rapid Deployment team. "They're better equipped to deal with all sorts of kidnapping cases."

A beat. "CARD would've been my first choice too," Pearson said. "You were requested."

"Me?" Her voice climbed in pitch. "Who requested me?"

She thought she heard Pearson sigh. "The parents. More specifically, the father of the victim. He, um, knows you. It's Darrel Joyce, Winnett."

"The district attorney? That Darrel Joyce?" That better not be happening. "You have to be kidding me, sir. He would've never requested me."

"And yet he did," Pearson replied coldly, probably not amused by her attitude. "By name. Against my advice."

She breathed, forcing herself to think. "Tell me about the victim."

"Paige Joyce, the eight-year-old daughter of Darrel and Miriam Joyce. The parents are divorced, the mother since remarried."

"How was she taken?" Tess asked, remembering the venue. "At gunpoint?" She started changing her attire, shifting the phone from one hand to the other as she took off her bar clothes and put on a clean shirt and some slacks. She always kept a change of clothes on a hanger behind the door. Bartending was a dirty business.

"The manner of abduction speaks volumes about these unsubs, Winnett. They managed to grab the kid from a theater filled with over a hundred parents and not be seen. It happened less than two hours ago."

She paused, letting the distant ruckus of the barroom fill the air for a moment. She wondered if anyone had actually interviewed those witnesses the right way. Someone always noticed something, only most times they didn't know they did. "Still, why me? This is not what I normally do, you know that. Give me a serial killer any day, but a missing kid?" She swallowed hard, her throat suddenly dry. "Not to mention whose kid this is."

"Yes, the child happens to be the DA's daughter, but that only looks like a lead to me, nothing else." Pearson's words had turned cutting, cold, hurried. He was visibly losing his patience with her objections. The almighty Special Agent in Charge Pearson was used to hearing little else than "Yes, sir," when he was handing out case assignments, and he was right to be pissed. After all, this was a crime, and she was an FBI agent with a sworn duty to fight crime. "Can't blame the man for wanting the best agent in this regional office to investigate the abduction of his own child." She could hear the frustrated reluctance in Pearson's voice as he said the words, so clear it almost made her laugh.

"But that's just it, sir," she pushed back, although she could imagine Pearson's forehead creasing at the sound of yet another objection. "He doesn't think so highly of me... quite the opposite."

"What do you mean?"

"Last time we spoke, I was on the stand for cross in a murder case, and he wiped the courtroom floor with me." A moment of heavy silence on the line, as Tess already regretted the words she'd shared with her boss. Maybe it was stupid to let him know how badly she and the DA were getting along, after he'd given her multiple warnings about the professional relationships she needed to nurture, both in the office and interagency. She'd conveniently omitted to say that after that cross-examination, the DA had caught up with her in the hallway and ripped her some more, calling her incompetent because he believed she'd jeopardized his case. Darrel Joyce was nothing but a bully of the worst kind, the kind that wields considerable power and knows it.

"Nevertheless, Winnett, he asked for you, and this is it. End of story. We owe him the courtesy." A dog barked somewhere in the background, and a child started crying. Pearson was probably at home.

"What were his exact words?" Tess grabbed her keys and wallet, getting ready to leave.

Pearson muttered an oath under his breath. "He said, word for word, 'Get me Winnett and no one else.'"

4

DARK

"What the hell were you thinking?" Mark paced the small room angrily, his fists plunged inside the pockets of his sweatshirt as if to keep them from smashing Gavin's stupid face. "Who told you it was okay to drug her?" He stopped pacing, his feet apart and his knees slightly bent to counteract the slight swaying of the floor. Water sloshed against the dock in the wake of a large boat. It had passed by ignoring the speed limit, a drunk asshole behind the wheel most likely. After all, it was a Friday night in Miami.

His head almost reached the light fixture hanging from the ceiling, probably the cheapest Walmart could offer. A diagonal hiatus in his right eyebrow always itched, a scar from a squarely landed punch he'd received for no reason whatsoever, a memory from his time behind bars. His goatee was in need of trimming, but he had bigger worries that day, like his partner's recklessness.

Gavin didn't seem fazed by Mark's shouting. Chewing casually on yesterday's leftover popcorn, he slouched on the dirty sofa littered with socks and T-shirts and candy wrappers and all sorts of things that didn't belong. "What the heck was I supposed to do, huh? Risk her screaming her lungs out as I hauled her ass from the car?" He spat an unpopped kernel with an arch. It hit the TV screen, then fell on the dirty carpet. "What would you have done, hotshot?"

"I wouldn't've drugged her, that's what. She's an eight-year-old, for cryin' out loud. You're telling me you can't subdue an eight-year-old kid without drugs?" Mark stopped abruptly in front of Gavin, propping his hands on his hips and leaning forward. He was seconds from wrapping his hands around the idiot's neck and snuffing his worthless life out of him. "We don't do anything unless specifically instructed, you hear me?"

"Yeah, yeah," Gavin waved him off and leaned sideways to see the TV screen. He clicked the remote a couple of times to switch channels until he found a rerun of yesterday's football game.

"Did you feed her?" Mark asked, fuming. He inserted his body into Gavin's line of sight.

"Not yet," the man replied, not making the tiniest effort to hide his annoyance. "She's still asleep."

"It's almost midnight!" His voice faltered, slipping toward a higher pitch as if he were a teenage boy. Frustration did that to him sometime and it only made things worse.

Gavin promptly laughed. "What, you've gone soprano on me, now?" He threw a few more kernels in his mouth and chewed them loudly. "Come on, get real. She's not gonna die of starvation if she skips dinner one time." There was a weird glint in his eyes when he spoke of the girl as if causing her harm excited him somehow.

Curling his lip in disgust, Mark grabbed a couple of candy bars from a Walmart bag he'd left on the table and went into the girl's room.

It was windowless and almost completely dark, only the hallway light coming in through the open door, and a small sensor night-light plugged into the wall socket did its part. But the darkness wasn't going to bother her; Gavin had blindfolded her as instructed, using a long, beige scarf he'd wrapped around her head twice and tied up with a hefty knot.

The girl was sound asleep, lying on her side on the small, stained mattress. Her wrists and ankles were bound with zip ties. The room, devoid of any other furniture, was the perfect place to keep her; they couldn't risk her being seen through a window by passersby. Mark reached down and touched the girl's shoulder, then shook her gently. She didn't wake up.

Closing the door behind him, candy bars still in hand, he didn't wait to reach the living room before shouting, "How much did you give her? She's out cold!"

"I gave her one dose, not more," Gavin replied, chewing with his mouth open, sending crumbs flying through the air as he spoke.

The man couldn't've been more disgusting if he tried. His eyes were narrow and close together, his pupils drawn to each other or perhaps both drawn to the root of his nose. His mouth had a permanent curl, as if contempt never left him, imprinting a snarl on his facial expression his trim beard didn't cover. One eyebrow was angled upward as if surprised, and his chin bore the mark of a fist that had shattered it during his first prison stint. And yet, people didn't seem to notice all that and took an instant liking to him.

Since Gavin got out the last time, he got smart, committed to make a life for himself that didn't include another stay behind bars, knowing he'd probably be looking at life if he got busted again. He'd taken a fake identity, then he changed cities, moving south, and slithered his way into a decent job. People must be idiots, Mark thought, if they bought this guy's résumé and sob story about a wife who'd died of cancer and him having to sell everything he had to pay for her medical bills. They even gave him housing assistance... unbelievable. How could they not see the way the slimeball looked at kids?

It wasn't as if Mark had much of a choice; given his current task, he needed someone who'd be up for the job and ask few questions, and no man had ever been less curious than Gavin when it came to making a quick buck. Apparently, curiosity required some degree of intelligence. He didn't have any, but could smell cash a mile away. He'd given an eight-year-old girl the entire adult dose of street-bought ketamine. They were lucky she was still alive. He had to keep Gavin away from the girl at all times.

But that wasn't even the hardest thing he had to do. Keeping himself from killing the asshole was going to take a lot of willpower.

"Did you call him?" Gavin asked, seriously stepping over the line.

Mark scowled. "Sure, I did."

"How did he take it?"

"As expected. By the time Big Man calls with instructions, he'll be ready, softened up like a pussycat and eager to please." Imagining his good old friend, the Broward County district attorney, shitting bricks at the thought of his sweet little girl in the hands of faceless thugs brought a wide grin on his face. He deserved everything he was going to get from the Big Man, and then some.

"Then go to bed. I'll stay up and watch the kid." His eyes glinted weirdly again.

"The hell you are," Mark hissed, grabbing a fistful of his shirt collar and twisting it until it choked him. He slammed Gavin against the couch, then released his grip. "Don't you ever forget who calls the shots here. If I don't tell you to, you don't eat, you don't take a shit, and you don't breathe. You feel me?"

A known coward in two state penitentiaries and one federal prison, the man nodded quickly, dropping the popcorn he'd grabbed with slimy fingers and wiping his hands against his stained jeans.

"Tomorrow, we make the fake ransom call, as discussed," said Mark, stepping back from Gavin, afraid he'd punch him after all if he so much as breathed the wrong way, and that would only make things worse. He looked outside, scrutinizing the darkness sprinkled with distant city lights toward the south, where Miami Beach lit the sky with a million fuzzy diamonds. It was a moonless night, the cloud cover thick and low, mist rolling in from the ocean in a thin layer that would be thick fog by sunrise.

"But why fake the ransom call, bro?" Gavin shifted sideways to look at him, folding his left leg underneath his body and resting his elbow on the sofa back pillow. "Why not take the money?" His eyes sparked when he said take. "Why not double-dip? Money never hurt anyone."

A million different ways things could go wrong if Mark didn't toe the line, many of them ending with him dying slowly and painfully in the hands of a man known for his creative vengefulness, bloody Aquila himself, known on the streets of Miami only as the Big Man. Few knew his real name and even fewer dared to speak it, as if only that was fault enough to draw the wrath of the man who owned all drug trafficking south of the Carolinas and east of Texas. Despite his Spanish moniker, it was rumored he was American, born and raised, not imported from one of the cartels that blossomed south of the border. Mark never met him face to face; he'd only spoken with him on the phone a couple of times.

On the flip side, a million dollars... or more. The things he could do, the places he could visit swirled in his mind, dizzying him, getting him intoxicated on dreams of freedom and fumes of endless debauchery. He would be set for life.

"The man said we do this his way, Gav. Remember, we're hired help on this one, and he's not the man you live to disobey." As he said the words, his voice trailed off, waning as the thought of what a million dollars could buy filled his mind and enslaved his senses like a drug.

5

SCENE

Four hours missing

By the time Tess reached the theater, the place was swarming with cops. Red and blue lights flashed eerily in the misty air, casting long shadows on the impressive building. Most of the police cars bore the insignia of Miami-Dade police, but there was one from Palm Beach County that drew her attention. A crime scene van was pulled close to the stairs, with its back doors wide open.

She approached a young officer who busied himself with cordoning off the area. "Who was first on scene?" She held her wallet open for a moment in front of the man's eyes. There was a flicker of surprise when he recognized the FBI credential. She wondered why; feds were a routine presence in kidnapping cases.

He looked around, squinting against the flashers from a nearby vehicle. "That would be Officer Carter." He pointed with his flashlight toward the theater entrance. "He's the tall guy over there with a mustache."

She nodded and rushed toward the entrance, where Officer Carter was talking with a dark-haired woman who was clasping and unclasping her hands nervously. She was wearing evening attire, probably what she'd worn for the play or maybe for the evening she had planned.

"Special Agent Winnett, FBI," she introduced herself after checking the man's name tag. The woman turned a lighter shade of pale. "You were first on the scene?" He was young and one of the very few men who looked decent wearing a mustache, neatly trimmed and symmetrical.

"Y—yes. The theater door triggered an alarm. We came to check it out and found Mrs. Joyce on the steps, looking for her daughter." He tapped her elbow to draw her a little farther from the woman and whispered in her ear, "Not sure if you already know, but the missing kid is the DA's daughter." A simple gesture of professional camaraderie that she rarely encountered.

"Thanks, yes, we already knew that." She approached the witness. "And you are?"

"Jolene Langhorne." Her voice croaked, and she quickly cleared her throat. "I organized the play and secured the venue."

"I took her statement," Officer Carter added. "She didn't see anything." Tess doubted Officer Carter had asked all the right questions before concluding that.

Through the theater lobby's imposing windows, she saw the DA hugging a red-haired woman who sobbed heavily and occasionally hit the man's chest with her clenched fists. "Please make sure you have her contact information and email everything to me." She handed Carter one of her business cards.

"Ten-four, Agent Winnett. Should I let her go home? It's getting late."

Tess hated when men talked about the women in their presence as if they weren't there. She turned to the woman. "Could you please wait a little longer? I might have urgent questions for you in a few minutes. You're welcome to come inside if it's too cold out here."

"Um, yes, sure," she replied. She seemed terrified, not guilty. Just scared of the enormity of what had happened, of having to deal with the police most likely. She turned to Carter. "Who else is here?"

"The theater manager. He was on our emergency contact list for the location. Over there, with his arms folded at his chest," he checked his notepad quickly, "Francis Brassfield." He wore a suit and a white shirt, undone at the top buttons, and his face reflected apprehension. From outside, the people standing in the lobby were like actors on a stage, well-lit while she stood engulfed in darkness, but she wasn't a spectator. Her lines hadn't been written yet, and her role was just starting.

"He's the one who helped us get this venue," Jolene Langhorne said. "On a Friday night, can you believe it?"

That piqued her interest. "How come? He must've forfeited a lot of revenue for a school play. It doesn't seem likely."

"His son is our student." Langhorne blushed and looked away for a moment. "He just made it happen."

"I see." Probably there was nothing worth pursuing there.

After climbing the front steps quickly, she entered the lobby and headed straight for the DA. Several other deputies were swarming, collecting evidence, and assisting the crime scene technicians who traveled back and forth down a long corridor that led to a closed coffee shop.

Darrel Joyce recognized her. He gently pushed the redhead away from his chest and said, "Miriam, this is Special Agent Winnett with the FBI." He pressed his lips tightly for a brief moment. "My ex-wife, Miriam Walsh." Then he gestured toward a handsome man who stood a few feet away. He had a tall forehead and tousled black hair, as if he'd just got out of bed, but wore an expensive charcoal suit and a solid gray tie. He seemed dark, deeply bothered by something. "And her husband, Maxwell Walsh." The man nodded but stayed away, his hands shoved into his pants pockets, his jacket open. Seeing his wife in her ex's arms might've been infuriating for him. Or perhaps something else was on his mind.

Miriam's swollen eyes were a stunning green, darting everywhere as if she desperately sought help or maybe was still hoping to see her daughter appear out of nowhere. She was tall and dressed in a black, fashionable top with silver zippers on the sleeves and black slacks and wore high-heeled boots. Tess was tall, but Miriam Walsh towered over her by at least four inches. Her hair, a shiny dark auburn that looked like silk and almost waist long, was brought forward over her right shoulder in a simple do that enhanced her silhouette. Yet she cared nothing about her appearance; her makeup was smudged, and a fine trail of blood had dried on her temple, smeared.

Her frantic gaze locked with Tess's for a brief moment. "You're going to find my daughter?"

"You have my word I'll do everything—"

"You and what army?" she replied bitterly, then turned to the DA. "That's all you could do, you, the powerful and respected district attorney for Broward County? Just one fed?"

Joyce looked at Tess, pleading silently.

"We could bring an entire team," Tess replied calmly. "If you're adamant about it, we will. But this is the best approach we can take, and that's what I'd do if my child were missing." She looked at Miriam, then at the DA. "Ultimately, it's your call. You can ask the FBI to deploy the CARD team, and they'll be here in minutes."

"Yes, let's do that," Miriam said, fresh tears brimming in her eyes, her voice breaking up, shattered by gasps of air that didn't seem to fill her lungs. "I want everyone looking for her. Oh, my baby," she sobbed, dry heaving, holding her stomach as if she was about to throw up, bent in half, unable to stand.

Joyce helped her to a chair her new husband brought quickly. She sat, sobbing hard, with her mouth open. "How could I have been so stupid?" she cried, hiding her face in her hands.

Tess crouched in front of her chair to be at the same eye level. "Tell me what happened."

She lowered her hands and clutched them together. Her eyes darted again, first at Joyce, then at the main entrance, then at the crime scene technicians who were coming and going on that corridor. "I was watching Paige's play when this man came and said he bumped my car or something. I didn't want to go, but—" she whimpered, agonizing, "I was stupid, and I should've seen it coming."

"Why?" Tess asked. "Why do you blame yourself?"

She heaved again, her breath shaky, her voice brittle. "He said the usher told him where to find me." She looked at Joyce with a loaded look, guilt and shame and something else. "The usher had no idea who I was... how could she know me? Oh, God... I should've known."

DA Joyce squeezed her shoulder while Walsh glared at him from a few feet away. "It's all right," Joyce said. "You couldn't've known, not really. Under stress—"

"You should've been there!" she snapped, taking Tess by surprise. She stood quickly, almost thrown off balance. "None of this would've happened if you had been here on time, just this once." Her voice trailed off as she broke down in bitter sobs. "Now my baby's gone."

Joyce lowered his eyes, distraught, ashamed. "I just couldn't leave on time. Something happened—" He stopped mid-phrase and looked at Tess.

She picked up on it. "What happened, sir? Why were you delayed?"

He ran his hands through his crew-cut hair, a legacy he kept from his days in the military. "There was this tow truck with a broken chain. It was blocking my car in the office underground parking." He shook his head. "There was nothing

I could do. I even had security lift the towed car with their bare hands and set it aside so I could leave. By then, it was too late. The interstate was at a standstill."

Classic delay tactic, and a bold move, to block the DA from reaching the theater in time. This kidnapping had been done by professionals. "I'll pull video for the garage," Tess replied. "It's a start."

Joyce nodded, still holding his gaze down. "I should've left the damn car and taken a cab."

But Tess had turned her attention to the silently angry Mr. Walsh. "Were you supposed to attend the school play, sir?"

He took his hands out of his pockets and fidgeted a quick moment, arranging his tie. "Yes, but I couldn't make it either." He noticed her unspoken question. "My car broke down in the middle of the interstate. There was no possible way I could've stepped away from it."

"Where was it parked the last time you used it?" She took out her notepad, ready to take some notes. She was discerning a pattern, although it made room for an intriguing question: why go through so much trouble to grab a girl from a crowded venue? Why not snatch her when she was at home or coming back from school?

Unless someone was sending a message.

"At my office, in Fort Lauderdale. I'm an architect; I work for the city."

She had two solid leads she could follow, but she wasn't done with Miriam Walsh yet. "Tell me about the man who approached you," Tess asked. "What do you remember?"

She wiped a tear off her face with the back of her hand. "Not much; it was dark. He had a dark jacket, some jeans, and a ball cap." She swallowed and looked at the DA for help as if he'd been there.

"Go on," he said, "you're doing fine." For some reason, his encouragement enraged her. She glared at him briefly before continuing.

"He had a beard, I think. Everything was dark." She sounded apologetic, her voice holding the promise of more tears. "I remember thinking, at least he had the common sense to admit he'd damaged my car. He walked behind me for the most part; I thought he was being polite."

"Was he taller than you?"

"N—no." She frowned, apparently trying to remember. "Two, maybe three inches shorter."

"Age? Race?"

"I'd say mid-thirties, Caucasian, dark-haired."

"He took you out of the auditorium, then what?" Tess visualized the events as she talked through them.

"I wanted to use the main entrance, but he said the car was parked closer to the side entrance. I agreed, although—" Tess waited patiently while Miriam was gathering her thoughts. "I remember thinking it wasn't really okay; I had a bad feeling about it, nothing tangible, but I kept going." Tears burst out of her eyes, and she wailed, covering her mouth with her hand. "I just wanted to go back and see Paige's play."

"Then?"

"Nothing." Miriam sniffled. "I woke up on the floor, bleeding, inside the janitor's closet." She whimpered again as if the urge to sob took too much effort to contain. "Everyone was gone."

"But you had your phone with you the whole time?" Tess asked.

"Y—yes. It was off for some reason when I came to. It was on when that man came; I remember getting text messages. He must've turned it off and put it back in my pocket."

Tess's brow furrowed. What perp turns off a victim's phone instead of taking it? One who's planning to call that number later with a ransom demand? Or one who wanted Miriam Walsh to have the means to call her ex-husband right away? In any case, the unsub might've wanted to keep the phone silent for a while. She locked eyes for a brief moment with the DA and realized he must've been asking himself the same questions.

Tess beckoned the theater manager, who watched from a distance. He hadn't moved an inch since she'd arrived but approached quickly with a worried yet polite expression on his face.

Tess showed her badge. "Special Agent Winnett. You are?"

"Frank Brassfield. I'm the manager of this venue. What can I help you with? Please rest assured we'll do anything in our power to assist in any way we can."

Tess nodded. "I'll need your surveillance recordings for tonight, sent to this email." She offered him Donovan's card. Her analyst was the best in the entire regional office. If there was anything usable on those recordings, he would find it.

"I'd be happy to," he replied with a quick, professional smile. "I have the video cued up for you if you'd like a look."

"Excellent." Tess turned to Miriam and Darrel. "One more question, ma'am. What was the last thing you remember seeing on stage when you left the auditorium?"

Her eyebrows shot up. She turned to her ex and whispered, "This is who you found to look for your daughter, Darrel? What's she going to do, by herself, when she's asking such senseless questions?"

The man's jaws clenched for a moment before he replied, his voice tinged with embarrassment, although he'd said worse things to her face the last time they met in court. "She has an entire team behind her."

The woman sighed and lowered her head, seeming defeated. "My goodness, Darrel, I hope you're right. But why not have more agents here to look for Paige? Why?" She paced restlessly back and forth like a caged animal, wailing like one.

"Trust me on this one, babe, please."

Her eyes glinted with rage. "I'm not your babe anymore, not since your paralegal took my place in your bed. Don't you ever forget it."

Max Walsh approached them and placed a firm hand on Darrel's shoulder. "I think it's best if you leave."

"Yeah, Darrel," Miriam interceded. "Leave. Because you're never there for your daughter anyway. Why should today be any different?" She shook her head while Darrel stood there, seeming at a loss for words, which Tess had never thought possible for the Broward County DA. Then, as if remembering what she'd asked earlier, Miriam caught Tess's glance and said, "She'd just started sprinkling breadcrumbs through the forest. Just white confetti Paige took from my office hole puncher."

"Thank you," Tess replied after taking a brief moment to understand what she was talking about. Paige, in her play, Hansel and Gretel, leaving a trail of breadcrumbs through the forest to find their way home. Now she had a memorable event timestamp to cite whenever interviewing witnesses from the auditorium because everyone had been watching the play and probably had lost track of time.

"You have until tomorrow morning," Miriam added coldly. "If I don't have my daughter by then, I'm calling everyone. I don't care what he has to say about it."

"Understood." Tess looked at the DA, who veered his eyes to avoid her scrutinizing glance. She was on her own, and DA Joyce was getting ready to leave.

"Call me as soon as you know anything?" he asked Miriam, but she didn't acknowledge him in any way. Then he looked at Tess.

"Will do. One more question: how did you find out your daughter was missing?"

The question seemed to surprise Joyce. His mouth agape for a long moment, he seemed to search his thoughts. "Miriam called me."

She didn't buy it for a second.

A district attorney should know better than to lie to a federal agent during an investigation.

6

SURVEILLANCE

Leaning into his elbows on the cluttered desk, Mark watched the screen of his laptop closely. A tense, excited smile stretched his thin lips as he heard Miriam snap at DA Joyce over his affair with his paralegal. "Ooh, Mr. District Attorney, how does it feel to be in the doghouse?" He clapped his hands, then rubbed them before settling back in front of the screen for some more captivating entertainment.

Prime-time reality TV had nothing on his own personal show.

Mark's only regret was that the camera wasn't capturing the DA's face, only his profile. If the asshole would only turn a little, then he'd see the fear written on his face, the cowardice, the submission, the defeat. But Gavin only had so many places where he could put that camera, and the same went for the audio bugs he'd scattered with generosity behind the lapels of about twelve different suit jackets he'd found in the DA's closet yesterday when he'd visited his posh residence during his gym hour.

But even so, he was able to catch most of the dialogue between him and that FBI agent. She didn't look that much, just a blonde chick with the unnerving habit of slightly tilting her head sideways when she was thinking. She squinted when she thought she was on to something, the corners of her mouth twitching just a little as if resisting the urge to smile. She'd asked some interesting questions, but nothing they hadn't anticipated.

Mark had planned for everything, including that fed. Not for her in particular, but for one fed. Those were the terms he'd dictated to the DA when he'd called him, albeit earlier than planned because Gavin did everything wrong with Miriam as well. He was supposed to hit her enough to get her dizzy, then give her a shot of ketamine to keep her out of it until morning. If he'd done that, his call to the DA would've sounded differently. He would've said, "We have your daughter and your ex-wife. As a gesture of goodwill on our part, you can find your wife in the janitor's closet, inside the Universal Stage Theater." But no… the knucklehead had to smack her in the head hard and crack her skull, then leave her there like that, bleeding on the floor in the closet, where she could've died, incurring him a murder charge he didn't deserve.

Even so, by waking up earlier than anticipated, Miriam almost blew up their entire plan. Gavin had just arrived with the kid when she was already calling her ex, only twenty minutes after Joyce had been by the theater himself. Good thing they had the bugs in place, and he heard the call; otherwise, they would've been taken for the most incompetent kidnap team in the history of first-degree felonies.

As soon as he'd heard Miriam's call, he called the DA with his terms. And so far, he'd been obedient, not willing to take unnecessary risks with his daughter's life just for the sake of playing cowboy. Darrel Joyce seemed to be levelheaded under pressure and had kept his cool beautifully, even when his former wife had wiped the floors with him in public.

So far, so good. Joyce had managed to send most of the cops on their way. It would've been senseless to demand that he didn't get the police involved, especially when dear old Gavin had managed to screw things up and Miriam had waltzed out of the theater, triggering all sorts of alarms and gathering more cops in five minutes than the United California bank heist. So, he'd improvised and accepted the idea of cops sniffing around, of the feds getting involved. Choosing to appear in control, rather than at the whim of fate through the incompetent hands of a lame partner named Gavin, he'd told the DA he could have whatever fed he wanted, as long it was only one. Not a team of gun-wielding, badge-flashing assholes he couldn't keep track of, just one. Because he didn't have the resources to bug an unknown number of cops, nor the time to listen to so many channels of surveillance audio.

DA Joyce had obeyed and chose, much to Mark's liking, a squinty-eyed blonde with a twitchy smile and rather weird interrogation techniques. He'd seen better in movies, he thought, chuckling when he heard her asking at which point in the play did Miriam leave the auditorium. If there was ever a stupid and pointless question, that had to be it.

His laughter died when he heard Miriam pleading with her ex over involving way more cops in the investigation. Joyce wasn't allowed to say a word to her, and he was doing just fine keeping his trap closed, but Miriam's insistence could prove an issue. That woman was fiery as hell. After all, she could pick up the phone at any time and call the feds herself, and they would come running. He needed to contain that risk and pronto.

Leaving the desk for a brief moment, Mark opened a window and watched the foul-smelling air escape into the night in rushed swirls, replaced by the misty chill of the Miami winter night.

The air had grown thick with fumes of stale food, rotting leftovers in old pizza boxes, and cheap cigar smoke. Seemed that Gavin, after playing the part he did at his job, where he was well-behaved and neatly dressed, turned into a slob the moment he walked through the door. Behind those walls, he could be his true self, an insensitive, foul-mouthed sloven.

He shot Gavin a disgusted look; he was still slouched in front of the TV, watching sports reruns and getting excited over what was happening on the screen, hollering and cussing as if the game hadn't been played already and he could cheer those players into a different outcome. Yet every time he felt like wringing Gavin's neck, he remembered how he came to be partners with a slimeball like him.

Mark never wanted to do this, to get involved in such a mess, but he hadn't had much choice, and it all had started with the DA himself, almost ten years ago. He'd just finished loading groceries in the car, when a drunk driver ran over the sidewalk and slammed into the parked cars in the Walmart lot at full speed. When he woke up, he was coming out of surgery and had to learn how to walk again. Three short weeks later when they released him, life had left its tread on his soul; he was already addicted to drugs.

It had started with doctor-prescribed opiates after his first surgery. By the time he could walk straight and set his entire weight on the scarred calf again, he would've done anything for another fix of oxycodone. He wasn't in pain anymore, not physical pain, and not real, anyway. His pain was now excruciating, worse than the wound had ever hurt, worse than he remembered agonizing on the asphalt, bleeding, pinned down under a crushed truck bed.

Within two months, his job and his girlfriend were gone, his college ambitions forgotten, his entire life destroyed. He moved in with his parents, but within weeks, he'd burned through everything he could get his hands on for cash. Until now, he'd never sunk so low in his entire existence as the day he pawned his mother's wedding ring for a few grams of white powder.

His dealer, a mousy teenager with a permanently running nose and darting eyes, had been busted minutes after selling to him and quickly turned state's evidence in exchange for a suspended sentence. The cops probably wanted his bosses and his bosses' bosses, but he must've given them his client list as gravy on the side. For free, most likely, because that's how lives get destroyed sometimes, for no good reason.

He was picked up that same evening and charged with possession with intent. Sadly, it wasn't his first encounter with the legal system; he'd been nabbed before, the first time for joyriding in a car he was supposed to valet for an upscale restaurant, although he only took it once around the block. The second time was for punching a drunk asshole in a bar, but he was a rather large man, and the judge saw that as an aggravating factor. Even so, he was sentenced to community service. He'd swept the floors at the local VA Medical Center for two months, getting the occasional doobies on the side from some of the vets.

Turned out possession with intent to distribute is an entirely different ball game when you're a third-time loser and the DA's reelection is due in only a few months. Instead of turning a blind eye like many in his place might have done, Darrel Joyce chose to make him the poster child for the war on drugs, especially in the local veterans' organizations like the VA where he still worked, on and off. While he was rotting in jail, his own mother refusing to post bail, the DA was on TV almost every day. He spoke about how returning heroes deserved to live a clean and healthy life and reintegrate into society without the risk of being exposed to criminal elements from within their own community, yadda, yadda, yadda... rabid son of a bitch. After finishing the spiel Mark had seen so many times he'd learned it by heart, the DA would invariably wave at the public, then put his hand above his heart and add, in a low, somber voice, "That is my solemn promise to you." And the crowds always cheered.

Darrel Joyce got reelected that year, a few months after Mark was sentenced to serve five years in a state penitentiary. A few years later, he was paroled and left the joint clean, scarred, and with no future. But life was filled with unexpected twists, much like a book. Every page one turns could take their breath away, sweep them off their feet, and land them into a different reality.

Who would've known I'd end up having to snatch a kid to save my life? And whose kid? The fucking DA's, out of all people. He laughed out loud as thoughts spun in his head, watching the DA being asked to leave by his ex's new husband. Gavin looked at him briefly before returning to his game. He ignored him.

The DA's kid... I better not get caught. On the flip side, isn't karma a bitch, Mr. District Attorney? Who's laughing now?

7

On the

Screen

Seven hours missing

It was almost two in the morning when Brassfield, the theater manager, led the way to the security office. Small and windowless, it housed top-notch equipment with inputs from high-resolution cameras equipped with color night vision and audio recording. Nine screens were set in rows of three, several frozen on still during playback of recordings, while the others were live monitoring the lobby, the stage, and several corridors.

Their small procession had Tess and Miriam leading, while others trailed only slightly behind. Mrs. Langhorne and another teacher had tagged along, and Officer Carter was at the tail end. He stood so far from the screens Tess doubted he could see anything.

A chime on her phone drew her attention. The AMBER Alert had gone out. Maybe they'd catch a break.

Brassfield pressed a few keys on the keyboard and clicked the play icon with the mouse. "I figured we could start here." The screen showed a view of the lobby, invaded by children and parents that were all heading toward the exit, chatting excitedly. Paige was among them, head on a swivel, looking everywhere for her mom.

"Oh, baby," Miriam whimpered, right next to Tess. The woman was doing her best to appear calm and tough, but she was crumbling inside.

Tess watched Paige on the screen as she slowly fell behind the rest, seeming lost. Then Mrs. Langhorne had approached her and said something to her, then clasped her hand and walked with her toward the exit. The recorded sound was unintelligible, the background noise echoing in the vast lobby drowning whatever the teacher had said.

"This is where I told her that her mother might've been outside, pulling the car to the curb," Mrs. Langhorne said as if reading Tess's mind.

Miriam turned at her, scowling. "You had no business telling her that," she said. "You didn't know that! Your duty was to stay with her until a parent picked her up."

Mrs. Langhorne lowered her gaze and whispered, "I—I'm really sorry. I didn't know—"

"Exactly." The word snapped in the electrified air like a crack of a whip. Then Miriam turned her attention to the screen, where Paige exited the lobby after Langhorne had let go of her hand and had gone ahead, leaving her alone with just a few other children and their parents.

"Let's switch to the outside view," Brassfield said, clicking the play button on another cued video. The camera was installed high from the ground, at least ten or twelve feet, and it covered a large section of the driveway and the stairs that led to the entrance. A long line of cars was moving slowly, stopping and picking up children and family members. Most of the families waited there to be picked up, leaving only one member of each family to walk across the large parking lot and bring their car over through the light drizzle of the chilly evening.

Miriam gasped. "That's my car," she pointed at a burgundy Subaru Forester that approached in line with other cars. Difficult to make out against the Subaru's shining headlights and rain-covered windshield, the driver seemed to be a Caucasian male, but no other distinctive feature could be seen.

"I'll need these videos sent over," Tess said, wondering if Donovan could do anything with the blurry image of the male driver.

"Already done," Brassfield replied.

In the video, the Subaru was drawing closer, the man behind the wheel a little more visible. Paige, standing at the top of the stairs and shifting her weight from one foot to the other, had recognized the car and started walking toward it with a spring in her step.

Tess paused the video. "Does anyone recognize this man?"

"No," Miriam answered, her voice strangled. No one else offered anything, and Tess resumed the playback.

She watched Paige step down the wide marble steps and open the door to the Subaru, then pull back slightly, startled, probably when she didn't recognize the man behind the wheel. She seemed to talk with the man for a while, leaning forward to look at him but not letting go of the door handle. Only two cars were still waiting behind the Subaru when Paige seemed to be convinced by something the man was saying and climbed inside.

"Oh, no," Miriam cried, touching the screen with her hand as if trying to hold on to her daughter's image for a bit longer. "No, baby, you know better than that." She sobbed heavily, still watching the screen where the Subaru had vanished.

Tess took down the time stamp: 7:12 P.M. Was the driver a complete stranger? Or someone Paige knew? "Would Paige have climbed into the car with someone she didn't know?"

Miriam looked at her through a veil of tears, her mouth agape. "I—I don't know. Not with a stranger, no... I don't think so."

"Where were you at this point, Mrs. Langhorne?"

The teacher's scared eyes brimmed with tears. "I was, um, I had left already. The white Toyota was mine; my husband brought it to the curb."

"You left her alone," Miriam shouted, grabbing the woman by the lapels of her jacket and slamming her against the wall. Her voice was brittle under the load of tears, her breath ragged. It must've been excruciating for her to see her daughter being taken. Tess would've never allowed her to see the recordings if it wasn't for the hope she'd recognize someone.

Tess put her arm around Miriam's shoulders. "Please, Mrs. Walsh, you're not helping things." The woman's anger dissolved into tears and a long wail. "Maybe it's better you don't see these recordings. Let me take you home."

Miriam sniffled and raised her eyes to meet Tess's. "No. I have every right to be here."

"All right, but I have to warn you I won't allow you to assault people, no matter how guilty they are. We will deal with everyone's role in due time, I promise."

The teacher turned pale as a sheet, her chin trembling visibly. "I'm really sorry, I didn't know... I saw her car, and Paige recognized it, and I thought—"

"Let's watch the other one," Tess interrupted. Her patience was wearing thin. The teacher had responsibilities she had chosen to ignore, but there wasn't time to deal with that now, not while Paige was missing.

Brassfield clicked, and the third screen displayed a view of the lobby area, where the man had entered calmly and quickly through the main doors and went straight into the auditorium after a quick nod to the usher. A few minutes later, Miriam exited the hall with the man. He carefully hid his face from the cameras the entire time. Brassfield changed the view when the two entered the corridor leading to the back entrance, but the man didn't hit Miriam until he was out of camera view. Then he disappeared through the door, only his feet visible on the screen for a brief moment. That had happened at 6:27 P.M.

"Okay," she acknowledged. "Thanks," she said to Brassfield and turned to leave.

"No, wait, there's one more video." He clicked, and the frozen screen in the middle of the second row of displays came to life, showing a deserted area of the parking lot where very few cars had been parked. "I tracked down where the driver of the Subaru was coming from." He clicked, and the images fast-forwarded, nothing really happening on the screen. "At first, I thought the man had walked to the Subaru from the street or maybe another car had dropped him off." He slowed the playback to normal speed as a man approached the Subaru. He walked calmly and fast, his gait determined and elastic, not hesitating at all, and unlocked the Subaru with the remote.

He had keys.

"Wait. Go back," Tess asked. "Where is he coming from? Where does this alley lead to?"

"Backstage exit," Brassfield replied.

Tess wrote down the time stamp, 7:03 P.M. Between 6:27 P.M. when he'd hit Miriam and 7:03 P.M., the man had ample time to leave through the side door and pull the car around to load Paige up without too many witnesses being left to see him. He must've taken Miriam's keys when he'd turned off her phone.

A jingle of keys drew Tess's attention, right when Miriam said, her voice a stunned whisper, "I still have my keys." She was holding them in the palm of her hand, her fingers trembling slightly in the pale light that came from the screens.

That simple cluster of everyday objects changed things. The unsub had been inside her house and had shown enough familiarity with the school play venue to not hesitate for a single moment. The kidnapping had been thoroughly planned, the level of detail in execution making her think of numerous scenarios, none of them good.

"Is EMS here yet?" she asked Officer Carter.

"Yes, ma'am. They've been waiting for a while."

"All right. I need a BOLO on that Subaru if you can," she said, speaking with the police officer but looking intently at Miriam. "Make it statewide."

"What is it?" the woman whispered, seemingly scared.

"Let's take you to that ambulance now," Tess said, grabbing her arm gently and leading her outside. "That concussion needs to be looked at." They walked quickly down the corridor toward the main entrance, where the red flashers of the ambulance were still on. Once they were out of everyone's earshot, she added, lowering her voice to a whisper, "I'll need you to change into a hospital gown or something. Your clothing is evidence."

8

NEIGHBOR

As soon as the AMBER Alert went out, Mark dozed off in the beat-up, stained recliner after he'd pushed himself backward until the foot support extended with a thud. He'd closed the window after an hour or so; the fresh air brought a little too much moisture, and the chill he'd welcomed at first had turned into an unpleasant basement feeling that brought up the smell of mildew from the old carpet and wall joints.

Gavin was snoring loudly, his mouth wide open and his head tilted backward on the sofa arm. He'd slid there after he'd fallen asleep watching TV, with the sound blaring and obnoxious commercials in annoyingly happy voices playing every five minutes, the hallmark of free television. Mark had to get off his butt to turn down the TV sound, but ended up switching the channel too. Then he half-watched an old episode of Criminal Minds until the AMBER Alert buzzed on his phone. Now he could sleep; the Big Man would also get the alert and know the job was done. Half of it, really, but the essential half.

A loud knock on the front door had him startled awake, on his feet, ready to run. It was still dark outside. He grabbed the gun he'd placed on the small table by his recliner and slid it into his belt, then checked the time. It was almost four in the morning. Who made house calls at that time of the night?

Covering Gavin's mouth with one hand, he shook him awake. When his bloodshot eyes focused on him, he let go of his mouth and gestured with a vertical finger against his lips to keep quiet.

"What?" Gavin whispered.

"Someone's at the door."

"Oh, crap." Gavin stood, his Glock in his shaky hand aimed at the door.

The burst of knocks repeated, this time followed by a female voice with a raspy voice and a touch of New York accent. "Come on, you guys, I know you're in there."

Mark looked at Gavin, then took position next to the door, ready to open it. Whatever it was the woman wanted at four in the morning, it was better he dealt with it. Gavin went into the hallway, out of sight but just around the corner, ready to shoot.

"Yeah, okay," Mark said as if responding to the visitor's request. He unlocked the door and opened it. "Can't blame a guy for sleeping at four in the fucking morning, can you?"

"Ha, sleep, my ass," the woman laughed. Her voice was gruff and grating. She was a thin, almost gaunt bleached blonde with dirty, clumped hair that reached her shoulders in uneven wisps. She smelled of cigarette smoke and stale booze, not that the stench on her breath didn't fit the room's general odor. But on her, the smell was intense and acrid as if she'd recently thrown up.

She shot him a quick dart of her eyes then wiped her nose with her finger in a lightning-fast move while she inhaled. Mark recognized the signs; she was a drug addict. "I'm Randi," she said, extending the hand she'd just wiped her nose with.

Mark ignored it. "Tell me why the heck you're banging on my door at four in the morning and get lost."

"Oh, I'm not going anywhere," she laughed, the coarse cackles coming from a throat overexerted by cheap smokes and who knows what else. She let go of the small duffel bag she was carrying; Mark hadn't noticed it before. It hit the floor with a loud thump. Then she walked past him and let herself drop into his recliner while grinning at him the entire time with an air of secretive superiority. Her teeth were stained yellow, although she was about twenty-five, maybe even younger. Drugs aged women very quickly. "I'm here to stay," she announced as she gleefully crossed her skinny legs at the ankles.

She wore Daisy Dukes on top of black leggings and a flimsy top that exposed a few inches of her emaciated abdomen where a navel piercing hung sadly.

Mark approached the recliner menacingly and stopped squarely in front of it, arms folded at his chest. "Yeah? And what makes you think I won't sink you to the bottom of the bay right this moment?"

She didn't seem fazed by his threat; she kept on grinning while her grimy fingers dug through her shorts pocket until they fished out a phone with a pink, glittery case. She showed it to him, although the screen was still dark. "This," she laughed coarsely again, "the AMBER Alert that just woke me up."

Mark felt the blood draining from his face. "What the hell are you talking about, woman?" He took one step closer, towering over her. She didn't flinch. He remembered the times when he was looking for a fix, just like she most probably was. He would've done anything, fearlessly and recklessly, just to score one more time.

"You and I are gonna become besties, you'll see. What's your name?"

Gavin appeared from the hallway, gun in hand. "Let's whack this broad and get back to sleep."

She laughed at him. "That's the guy I saw. I was wondering where you were, 'cause it wasn't you," she pointed at Mark, "who carried that kid in here last night."

Mark and Gavin exchanged a quick, worried glance. Maybe whatever it was she'd seen, others had too, and things were about to head south with a tailwind.

"Who are you, again?" Mark asked, frowning and scratching the roots of his hair. What the heck was he supposed to do now? Run? Where? They had nothing arranged; they were sure they'd be safe on the houseboat.

"I'm your next-door neighbor." She held a long, thin finger in the air, then pointed toward the south of the bay. "That way. I live in that converted pontoon you always pass by when you come home." Mark was dumbfounded. Researching the marina had been Gavin's job. The turd couldn't get anything done right. As if reading his thoughts, Randi said, "It's not easy to see if someone lives there or not. I made sure of it." She laughed again, a quick, resounding cackle. "But you guys should learn to keep your voices down. Sound carries over water, you know."

"What do you think you heard?" Mark asked, still hoping it was some confusion he could sort out and send the girl away.

"Oh, I heard plenty," she replied, patting the arms of the recliner with a satisfied grin. "You were arguing over drugging an eight-year-old, remember?" Her words hit Mark in the gut like a fist. "I didn't think much of it at the time, but then I got the AMBER Alert, and I started to put things together." She stared at them, her grin gone, her brown eyes turned to steel. "You guys are in it for the money, and I'm your new partner."

"The hell you are," Gavin replied. With a few quick and angry footsteps, he reached her and grabbed her arm while he shoved the barrel of his gun in her temple. "This is the day you die, bitch."

Randi laughed again. "Nah, I don't think so. My homies know where I am and what to do if I don't show up when I said I would."

Gavin let go of her arm as if her skin burned his fingers. He shot Mark a quick, inquisitive glance.

"What do you want?" Mark asked.

"You're not very smart, are you?" Randi asked derisively. "I told you already, I want in on your little kidnapping scheme, so, yeah, I want a third of what you'll be getting." She sucked her teeth while looking at them inquisitively. "And don't even dream of screwing me on this."

Unexpectedly, Mark felt the searing urge for a hit of white powder. He hadn't felt that in a long time. It was so bad it knocked the breath out of his lungs. He stared at the woman, fighting his own betraying body, aching for the release brought by a good fix. Grinding his teeth, he forced some air into his lungs, instantly hating the woman who'd brought his own past onto his doorstep and wishing he could snuff the life out of her slowly, with his fingers digging deep into that skinny throat of hers until her windpipe broke.

Jaws clenched until they hurt, he managed to resist. Part of his inner angst made it across to the woman, maybe in his eyes, because she said, "Whoa, there, buddy, don't get any crazy ideas, all right? My homies don't have a sense of humor." The laughter was gone from her voice, replaced by the strangled, gurgling sound of fear.

How was he going to tell her he wasn't doing this for the money? He couldn't share anything with the woman, and she wouldn't've cared anyway. She was after money, enough money to kill herself in a storm of white snow, either slowly or quickly, in a massive overdose like he'd seen happen so many times before. No; even if she learned about Mark's motives in the kidnapping, she'd just subscribe to Gavin's agenda and demand they take the ransom too.

The more he thought about it, the more it seemed they were headed that way. He just hoped the Big Man wouldn't care about a measly million dollars he'd take from the DA when he'd specifically said to make the ransom call then not show up, to create confusion and vulnerability in the DA's family and buy them time. Yet strangely, the thought of fleecing the DA made him irrationally happy.

He grinned. "Okay. You're in."

"Really?" she asked, springing to her feet with the agility of a twitching crack addict. "I'll pull my own weight, you know," she continued selling it, although it made no sense. "I'll take the kid potty, wipe her nose, shit like that."

He wondered if she knew who the kid was, or if she didn't, would it make a difference when she found out?

"Be careful what you're getting yourself into," he warned her, but her glassy eyes were not focused anymore, darting all over the room. "You can still walk away right now, no hard feelings."

She scoffed. "Hey, you think I'm stupid or something?"

Mark refrained from telling her what he thought about her. Instead, he gave her one last warning in a somber and honest tone of voice. "There's a strong chance we might all end up dead after this."

9

AT HOME

Nine hours missing

There was a hint of light toward the Atlantic, coloring the sky in deep shades of purple, so dark it barely seemed like the promise of daybreak soon to follow. The ambulance flashers still colored the theater in bright reds, every now and then underlined by shimmers of blue coming from the remaining police cars. The air was thick with fog, the smell of salty ocean mist and seaweed heavy, the moisture quick to dampen clothing and bring a sense of cold, heartless misery to all those still working the early morning hours.

Tess waited for Miriam to finish changing behind an improvised screen made from two gurney sheets in the back of the ambulance. She whimpered as she disrobed, crying softly.

"Right after this, we'll take you home," Tess said, wishing she could tell her to move faster, but she didn't have the heart to rush her. "For anyone who asks, I'm your cousin from Orlando, and my husband will be joining me." She checked the time. "I believe he's already there. His name is Donovan."

"He is?" Miriam emerged from behind the sheets, dressed in a paper-thin disposable coverall, the kind EMS and crime scene technicians used. The white of the coverall brought up the pallor of her face and the bright red of her shiny, long hair. Dark circles had appeared under her swollen eyes.

"He should be there by now," Tess confirmed. She crouched by the abandoned pile of clothing Miriam had dropped on a broad sheet of paper. Slipping on a pair of fresh gloves, she felt the fabric of each item looking for anything that didn't belong, then packed each item in an evidence bag. She anticipated bugs, mics, or pinpoint cameras even. There weren't any, but something rustled inside one of the jacket pockets. "He will be scanning your house for any surveillance devices." She unzipped a fancy sleeve pocket and pulled out a piece of paper folded in four.

"What's that?" Miriam asked.

Tess carefully unfolded it and read it herself before sharing. It was scribbled in block letters on plain notepad paper using a ballpoint pen that had been pressed on the paper firmly. The handwriting seemed rushed and lacked the luster of practice, of a routinely used skill. "It's a note from the kidnappers." Miriam gasped. "I was expecting that," Tess added reassuringly. "It says, 'Go home and wait by the phone until you hear how much money your daughter will cost you. No media, no drawing attention to yourself, no wiseass moves. Keep this quiet and do as you're told, or she dies.' It's not signed in any way." She slipped the note into an evidence pouch and sealed it.

Miriam covered her mouth with a trembling hand, sobbing again, hard, heaving sobs that shook her entire body. Tess squeezed her shoulder gently. "We'll get her back. Just let us work, and we'll get your daughter back."

Miriam nodded but continued to cry, her wails coming through the hand she pressed hard over her mouth as if trying to force them to stay inside, captive in her chest. Carrying all the evidence bags, Tess opened the ambulance's back doors and climbed down, then extended a hand for Miriam. She took it.

Her fingers were frozen, and she shook badly in the cold morning wind, the rustling coveralls she wore thin as paper.

Her Suburban was parked a short distance away, and she led Miriam over there in a quick pace, speaking to her in a gentle voice. "Soon, all this will be over, I promise. I'll turn up the heat for the ride home, then you'll get some rest while we work." She squeezed her hand gently but firmly, trying to instill a little confidence in her. "We'll find Paige; we won't stop until we do."

Seemingly at the end of her strength, Miriam let herself be loaded into the Suburban like an obedient child. Tess clicked the seatbelt for her, then circled the SUV and climbed behind the wheel.

"Where's Max?" she asked, realizing her husband wasn't there. He'd been absent for a while, but she hadn't asked about him until then.

"He went home to work with Donovan." Tess shot the woman a quick glance. She seemed so tiny in that seat, fragile, still shaking despite the flow of hot air coming from the vents. "He's screening your home for any surveillance equipment, bugs, or cameras."

"Who is this Donovan?" she asked, her voice barely above a whisper. "You keep mentioning him."

"He is the best analyst one could hope for in a case like this," Tess said, her voice sounding just as confident as she felt. "He works with me at the regional office of the FBI, here in Miami. He's very bright, about thirty years old, and a little nerdy, but he's the guy you want on your team. He'll make a fine field agent someday." She didn't believe it was necessary to mention that Donovan would probably never make field agent, despite wanting that very much; he'd already tried twice and failed. Rumor had it that senior management discouraged it because he was the best analyst the field office had seen in decades. Despite the rumors, she knew why Donovan had failed the test twice. He was fabulous with anything and everything data and technology, but when it came to pure, instinctual action with a gun in his hand, he overthought things, and his responses were slow.

"And if he finds bugs? What if the kidnappers get mad if he removes them and they hurt my little girl?" Panic streaked her voice, acute, high-pitched.

"He won't remove them. We'll just work a little differently. We'll know where they are and where in the house we'll be able to speak freely, that's all."

"Oh," she acknowledged, then closed her eyes and seemed to slip away.

The drive was short on the almost deserted interstate, too early for rush hour. The sun was about to rise when Tess pulled into the driveway in front of the Walsh residence.

It was a single-story house in sand-color brick matching the shade of the roof tiles to perfection. The interlocking stone driveway led to a double-car garage with a wood finish door. Tess pulled in front of the bay closest to the entrance. The landscaping was neat and elaborate, the sign of an expensive lawn service doing weekly calls.

The moment she cut the engine, the front door opened, and Max rushed to the car, followed closely by Donovan. There was a resemblance between Max and Donovan; Max could've been the other man's older brother. Both were attractive men, dressed in dark business suits and white shirts, Max looked disheveled and visibly upset, while Donovan seemed uncomfortable with the situation. He'd never been one to know how to handle intense emotions, even if they belonged to other people, not himself.

Miriam climbed out of the Suburban, holding on to the door for balance, then Max wrapped her in his arms. Face buried in his chest, she wept quietly, clasping fistfuls of his shirt sleeves with trembling fingers.

"Come on, let's get you inside."

Tess stayed behind for a moment, then asked Donovan, "Any bugs?"

"Nope, all clear."

"Good." She entered the house, and Donovan followed, closing the door behind him.

The large lobby was lit by sunrays coming in through the beveled front door glass panels. White marble tiles with webs of gray fracture lines reflected the light, filling the room with sunshine. The living room was letting the backyard colors in through wide and tall windows overlooking a white wood deck set around a large pool and decorated with sail shades in bright colors and stylish patio furniture. A sectional sofa in grayish blue took most of the living room space. Tess gave it a moment's consideration before opting for the formal dining room, where the large oak table was better suited for her needs.

His arm wrapped around Miriam's shoulders, Max helped her toward the back of the house. "Let's run you a bath. It will warm you up."

"I have a few more questions," Tess said, hating herself for prolonging the woman's misery. "The sooner we get all the facts, the better our chances of finding Paige."

Miriam approached the dining room table without saying a word, then sat on a chair that Max pulled out for her. She stared into thin air, not making eye contact with either Tess or Donovan.

"Let me make you a cup of tea," Max offered, then filled a cup of water and warmed it quickly in the microwave. Then he tore the wrapping off a chamomile tea bag and sunk it into the hot water. "There," he said, setting the hot drink on a coaster and pushing it toward Miriam. Miriam wrapped her fingers around the cup, probably to warm them up.

"Tell me what you want to know," she whispered.

"What do you do for a living, Mrs. Walsh?" Tess asked. The DA might've been a target in the kidnapping, but she had to cover all the bases.

"I own a pharmacy. It's on Grand Concourse," she replied, her words barely intelligible as if speaking drained more energy than she had left.

"Which one?" Donovan asked.

"Life Rx. It's by the small outlet mall where the cleaners and the Chinese restaurant are."

"I know it," Tess replied. The pharmacy was large, about half the size of a CVS location. Could this have been about drugs? If the kidnappers called with a tall order of oxy or morphine, she'd know.

"How about you, sir?" she asked, looking at Max.

"I'm just an architect who works for the city," he said, seeming surprised by the question. He wasn't Paige's father, and any connection with him was a long shot.

"Anyone else in the family who might have been involved in this?"

"N—no, there's no one else in the family," Max replied. "I have a daughter from a previous marriage, but she lives in Europe. And Miriam has a brother who lives in Texas."

"Any disputes with anyone, family members included, in the past twelve months?" Tess pressed on, although she could see in their behavior, in the unspoken questions in their eyes, they had no idea who could've taken Paige and why.

"No," Miriam whispered, closing her eyes for a long moment. A tear emerged from the corner of her eye and started rolling down her pale cheek. She ignored it.

"Any disgruntled employees? People you might've fired?"

She shook her head slowly. "I haven't fired anyone in five years. We're like a small family."

"How about customers? Did anyone try to get a fix of something and was turned down?"

She smiled sadly. "Those we get every day, Agent Winnett. Not one day goes by that someone doesn't try to squeeze a couple of pills out of us without the right prescription. They try, they fail, then they go on their way and try someplace else."

"You don't believe any of them could—"

"No, I don't believe so." There was firmness in her voice, a trace of the strength she had. There was something formidable in the red-haired woman. Still dressed in the rustling, white coveralls and barely able to speak, she had the tenacity to endure through endless questions and remain focused. She looked at Tess through a blur of tears. "Those addicts are small-time losers, Agent Winnett. The man who took my daughter wasn't an addict. His speech was articulate, his eyes weren't glassy, he wasn't twitching." She lowered her forehead into her hands, slowly shaking her head. "I think they're after money. As a business owner in this city, I might've been targeted."

That was a possibility. "How much money are we talking about here, Mrs. Walsh?"

She seemed intrigued by the question. "You mean, the pharmacy?" Tess nodded. "Last year, revenue was almost fifteen million dollars."

Donovan whistled, and Tess threw him a quick, disapproving look. With drug prices gone haywire and a location in an affluent area, that number wasn't surprising at all. Maybe this kidnapping was about the money after all. Perhaps the unsub didn't even know Paige was the DA's daughter, or he would've tried his luck elsewhere.

"There's nothing to whistle about," Miriam said. "The cost of drugs drives this number and almost all of the money goes to the pharmaceutical companies. For me, it's a paycheck and a lot of hard work."

"Mrs. Walsh, how long have you and Mr. Walsh been married?"

They briefly looked at each other. Max reached over the table and squeezed her hand.

"Almost four years," she replied.

At the same time, Max said, "It will be four years in the summer. We were married in June."

"And when did you divorce Mr. Joyce?"

She scoffed bitterly. "Paige wasn't even one year old when I caught him cheating on me. I called my attorney the next day."

That meant three years before she married Max Walsh. Even an unsub who was above average in doing his diligence might've missed the fact that Paige was the DA's kid.

"Do Paige and her biological father spend any time together?"

She shrugged and veered her eyes, seeming saddened and aggravated at the same time. "He has visitation rights, one weekend per month, and I've always encouraged him to build a strong relationship with his daughter. But my ex-husband is a selfish, womanizing prick who doesn't bother himself to spend time with Paige." She wiped a tear from the corner of her eye with a quick swipe of her finger. "My daughter loves him and cherishes every minute she gets to be with him. He just sends her letters and gifts but rarely visits."

"How often, though?"

"Last year, he came three—no, four times. One time, in May I believe it was, he took her away for a week. He rented a ski lodge in Colorado with some friends of his, maybe a mistress too, who the hell knows." She sniffled, lowering her eyes. "My poor baby wouldn't stop talking about that vacation, and Daddy," she made air quotes with her fingers as she spat the emphasized word, "and how fun it all was." She sighed, her breath ragged as if it hurt her lungs when it came out of her chest. Then, as if she'd been injected with a shot of energy coming from her pooling anger, she raised her eyes and shrugged everything off. "Paige kept begging me to speak with Darrel to get his permission to post their vacation photos on Facebook. Apparently, he'd forbidden her to do that, probably concerned with his ability to pick up women if he appeared in photos with his little girl." Her voice was different when she talked about her ex, loaded with deep, unresolved, raw pain. "Of course, I didn't speak with him about the photos. She'll grow out of it, of her infatuation with him. We're taking her to the Bahamas this year, in a speedboat." She stopped speaking as if something had kicked her in the stomach as soon as she remembered Paige was gone. "Oh, God... my poor baby." She wrapped her arms around herself and bent over, her face almost touching the table.

Max stood, the legs of his chair scraping against the gleaming hardwood floor, then took Miriam's hand in his. "Are we finished here, Agent Winnett?"

"One more question, please," Tess replied, then looked at Miriam. "Is there a spare set of keys for your Subaru? This will tell us if the kidnappers were in your house."

Her jaw slacked as she lifted a shaky finger, pointing toward the kitchen. Max rushed over there with big strides, his footfalls sending echoes in the deathly silent house. He opened a drawer, the closest one to the garage entrance, and rummaged quickly through the items stored in there. Then he turned and said, "They're gone."

10

PEARSON

Eleven hours missing

Miriam had finally gone to her bedroom. For a while, Tess could hear her heart-wrenching sobs through the closed door. She'd refused to take a sleeping pill, wanting to stay alert and clear-minded if the kidnappers called with their demands. Max seemed to need the medication more than she did; he was falling apart quickly, his eyes welling up whenever Miriam wasn't looking, and he thought Tess wouldn't notice. He'd probably raised Paige as his own.

Donovan had set up the equipment needed to trace the ransom call on the dining room table. The devices, packed conveniently in thick briefcases laid open, were plugged in and connected to the internet. One was already wired into the landline phone circuit. The second one held Miriam's cell phone in a slot, and displayed battery and signal strength status on a small, green screen.

Now they waited.

The sobs behind the closed bedroom door had waned, replaced with an eerie, heavy silence. Tess filled herself a cup with coffee from the pot and asked Donovan if he wanted some with a simple gesture of her hand. He shook his head.

"I'm lining up all the videos taken last night during the play," he said, keeping his voice lowered, a quiet whisper. "I bet there are tens of hours of video we could sift through, and maybe we'll get a better angle on the unsub's face." He raised his eyes to look at Tess. "That was one bold move, I have to admit."

"Yup," Tess replied. It was precisely what she was thinking of. The boldness of the attack, the seemingly unnecessary risk the unsub had taken by snatching the girl when she was surrounded by more than a hundred potential witnesses. Why would anyone take that kind of risk? It felt defiant, like the deed of a showoff, a demonstration of skill and courage, a show of strength.

"Any word on social media about the abduction yet?" She took another sip of coffee. The aroma reminded her of Starbucks and her favorite blend of latte. The teachers had been told to keep the abduction a secret, but people talked anyway, sometimes even if they risked an obstruction charge. Sooner or later, word would get out.

"Strangely, not a peep," Donovan replied.

"The note from the unsub says specifically no media. I wonder why." She slowly paced the dining room, absentmindedly looking at the call tracing equipment. "I've never met an unsub who wasn't craving attention."

Donovan leaned back in his chair and interlocked his fingers behind his head. "There's a first time for everything, I guess."

"Yeah, but why?" She leaned against the table and crossed her ankles. "I don't believe this is random. I believe whatever he's after requires that the kidnapping is not known to the public."

Donovan laughed quietly, his eyes sparkling. "Maybe he's afraid his buddies would come after him once they find out he cashed in on a big ransom?" His grin widened. "Maybe they're a team, and the unsub who left the note is planning to rid himself of the others. It's known to happen in criminal groups."

She pressed her lips together for a brief moment. It made some sense, but it didn't feel right. The note spoke of a ransom, but it felt as if she was missing something. She'd know more when they finally called. If they would only call already.

She'd instructed Miriam on how to handle the incoming call, and she had every confidence the strong woman would play her part brilliantly. But the waiting was killing her. While Donovan was gathering video recordings from the attending parents and teachers under false pretenses with Mrs. Langhorne's help, she'd worked with the Real Time Crime Center in Miami to get information about the burgundy Subaru after it had left the theater. The RTCC had access to all the cameras and automatic license plate readers across town and was staffed with round-the-clock analysts and technicians ready to assist with cases like Paige's kidnapping. After successfully tracking the Subaru for a few blocks after it left the theater, they lost it. The vehicle vanished in an area not covered by cameras. Seeing that, Tess believed the kidnapper knew very well what he was doing and had spent an ample amount of time preparing the hit.

When the phone rang, she jumped out of her skin before she realized it was her own cell phone. The unsubs would've never called that line. She took it out of her pocket and recognized SAC Pearson's name on the display.

"Winnett," she said, keeping her voice low for the Walshes' benefit and checking the time. It was almost eight-thirty.

"What can you tell me?" her boss asked, cutting straight to the chase.

She walked briskly toward the patio door and stepped outside, carefully looking left and right before speaking. "This case has ramifications in a dozen different directions." Her voice was low and tense. She hated not having results to share with her boss. "The mother owns a pharmacy; this could be about drugs or money." She recalled she hadn't had the time to brief him about the note. "The unsub makes reference to a ransom call we're waiting for."

"There's a note?" He seemed unexpectedly surprised.

Why would a note mentioning a ransom call be so unusual in a kidnapping case? "Y—yes. What am I missing?"

"Being the kid is the DA's daughter, I thought... Never mind, Winnett, just tell me what you have."

"Yes, there's the DA angle. It could be they are targeting DA Joyce with the kidnapping of his child. From what I'm hearing, he and Paige weren't that close. If they were targeting him, they didn't do enough diligence, although everything about this kidnapping spells professional team."

"What does that famous gut of yours tell you, Winnett?"

She listened for sarcasm in his voice, but there was none.

"While we're waiting for the ransom call, I want to know what cases the DA is currently working on. Even those in preliminary stages." She paused for a moment, unsure if she should further complicate things at that point. With a repressed sigh, she added, "We have a procedure manual thick as a brick and just as unpalatable when it comes to any crime against a DA's family. What do we do? Follow that?"

There was silence on the line, a few long seconds of it, heavy, loaded with unspoken questions and unfathomable scenarios.

"You're thinking organized crime?" Pearson asked, his voice tinged with concern.

"It's too soon to be sure, but we can't ignore who the father of the victim is." She paused, looking at the sparkling pool water sloshing gently a few feet away under the morning breeze. The air was still chilly after one of the coldest nights of the season, but the sun was shining, and the sky was perfectly blue. "We need discreet surveillance on the DA around the clock, and I repeat, it has to be discreet. If the unsubs are after him, they can't know we're watching him."

"What are you expecting? An attack of sorts?"

She thought for a moment. It made no sense to physically harm the DA after they'd taken his child. "I don't believe they'd go after him physically. I believe if they wanted that, they could've done it already. They were bold enough to delay him at the office, and I'm willing to bet a month's pay they had a backup plan in place for every juncture where he could've decided differently."

"What do you mean?"

"They blocked his car in his office parking lot. What if he took an Uber instead of working with them and garage security to have his car pulled out? I don't believe a professional team such as this would've left that option to chance. If he had called an Uber, something would've happened to further delay him; we just don't know what." Frowning and staring at the interlocking bricks that lined the pool patio, she tried to visualize scenarios. "I'm not sure what they would've done, but I don't believe they left anything to chance."

"Are you looking into what happened at that garage?"

"At both garages, yes."

"Both?"

She put her hand at her forehead, shielding her eyes from the sun's piercing rays. "Turns out both men were supposed to attend the school play: the girl's biological father and Maxwell Walsh, the girl's stepdad. Max Walsh didn't make it either. His brand-new BMW X3 suddenly died on the interstate." She rubbed her forehead, feeling the seeds of a migraine germinating under the bright sunlight. "We're having it towed and examined."

"So, the unsubs kept both men from reaching the play without arousing any suspicion, attacked the mother, and managed to get away with the daughter?" The unspoken conclusion came across clearly in the tone of his voice.

"Precisely my point. They're experienced, skilled, perfectly coordinated, and we have no idea what they're after."

"Didn't you say they're planning a ransom call?"

"Two ex-cons with a drug or a gambling habit would nab a kid for ransom money and would make it simple, passing by the schoolyard in a stolen vehicle or grabbing one of the kids waiting for the school bus by themselves. That's what a ransom kidnapping would look like. This, I have no idea what this is. But I'd like to look at every single case the DA is working on, just to cover my bases."

"Yeah, makes perfect sense, Winnett. I'll arrange it."

"Joyce can't know about it."

"Why?"

"The fact that he asked for me doesn't feel right." She closed her eyes for a brief moment, remembering the heated exchange of words they'd last had on a poorly lit courthouse corridor, the condescension in his voice, the contempt glinting in his eyes. "What if we're missing something critical? What if they're after him, and they're closely watching every move he makes, and by reaching out to him, we might put his little girl's life in danger?"

A brief moment of silence on the call, ended by a long breath of air leaving Pearson's lungs. "Not everything that happens in this world is personal and has to do with you, Agent Winnett. I wish you understood that."

"I'm not saying it does." She closed her eyes again, willing herself to stay calm and not further aggravate her already frustrated boss. "All I'm saying is they might be watching him, and until we know for sure what's going on, I won't do a thing to jeopardize Paige's life."

"You're not being fully honest here, Winnett. What are you keeping from me?"

"Nothing," she blurted like a kid caught hiding stolen candy in the palm of her hand. "I just don't have enough evidence to prove my point, that's all. It's just speculation for now."

"Noted. Now share."

She drew a long breath, feeling her body reinvigorated by the chilly air. "If they're after something in particular, and we somehow jeopardize the DA's ability to deliver what they want, we'll put Paige's life in serious danger." Frowning, she stopped talking for a beat, wondering how much she should share. Half-baked theories, wild suppositions, and unsubstantiated statements could cause more harm than good. But so would withholding critical information from the only FBI senior agent involved in that case. "I think that's why the unsubs demanded no media involvement. Otherwise, who would stand to gain from it? Most unsubs advertise left and right, to drive the parents to pay the ransom under the pressure of public opinion."

"You better be sure about this, Winnett." She heard a muffled groan on the line. She could visualize him sitting on his leather chair behind his desk, running his hands over his shiny scalp as if to smooth the many lines running across his forehead. "You're choosing to work this case alone, without involving the DA, which is not the most logical choice and will limit your options. But you've always been a maverick, haven't you?"

She let a moment's silence be her answer. "I believe if we put discreet surveillance on Joyce, around the clock, just to make sure he isn't harmed, and I get clearance to pull up the cases he's working on, then we're good. I'll take care about the Walshes myself."

"What about the procedure manual you were referencing?" he asked in a low, menacing voice. "The one you're supposed to follow when a DA's family is attacked?"

After hesitating for only a moment, she lowered her voice even more. "I'll hold with those procedures for now. I'd rather not jeopardize a little girl's life. If she becomes irrelevant, they will kill her."

"I hope you know what you're doing, Winnett."

He hung up without another word, which she'd learned over time meant the ball was in her court now.

She slipped the phone back into her pocket and turned to leave.

In the doorway, pale as a sheet and trembling, Miriam stood tall, her green eyes drilling into hers. "What the hell aren't you telling me?"

11

HISTORY

Mark stood, leaning against the stained wall, watching Randi. She'd taken his recliner and had commandeered Gavin's remote, shifting channels like only a coke addict would, spending less than two seconds on each and not minding the loud sound one bit.

Only moments after wielding his Glock at the woman, Gavin had lain on the couch and was sawing wood loudly, mouth open, his head tilted backward in a grotesque position. Gavin always took him for granted. He counted on him to keep that opportunistic little bitch under control, and he did, watching her every move, although he ached for some shuteye.

But could he really sleep, not knowing what Randi would do, or if her homies would decide to take over the kidnapping altogether and keep all the money? No... he had to tough it out and stay awake, alert, trying to hear any noise coming from outside under the constant barrage of TV sound bites. If he heard them coming, at least he'd have a chance to pull out his gun and shoot his way out of whatever trouble that broad brought to their doorstep.

Gavin... he'd drunk so much after he came back with the girl, he couldn't stand upright even if Mark trusted him with the next shift watching Randi. He'd fall back on that couch after saying something like, "You wouldn't do anything stupid, would you, sweetie?" Or maybe he'd try to get laid first, and chances were Randi wasn't looking for that sort of action. Who knows what she'd do if Gavin pissed her off? With addicts, there's no telling, not ever.

"Son of a bitch," he muttered, looking at Gavin, who'd just choked on his own saliva and had briefly stopped snoring. Now he had two partners he didn't want, not one.

The truth was, without Gavin, he would've been in serious trouble, with no idea how to nab the girl and get the job done before the Big Man ended him like a bug, crushed under the heel of his boot.

The fact that he still had teeth in his mouth he owed to Gavin and the gang he'd introduced him to when he was doing his time at Florida State. He'd just started his five-year sentence and was barely getting grounded in the place when he got cornered in the showers by a group of large men who'd been doing little else than pumping iron their entire lives. He was still addicted at the time, shivering and trembling and throwing up from withdrawal, posing little threat to the men, especially to the one who seemed to believe that Mark would be better off without his teeth, so he wouldn't be able to bite during the activities they had planned for him.

One of the men had grabbed him by the throat with one hand and had pinned him to the tiled wall and was about to pound on him with a fist the size of a football when Gavin had entered the showers. Unfazed, he'd said, "I don't believe the Big Man would like that."

That was all it took to scatter the four men away, just the mention of a person he'd never met or heard of before, who wasn't even there, locked up with them at Florida State in Raiford.

Gavin had helped him out of the shower and said little on the way back to his cell. There, he sat on the bed and threw Mark a critical look. "You'll need a tattoo on your neck to survive in here. I'll arrange that. And some pills that will help with that," he'd said, pointing at Mark's trembling hands.

No one touched him since that day, threatened him, or even looked at him sideways, the only real break he'd caught since that fated accident that got him addicted to opiates a few years before. Two days later, he was sporting a new tattoo that established his affiliation with a well-known, powerful Florida gang, and Gavin's magical pills had taken his withdrawal ills away overnight. On his way to becoming sober and with a real chance to survive his sentence, he wondered when the piper would have to be paid. No one did anyone any favors for free in jail; the usual payment was in blood.

About a month later, a rather scrawny inmate approached him, while five others kept a respectful distance. He had a tall forehead and hollow eyes, with pronounced brow ridges. He didn't introduce himself, but later, Mark had learned people referred to him as Mr. Erwin.

"Aquila sends his regards," Mr. Erwin had said in a low, conspirative tone. The pitch of his voice was unusually high, even if he spoke softly.

"Who?" Mark had asked. He'd never heard the moniker before.

"People who don't have the privilege of belonging to his inner circle only know him as the Big Man."

"Ah." That explained everything, except how he'd made it in the powerful individual's inner circle when he didn't even know who he really was. "Please thank him for—everything." He raised his arms in a gesture of gratitude.

"He'll be glad to hear you feel this way. There will come a time when he'll need a favor from you." Mr. Erwin approached him even more and planted a firm hand on his shoulder, then whispered in his ear. "Whatever he asks, don't hesitate for a moment to make Aquila happy." He withdrew a few inches. "You'll be a made man for life." Mr. Erwin never smiled.

A jolt of fear stabbed Mark in the gut. There it was, the payday he'd fearfully anticipated. He nodded, his mouth too dry to articulate any words, not that anything came to mind at the time. But the conversation had ended then, and nothing was asked of him while he was jailed. Mr. Erwin left the prison soon after that, although he'd served fewer than thirty days.

Surprisingly, his name was on an early parole list, and he suspected the mighty Aquila was behind that as well. It shaved more than three years of his sentence, and when he finally walked out through the prison gates, he swore to himself he'd never break the law again.

That was his good intention, but the road to hell was paved with them, wider than the interstate.

Gavin had suggested a place for him to stay, where they would take parolees. Lacking other options, he went there and found the rent was paid in advance for a year. Then his parole officer came to visit. She was about thirty years old, her hair tight in a nape bun and her glasses thick-rimmed. Her beady eyes studied the small apartment critically, but she didn't say much; she just scrutinized everything, hands behind her back, like an Army sergeant. Then she'd said, "Get yourself a job and report to me when you have it. This will help you get started. Don't even think of getting high; I'll test you every two weeks." She deposited a thick envelope on the kitchen counter and left without saying another word.

For long minutes after his parole officer had left, he stared at the envelope, afraid to touch it, as if opening it would unleash some unseen evil. But evil had already taken hold of him the moment he'd moved into the paid apartment, the moment the woman had left the envelope with him. The moment Gavin had intervened in his favor in the prison showers.

Twenty thousand dollars and nothing demanded of him in return except to stay sober and clean.

For days, he continued waiting for Aquila's orders, but nothing came. Petrified in fear, he didn't leave the apartment, didn't look for work, and spent as little money as he could, buying only the cheapest food and paying the utility bills. But Aquila didn't call.

He didn't for years, but when he did, he had a tall order, delivered calmly and sternly by Mr. Erwin.

He was to kidnap the district attorney's daughter and wait for instructions once he had the kid. He was supposed to fake a ransom call then not show up to pick up the money, the call being nothing but a divertive tactic, something to throw the feds off the scent of Aquila's real intentions.

Neither Aquila nor Mr. Erwin had shared the end goal of the operation, but Mark wasn't some idiot. It had to be related to one of the cases the DA was prosecuting; otherwise, why kidnap the DA's child if the ransom call was supposed to be for nothing? But he knew better than to ask the dangerously calm Mr. Erwin, who'd visited the seedy Upper Eastside neighborhood dressed in an Armani suit and driving a Mercedes-AMG GT four-door coupe in electric blue. No one would've touched him, Aquila's clout ensuring his safe passage everywhere he went.

Mark had a deadline; he was to take the girl before the end of the week. Mr. Erwin hadn't mentioned what would happen if Mark failed, but it wasn't something he needed to ask. Just thinking of it ran chills throughout his body, as if his blood had turned to icicles and no amount of cheap booze could warm it up.

The next day, still shuddering, he was stalking the girl's school in a car he picked up from a used car lot for less than two grand. It was a beat-up, green Honda minivan that looked good on the outside but had a crack in the engine block and burned through oil, leaving bluish smoke behind everywhere it went. But the minivan fit nicely on a school street, and no one gave it a second look.

He watched the kids leave the school in rowdy bunches, getting loaded in school busses that pulled to the curb, Paige Joyce one of them. He couldn't get close enough to grab her; the school was not an option, and he was running out of alternatives. He decided to wait and trail the school bus she'd climbed into all the way to her house; he waited patiently for endless hordes of kids to come out of the school.

That's when he saw Gavin, although he barely recognized him. He'd cleaned up nicely, clean-shaven and dressed neatly in a suit only a size too large for him, carrying a briefcase and a pleasant smile on his face.

That afternoon, instead of trailing the school bus, he followed Gavin all the way to the marina, where he lived in a houseboat at the far end, where the light was dim and few people ever ventured.

He'd turned ice-cold when he saw Mark approaching his houseboat, and for a long, embarrassing moment, pretended not to know Mark.

"Oh, come on, Gav, I won't blow your cover," Mark eventually said, standing in front of the houseboat and the still, pale owner of it. "Permission to come aboard?" he'd quipped.

"Yeah, whatever," Gavin had replied, then invited Mark in with a hand gesture.

"When did you get out?"

That's how their relationship had resumed, after a couple of years of hiatus. After Mark had sworn on his soul, he'd never burn Gavin's carefully constructed persona. He wouldn't, not for anything, not in a million years, because any man who managed to make a life for himself after serving time deserved a chance.

Gavin had stolen an identity; it belonged to some poor veteran dying in the hospital where he was admitted for surgery. His wallet was handy, and the opportunity too good to skip. That man wasn't going to miss it where he was going, and Gavin needed the money, the identity, everything he didn't have and desperately required to survive. He'd entered that hospital bent over and groaning in pain, as Gavin Martinez, a forty-six-year-old ex-con with a long rap sheet for B&E, assault, possession, and a bad case of acute appendicitis. He left two days later as Michael Brannan, a forty-two-year-old commended veteran, honorably discharged after twenty years of service and drawing a pension. The surprises continued when he found he now owned a houseboat and a certification as a teacher.

No, Mark would never damage Gavin's new, shiny persona. Without him, he would've been the mistress of any number of gangbangers in the joint. He'd saved his life back then, and he could save it again.

Only Gavin wasn't interested in helping him pull the job. Not until Mark mentioned the Big Man. He didn't mention Aquila by name because Gavin obviously wasn't part of the inner circle like he was, or he would've known it already. Even so, he showed no genuine interest until Mark mentioned the job involved an eight-year-old girl, at which point Gavin's eyes flickered with interest. Disgusted, Mark swore to himself he'd keep an eye on Gavin at all times and wished he could've done away with him one moonless night out at sea. He hated nothing more than pedophiles, and he'd met his share of the leeches behind bars. But the fact was, he still needed Gavin's help.

Yes, he was testing his patience with his snoring, his disgusting habits, and the way he veered from the plan at every juncture, but Mark couldn't handle everything alone. Maybe Randi would prove her usefulness too; they were stuck with her anyway. If for no other reason, she could at least keep an eye on

Gavin and make sure he didn't do anything stupid. Or touch that girl.

Aquila would hang him by his balls if anything went wrong with his plan. If he screwed up, there would be no saving him this time.

There was only one problem, one that seeded icicles in Mark's blood. Aquila never said it was okay to collect the ransom or bring a partner into the game.

Now he had two.

12

MAX

Fifteen hours missing

Miriam took a large step forward and slammed Tess against the wall, both her hands firmly clasping her shirt. "What the hell aren't you telling me, huh?" Her voice was high-pitched and brittle, tears rolling down her cheeks as her eyes drilled into hers mercilessly. "Tell me!"

Deeply resenting the woman's aggression and the way she felt being pinned against the wall, Tess willed herself to remain calm. Miriam wasn't a perp who deserved to have her arm twisted behind her back and a felony charge for assaulting an officer. She was just a desperate parent who had overheard pieces of only one side of a conversation and felt betrayed, vulnerable, lost.

"Listen, I don't know what you might've heard—"

"Irrelevant?" she shrieked. "My daughter could become irrelevant and be killed?" She shoved Tess again, just as Donovan and Max rushed out of the house and pulled her away. "Who speaks like that about a little girl? What kind of monster are you?" She writhed in their grip until Tess stopped them with a hand gesture and an unspoken no in her glance at Donovan.

"Why don't we sit down inside? I'll explain everything you need to know," Tess spoke calmly, reassuringly, but the woman needed much more than that to be convinced. Her arm still gripped in Max's hand, she followed Tess reluctantly into the living room and sat down by her husband's side. He let go of her arm and took her hand instead, but she wasn't paying any attention to him, her eyes still riveted on Tess, brimming with tears. She sat on the edge of the sofa cushion as if getting ready to run or pounce.

"Please, don't lie to me," she asked, "I can't take it anymore. I—I just can't."

"I'm not lying," Tess replied, cringing as she realized just how defensive her words sounded. "We're exploring scenarios, possibilities, that's all."

She looked at Tess in saddened disbelief, as if disappointed by her lies. Miriam didn't believe a word she was saying.

"We think your daughter might've been taken because of a case your husband might be working on, that's all."

Blood drained from her face. "What case?" Miriam's voice was barely a whisper.

"We don't know yet." Tess saw the doubt in her eyes. "I promise you we don't know. It's just a theory at this point, nothing more. Whenever the family of a judge, DA, or juror are targeted, it's only logical to consider the potential correlation with the cases they're working on."

Miriam lowered her head and pulled her hand out of Max's. She seemed defeated, her thin shoulders heaving with every sob, poking through the fabric of her terry bathrobe. She clasped her hands together tightly, wringing them until her knuckles turned white. "The only good thing that ever came out of that man was Paige," she whispered.

Tess approached her and crouched by her side, trying to make eye contact. She reached out and squeezed her hand. "You need to get some rest, and we need to work. Please understand

and let us do our job." A whimper was her only response. "Waiting for that ransom call is probably the hardest thing you'll ever have to do in your entire life, but we're not sitting on our hands. We have several leads we're following. We just need time, and you need to rest, to be ready for whatever they throw our way."

"I can't sleep," she muttered, as if in a trance. She was dissociating, her brain too weary and hurt to withstand reality.

"Just lie down," Max pleaded, taking her arm and leading her toward the back of the house. Max threw Tess a reassuring look and disappeared into the bedroom with her.

Tess straightened her shirt and groaned when she noticed a torn buttonhole. She needed a safety pin but didn't have one.

"Now that's something you don't see every day," Donovan said, keeping his voice low. "Agent Winnett pushed around, and the doer lived to tell the story."

Tess looked at him, frowning. "You know, D, this might be one of the reasons why you don't make field agent. You're not twelve anymore, for crying out loud." Seeing how her words might've been too harsh, she added, "That said, I'm safe to assume no word of this incident will make it back into the field office. Right?" She smiled and was glad to see Donovan smiling back.

"Mum's the word, Winnett."

She pulled out a chair and sat across from him at the dining room table, tension replacing the brief smile with clenched jaws and an obsessive time check. Paige had been gone for almost sixteen hours. "Show me what you have."

"The only thing so far is the tow truck at the DA's parking garage. It was a routine call, recorded as such on the dispatcher's logs. The particular truck that went out was her decision, not anyone else's, and had to do with the trucks available at the time." Donovan scratched the roots of his hair. "Trying to control that would be, like, impossible."

"So, what are you saying? That the broken chain or whatever it was on that truck was a coincidence? I'm not buying that for a second."

"Me neither. I asked the boss for help, and he sent SA Patto to interview the driver. He just reported back that while on-site, the driver had been called away for a few minutes, leaving the truck inside the garage, to deal with some bogus paperwork at the front gate. When he came back and resumed work loading up the busted vehicle, that's when the chain broke."

Her eyes lit up. "That's how they did it. It takes a mere minute to spray liquid nitrogen on a chain and hit it with a hammer. It will break like it's made of glass and leave no trace."

"Precisely." Satisfied, Donovan rapped his fingers against the table as if playing the drums. "Patto spoke with the garage attendant, who remembers seeing a double-dipping, ride-hailing driver lurking nearby."

"Double-dipping?"

"Uber and Lyft. The vehicle the man saw had both logos displayed on his windshield. Patto just texted me he's bringing him in, to work with a sketch artist."

Tess cupped her chin in her hand, intrigued. "So, if DA Joyce had abandoned his blocked car and decided to call for a ride instead, he would've landed with one of the crew, huh?"

"Seems that way, yes."

"What if he would've called a regular cab company?"

Donovan shrugged. "No idea. Do you want me to follow up with his office, see who they normally used? Maybe the unsub found out somehow."

"I wonder if he's an Uber guy, our Mr. Joyce," Tess muttered, then refocused. "What else?"

Donovan didn't reply. Instead, he looked at something behind her. She turned and found Max standing by her chair. He seemed tired, drawn, and still wore the same clothes he'd worn all night. The white shirt was unbuttoned at the collar, and his tie loosened, both stained with smudges of Miriam's makeup and tears.

"She's finally resting," he said, lowering his shoulders a bit as if his arms had become too heavy to carry around. He pulled a chair by Tess's side and leaned against the table. "What can I help with, Agent Winnett? What do you need to know to find out who took our little girl?"

Outside of some basic information she could've obtained from state records, she knew very little about Miriam, Paige, and DA Joyce, about their families, their ties with other people, their friends, and potential enemies. "Tell me about Paige. What's she like?"

His eyes lit up, and a warm smile tugged at his lips. "She's an amazing little girl. As you know, she's not biologically mine, but I'm grateful to be her stepdad. Miriam doesn't want to have any more children, and I'm okay with that because Paige is an amazing daughter." He paused for a beat, staring over Tess's shoulder into the distance. "She's very bright, sometimes obstinate, and learns very quickly. She's playful and resilient." His eyes clouded with sadness. "She has what it takes to survive this, Agent Winnett, but I'm still worried. She—" His voice broke, and his eyes pooled with tears. He inhaled abruptly, willing the tears away. "She should never know this kind of traumatizing hardship. It will change who she is, possibly forever."

"Kids are strong," Tess replied, wondering if strong meant they could survive being held hostage without developing some kind of post-traumatic stress. She knew firsthand how that felt, how it changed one's life completely, how nothing was ever the same again, as if a dark cloud permanently dimmed the sun. "How about Miriam's divorce? Do you know anything about how that came to be?"

He smiled with bitterness, his eyes veering to the side, seeming ashamed. "It was quite simple, the way my wife told me. When Paige was about one year old, Miriam came home from the pharmacy for lunch and found a stranger in the shower. She was tempted to grab her by the hair and throw her out of the house wet and butt naked." He chuckled, but sadness tinged his voice. "Knowing Miriam, I totally believe she would've done that. Apparently, Darrel intervened, and she threw both of them out of the house that day, albeit fully clothed." He rubbed the root of his nose with two fingers, closing his eyes while at it. "Must have been a terrible heartbreak for Miriam; I can only imagine." He lifted his eyes and looked at Tess with a hint of pride in his gaze. "The next day, she filed for divorce; didn't waste any time."

"She's determined, isn't she?" Tess asked.

He nodded, a hint of pride lingering in his smile.

"How about her family? Have you met them?"

"At the wedding, yes." He cleared his voice and squinted as if trying to remember. "Her brother lives in Texas, and they rarely speak. When he was a teenager, something happened; I don't recall exactly what, he did something wrong. Their mother was mad at him, and Miriam agreed with her, but only to some extent."

"When's the last time they spoke?"

"Um, not in the last year, maybe even two." He frowned, thinking. "Could be more than that. Miriam gets upset when they talk. She feels the family was too harsh with him for whatever it was he'd done, but then he was also too proud to forgive his parents and come home. Every time she tries to reconcile them and begs him to come back, he ends up hanging up on her, and she ends up in tears."

There was nothing there. "How about you?" Tess asked. "Do you have any enemies?" His eyebrows shot up. "Would anyone have anything to gain if they blackmailed you?"

He shook his head. "I'm an architect; I don't hold anything of value in my office, and I can't think of anything anyone would kidnap Paige for. I lead the city zoning team, but I don't have a single zoning change request open right now."

Tess gazed at the man silently for a long moment. "Well, let me know if that changes out of the blue."

He nodded, then stood and started pacing the floor, staring out the window. After a few loaded moments, he stopped in front of Tess and asked, "When will they call with their demands?"

13

LIABILITIES

The cramped living room was silent. Sunshine came in through the windows facing the ocean, revealing the dust particles swirling through the stale air that smelled of dirty socks and leftovers. The piece of trash that had blown in the night before was fast asleep in Mark's stained recliner. Even in her slumber, Randi held on to her phone, tightly clasping the bejeweled pink case with thin, grimy fingers. The locked screen showed alerts for several missed messages and calls.

Mark had checked on the girl twice since the break of dawn, but she wasn't awake yet. Her breathing was fine, but the fact that she wasn't waking up worried him. As far as he knew, ketamine overdoses led to a slew of symptoms, but once she'd fallen asleep, the only visible symptom would've been slowed breathing. Hers seemed fine.

Gavin drew closer to him, filling Mark's nostrils with the stench of sweat and yesterday's booze. Mornings had a strange effect on Gavin; it was as if the rising sun brought clarity to his mind, a sense of decency even, that completely disappeared by nightfall. Or maybe it was alcohol turning his partner into an irrational and impulsive slob.

As soon as he'd awakened, Gavin had thrown the room a critical look, his stare lingering for a long moment on Randi's face as he sucked his teeth and crinkled his nose in disgust. Then he picked up the trash and dirty laundry littering the room, moving quickly and efficiently. At the end of three minutes, it almost seemed livable again.

He still needed a shower, though, just as badly as Mark needed a shave and a trim of his goatee that now tickled his nose every time he spoke. He scratched his upper lip, then touched the tattoo on his neck; he'd been doing that a lot lately, every time he thought of Aquila and what his future might hold if he screwed up the job, as if the eagle drawn on his skin in prison ink held all the answers.

Heads close together, both men were looking at the laptop screen, set on the small table they almost never used for dining. Gavin flipped through several views on an application that managed all the feeds from the video cameras he had installed until he stopped on the one hidden in the AC vent inside the security office at the theater.

On the low-resolution view, they saw two men who, in their turn, were staring at computer screens. The one standing was the theater manager, that arrogant know-it-all, Brassfield. The man sitting in front of the keyboard was not someone Mark or Gavin had met before, but he had to be some technician or analyst or something like that; the man typed so quickly they couldn't even see his fingers touching the keys, just a blur of movement above the keyboard.

Several stills taken from last night's surveillance recordings were displayed, all of them showing the burgundy Subaru from various angles. An image taken as Gavin had rolled up the Subaru at the curb and Paige had climbed into the car was zoomed in and focused on his blurry face on the center screen. That was probably the moment he'd come closest to the surveillance camera, and it had happened at a time when he had to focus on the girl, on persuading her to climb inside the vehicle.

It wasn't Gavin's fault.

Every few seconds, the man behind the keyboard typed something on a control panel, and the image refreshed with difficulty, line after line of processed pixels appearing slowly on the screen. But with each round of processing, the image gained clarity and contrast.

Soon, they'd have enough for a facial recognition match. Since Gavin was an ex-con, his mug was in the system, and they'd be onto him faster than a speeding bullet. His partner was becoming a huge liability.

Unmanaged, the situation could unravel quickly. One thing cops always did when investigating ex-cons was to run their known associates from their time behind bars. From identifying Gavin to figuring out that Mark was part of the kidnapping job would probably be a whole ten minutes or less.

Then he'd really be screwed, on the lam from the cops and Aquila, with zero chances of survival.

"You have to go back," he said, keeping his voice low to not awaken Randi, his other liability.

"You're kidding me right now?" Gavin stood and propped his hands on his hips. "I can't go back, not after the girl's vanished."

"They don't know it's you, Gav, but soon they'll figure it out. Unless you're there, to talk them out of what they're doing, to manage this somehow."

"Oh, so I'm supposed to waltz right into that theater and tell them, 'Boys, drop what you're doing because...' Because what, Mark? What the hell do you think I can say to them?"

"You'll think of something." There wasn't a better actor than Gavin that Mark had ever seen, in real life or on the big screen. The moment he stepped into character, he was believable, and it all came naturally to him. He wasn't the slob he knew well, not the moment he stepped out of the houseboat. Showered and well-dressed, he wore his head up high and smiled, that reassured smile of the man who's always in control, who's never bothered by small things, who people love to follow.

He dropped his hands from his hips and crossed his arms at his chest, biting his upper lip. "All right, I'll go. I'll tell them I recognize the guy or something, send them on a wild goose chase." He didn't seem too convinced, but with Gavin, it was a process. It took time until he wrote the script for the part he was going to play. "I'll tell them I left my phone there last night. That will open the doors for me."

Mark smiled and patted Gavin on the shoulder. "Attaboy."

The man frowned. "Screw you. I have no idea why the Big Man chose you for this job. You ain't got nothin' on me."

"Next time you see him, why don't you ask him?" Mark elbowed Gavin and cackled. Randi shifted in her sleep, muttering something unintelligible.

"What about her?" Gavin asked. "Do you think those homies of hers are real?"

Mark shrugged. "Real or not, she could've dialed nine-one-one, and we'd be toast right about now. But she wants money, and when people want money, they're the kind of people I like. You know why?" Gavin scrunched his face but didn't reply. "Because I can understand them. I can relate to them." He cringed, thinking of what he was about to say; it was almost true, and that disturbed him deeply. "You and I are the same, Gav."

Gavin looked at Mark for a moment as if to wonder if he was still sane. "Be careful with her, bro. She's nothing like us. She's a crackhead who just wants a fix and would kill for it. There's a difference."

That difference Mark knew painfully well. As Gavin spoke, the urge to feel that drug-induced high again had him grinding his teeth while beads of sweat emerged at the roots of his hair. "You're right. You go there," he pointed at the screen, "and manage this fucking mess. When you return, we'll make the ransom call."

14

LEADS

Nineteen hours missing

Since Tess and Donovan had gained access to DA Joyce's caseload, they'd been buried. Yet, every few minutes, Tess glanced at the two open call tracking briefcases and the phones connected to them.

Why weren't the kidnappers calling already?

Any unsub who took someone for a quick payday would be eager to get the money and run, be done with it, and out of danger. Holding people hostage was not an easy feat; they fought, they could be seen or heard screaming for help, they posed countless risks and challenges. Children were the most challenging from that perspective. Numerous people would ignore an ad about a missing forty-year-old but would see the face of a milk carton child everywhere they looked, and that's why AMBER Alerts worked because people's DNA is hard-wired to care about the young.

The AMBER Alert for Paige had generated few calls, all false alarms. That didn't worry Tess too much; the unsub team was so well organized, she didn't anticipate they'd allow anyone to see Paige or make any of the common mistakes inexperienced perps made, like sudden changes in established routines without a change in location, drinking and telling at the local pub, or—Tess's absolute favorite—braggart postings on social media.

Time was slipping by, dangerously close to the dreaded twenty-four-hour milestone, beyond which the statistics turned grim quickly. After she'd seen the note left by the unsub, she'd been confident the case would end with a positive outcome. Now, she wasn't so sure anymore. The unsub's behavior didn't fit; a crucial piece of the puzzle was still missing.

Swallowing a curse, she focused on the laptop screen, ready to sift through DA Joyce's caseload. After Pearson had reluctantly given his tacit approval, Donovan had accessed the cases without notifying the Department of Justice, using his unofficial hacking skills. Tess feared that if the DA was targeted and the DOJ learned about the kidnapping, it would throw a wrench in the gears of the entire operation. She hated to admit it, but she didn't know what to believe. Was the unsub after ransom dollars? Or was this a ploy to force the DA to do something about one of his cases? There wasn't enough evidence or data to reach a conclusion; only time would tell, and time was running out fast for Paige. The thought of that little girl held in whatever hole those unsubs had crawled out of made her sick to the stomach.

"Your man Joyce is one busy district attorney," Donovan quipped, earning himself a frown and a scowl from Tess.

"He's not my man."

"He's your biggest fan," Donovan pushed back calmly. "How many special agents can claim they've been requested by name like superstars?"

She just glared at him. "Show me the cases."

He pushed his laptop closer to her. "Most of his cases are drug-related. His team handles the possessions with and without intent to distribute. He keeps for himself the big ones, the major busts, the network leaders, and any possession case over one kilo." He shot her a quick look. "There are surprisingly many of those. It makes you think about how much of this poison is out there on the streets."

The list of case numbers was long, each name linked to the actual case file he'd already extracted and structured for review.

"He's got a couple of murder cases, an aggravated manslaughter, four sexual assault cases including a serial rapist, an aggravated kidnapping, and a RICO case." He paused for a moment as if giving her the time to process. "Which ones of these upstanding citizens would have had the stones to pull something like kidnapping the DA's daughter?"

She reached for the mouse and took it, sliding it over to her left hand.

"You're a leftie?" Donovan smiled.

"Ambidextrous." She clicked on a few of the drug case numbers, and quickly reviewed the status notes, displayed neatly with the username of the person who had entered the information in the system. "Most of these drug cases are small-timers who couldn't even post bail for themselves, so low down in the structure no one worried too much about them turning state's evidence and rattling up the food chain." She exited the drug case list and moved over to the homicides. As she'd anticipated, the aggravated manslaughter was an impaired driving vehicular homicide. A drunk driver lost control of his truck and killed an elderly man on the sidewalk. One of the murders was a burglary gone wrong, the other a mugging where the victim had fought back until the perp had hit him in the head with the butt of his gun and left him bleeding on the sidewalk. Both perps were repeat offenders who didn't look like they had the brainpower or the clout to organize a team like the unsubs they were looking for.

She skipped the sexual assault case list and hovered above the RICO.

"What about these?" Donovan asked, pointing at the list of four case numbers she'd skipped.

"Any of these perps would've kidnapped, intimidated, or eliminated their victims. Sexual assault cases are simple that way; without the victim's testimony, the case falls apart quickly."

"Then it's the RICO case," he stated convincingly as if he'd just uncovered evidence beyond any reasonable doubt to that fact. "It makes sense."

"It does," Tess admitted. "Everything we know so far about the unsubs points to the level of sophistication you encounter in organized crime. It fits." She frowned. It was too simple and, at the same time, immensely complicated.

She clicked on the case number and started reading, occasionally highlighting sections of text she wanted Donovan to pay attention to.

The Racketeer Influenced and Corrupt Organizations charge had been brought against a known crime lord, who'd never before been prosecuted before, by the name of Allan Curtis Mitchell. He was fifty-nine. He was charged with ordering two witnesses killed in the racketeering trial of his son, Edward. Mitchell's organization was vast and reached deep into the city's underbelly, rumored to have a finger in everything from drug trade to human trafficking to protection rackets skimming from countless restaurants and bars along the coast.

Out of all of DA Joyce's cases, that one was the only one that fit.

That was bad news.

With a long sigh, she abandoned the mouse on the table and crossed her arms at her chest. Infiltrating an organized crime network took months, if not years, of deep undercover work, time Paige Joyce didn't have.

"Now what?" Donovan asked.

She didn't get to answer, not that she had an answer anyway. Her phone chimed, and she spent a few seconds reading a message marked urgent.

This is Francis Brassfield. One of the teachers said he recognized the man in the surveillance feed and named a former janitor at the school who was recently fired. Please advise.

Finally, a break, although the janitor didn't fit the profile of a highly organized, professional abduction team. He could've been the unsubs' way in, though. He would've known his way around the teaching staff and could've known Miriam enough to pick her out from the theater crowd. Paige could've recognized him behind the wheel, and a well-spun lie could've persuaded her to climb into the car with him. Maybe the poor fellow was already fish food after having served his purpose, but it was a strong lead worth pursuing.

Feeling the adrenaline rush through her veins, she quickly typed a reply for Brassfield.

Mr. Brassfield, thank you for your help. Please ask the teacher to wait and give a formal statement to Agent Patto. He's on his way.

Then she texted Patto and, within seconds, got the confirmation he was rushing over to the theater to interview the witness. She breathed deeply, realizing she'd been holding air in her lungs for a while. Yet there was something undefined unfurling in her gut, something she'd felt some time ago right before stepping on a snake during a walk through the Everglades National Park.

Instinct.

A chime disrupted her introspection. It came from Donovan's computer and resounded loudly in the silent house.

"Hey, BOLO came back," he announced cheerfully. "They found the Subaru."

"Where did they find it?"

"In a parking lot on NE First Street. The parking attendant reported it abandoned."

Tess grinned. "I'm willing to bet there are no cameras anywhere near that parking lot. It's a short ride from the theater, makes sense." She stood, anxious to hit the road and start following the janitor lead, maybe even discover what caused the lingering uneasiness in her gut.

He leaned closer to the screen to read the annoyingly small font of the notification. "They recovered some evidence, and they're sending it here."

"What evidence?"

Donovan shrugged and loosened his tie. "The note only says you need to look at it with the family."

"All right," she replied, pacing the room impatiently. Why weren't they calling already? Waiting while that little girl was out there stretched her nerves to the point of snapping. She'd never been good at waiting or letting other people run the show she was cast in. Pearson was right; she lacked patience and had too much sense of urgency, if such a thing even existed. She was sure Paige didn't mind her exacerbated drive to bring her home, and neither did Miriam and her husband.

Removing the clip that held her hair back, she loosened and shook it, ran her fingers through it like a comb massaging her achy scalp, then tied it back tightly with the same clip.

"Come on, already," she muttered, staring at her watch for the tenth time in just as many minutes. Unable to sit still any longer, she rushed to the door, staring through the beveled glass until a white sedan displaying the USPS logo stopped in front of it. She recognized it; the sedan was an actual Postal Service vehicle the feds occasionally borrowed when they needed to make pickups and deliveries without raising red flags if the house was being watched by unsubs.

She unlocked the door before the agent had a chance to ring the bell and went through the entire charade of signing for the package, wrapped and stamped neatly as any legit postal delivery would've been. It was small, light, and rattled as if a loose object bounced against the box. She thanked the agent, then closed the door and rushed to the dining room table. There, she unsealed the package and pulled out a sealed evidence pouch that contained a small, silver crescent moon. At one of the ends of the crescent, a little eye seemed bent as if it had been torn from a chain by twisting it.

"We need Miriam." She walked briskly toward the bedroom, then knocked gently on the door. "Mrs. Walsh?" she called through the door. It opened immediately as if the woman had been waiting by the door for her signal.

Her eyes were swollen and red; she'd probably wept the entire time, unable to rest. Yet she stood straight, her chin thrust forward, a stern look of determination on her face. She was ready for whatever needed to be done and wanted everyone to know it.

She searched Tess's eyes with an unspoken question.

"They found your car, and there was something in it I'm hoping you might identify."

She followed Tess to the dining room table. When she saw the evidence pouch, she covered her mouth with her hand to stifle a sob.

"It's from my daughter's charm bracelet," she whispered between sobs. "She loves this bracelet so much, she won't take it off no matter what, not even at bath time." She sniffled and took the pouch in her hand, her thin fingers touching the object through the plastic as if to caress it. "Max has to clean it every now and then because it gets tarnished from the soapy water and stains her skin. It's sterling silver."

"Do you have a picture of it?" Tess asked, wondering how difficult it might've been to tear that charm off the bracelet. Had Paige been roughed up? Held by her wrists, causing it to fall?

Miriam fished her phone from her bathrobe pocket and sifted through the photos quickly. "There." The photo showed a wet-haired Paige wearing a swimsuit, grinning gleefully in the sun, and holding her hand out to show off the bracelet. The charm chain links were thick enough to last on an eight-year-old, active girl's wrist.

"She was wearing it in the pool?" Tess asked.

"In the pool, everywhere." Miriam wiped a tear from the corner of her eye. "She grew out of it, and we had it extended; she wouldn't stop crying." She touched the crescent moon again. "I made up a poem for her when she turned four, and I gave that to her on her birthday." Her eyes brimmed with fresh tears. She veered her gaze away for a moment and breathed, willing herself to stop crying. "It goes like this." She closed her eyes while her chin trembled. "The sun and the moon / In the month of June. / The lion and the unicorn / My little girl adorn. / The owl and the dog / Keep watch in the fog. / The monkey and the sheep / Watch my baby sleep. / Good night moon / We'll see mommy soon." She reached for the box of tissues on the far end of the table and pulled one, tapping her eyes with it. "It's not much, but it made her happy."

"So, the sun is the first charm in the poem?" Tess asked, wondering if it had been lost by accident or left in the car on purpose by a smart little girl who'd just played the leading part in Hansel and Gretel.

Miriam's eyes focused on Tess, intense, analytical, as if an idea had flashed through her mind. "It's because of the ending," she said, her voice no longer brittle but hopeful. "When I made up the poem for her, it used to be, 'We'll see you all soon,' but she didn't like it. She wanted mommy in there." Emotion fluttered over her face, shuddering her breath. "I think she's sending me a message." She clasped the evidence pouch in her hand. "It's a breadcrumb."

15

STANDOFF

Only Gavin could pull a bold stunt like that; he was one in a million.

Mark had watched his performance via the spycam feed on his laptop, breathlessly observing every move he made, his body language, the words he spoke that Mark couldn't hear. Some he could lip-read when Gavin faced the spycam, perhaps on purpose. Even without sound, the images were more than enough to remind Mark why he needed him.

He seemed casual, leaning against the doorsill and shooting the breeze with the theater manager for a while as if the entire day belonged to him with nothing better to do. For his character, that rang true; he was supposed to be the teacher who'd forgot his phone the night before, in the frenzy of everything that had happened. He must've been convincing because he disappeared for a while from the manager's office and returned moments later with his phone in hand and a wide grin on his face.

Then he seemed interested in what was on the security screens. He observed one closely, then pointed his finger at the man behind the wheel. "I think I recognize this man," Mark read on Gavin's lips.

The manager bought it. So did his security guy. Completely ignoring the man standing right in front of them, smiling confidently, who could've easily been the driver in the video.

That was Gavin's unique talent.

Then Mark started losing his patience when Gavin didn't leave the theater as discussed. Why was he lingering? Was he looking for trouble? When a fourth man appeared, showing an FBI badge, Mark's blood turned to ice. His shallow, raspy breaths marked each movement he observed on the screen as the fed interrogated Gavin. Yet his partner seemed unfazed, patiently answering questions, then thanking the fed and finally leaving.

Only then, Mark breathed fully, his lungs craving air, his entire body reeling from the fear.

He abandoned the laptop, deciding it was time to see how the girl was doing. The crackhead started to shift more often in her restless sleep; she was about to wake up. Her face was covered in sweat, something he remembered well, when every new day meant withdrawal, just for the taste of it, just for a few hours until he could get another fix. Even if the day started well in the afternoon.

Moving quietly, he went to the back of the houseboat where the girl was locked inside a windowless room and opened the door. The air was stale, and the dim light didn't allow him to see much. He flipped on the ceiling fixture switch and looked at the girl.

She lay on her side, her wrists and ankles bound tightly, the dirty scarf used as a blindfold wrapped twice around her head and secured with a double knot above her right ear. When Mark stepped inside the room and closed the door, the girl's feet twitched.

She was awake.

He stopped by the side of the mattress, frowning. Never in his wildest nightmares had he envisioned he'd end up like that, taking a child and partnering with a closet pedophile and a junkie. If he got caught, they'd lock him up and throw away the key; he'd never see the light of day again. The fact that he had no choice wouldn't soften a single juror's death glare.

Tears were escaping from underneath the scarf, soaked where it touched the girl's face. She'd been crying for a while, silently, probably scared out of her mind. Gently, he touched her shoulder.

She whimpered and tried to pull back. "Please, don't hurt me." Her voice was a brittle, tear-filled whisper.

"I won't hurt you, kid," he replied, also whispering. He'd read somewhere that voices can be easily recognized, but whispers can't. "Are you hungry?"

The girl held her breath, then sniffled. "A little."

"Do you need to use the bathroom?"

She nodded, sending ripples through the long, curly, red hair that escaped from underneath the scarf, clinging to the fabric of her white shirt. He helped her sit on the side of the mattress. She jumped out of her skin when he touched her, every time.

He stared at the plastic ties cutting into her flesh and muttered a curse. That animal, Gavin, must've been thrilled to pull those cable ties so tightly; it seemed that inflicting pain on little girls did something for him. Mark struggled with the urge to spit on the floor, to clear the taste left in his mouth by the thought of Gavin having his way with that girl. Then he reached inside his pocket and fished out a small wire cutter. With one swift move, he snipped the cable tie that bound the girl's wrists right below the silver charm bracelet she wore on her right hand.

"Thank you," she whispered, surprising him. She rubbed her wrists gently, wincing.

"Promise you won't do anything stupid."

"I promise," she replied, her voice tinged with fear and loaded with tears.

"All right." He cut the ankle tie and grabbed her forearm. The plastic had done less damage to her feet; she wore jeans and white socks, shielding her skin from the cutting edges of the cable ties. "Let's take you to the bathroom."

"Where are you taking that kid?" Randi's hoarse voice startled Mark.

"Shit, woman, don't sneak up on me like that." He cleared his constricted throat. "She needs to pee."

Randi scoffed, then examined her fingernails for a brief moment. "Then, that's my job, don't you think?"

He stared at her, speechless. Then he scratched his head, considering his options. He would've preferred to not leave the girl alone with either of his freak partners, but it seemed more appropriate for a woman to take the girl to the bathroom. "Sure." He pointed at a door down the hallway. "It's in there."

Randi took the girl's hand and dragged her down the hallway, not caring much if she bumped into walls. Paige held her hand out in front of her, instinct telling her what to do to protect herself while she couldn't see.

Once at the bathroom, Randi opened the door and turned the light on, then off, and chuckled. "You won't be needing that anyway." She pushed the girl inside, then closed the door. Mark stared at her from the hallway. "What? You thought I was going to go in there with her? What's she gonna do? Escape through the toilet drain?" She whistled her visible amazement, then leaned against the wall and examined her fingernails critically, this time with a nail file in hand she'd fished out of her purse.

A loud and annoying ringtone disrupted the silence just as Gavin was unlocking the front door. Mark recognized the burner phone Mr. Erwin had given him, along with the instructions to never turn it off, always keep it charged, and never use it to call anyone else but him, and that only in emergencies. He took the phone out of his pocket and flipped it open, just as Randi muttered, "Two phones, what do you know? I wonder what that's about."

"Yes."

"You can make the ransom call now," Mr. Erwin said, his dry, high-pitched voice unmistakable. Then he ended the call without saying anything else.

Mark folded the flip phone and slid it in his pants pocket, then crossed his arms at his chest.

"Who was it?" Randi asked. Her tone was stern, low, menacing.

Gavin popped his head in the doorway with an inquisitive gaze. He seemed relaxed, satisfied.

"Wrong number."

The toilet flushed behind the closed door. Then the sink water started flowing.

A small, pink gun appeared in Randi's hand. "Try again." Her eyes were glassy, maniacal. Withdrawal was starting to take its toll.

"Whoa." Mark took a step back, holding his hands up in the air. "Take it easy there, sweetie. It was a wrong number, that's all."

"Did you make the ransom call yet?" Her lips were a sickly pale purple without makeup, her face stained with liver spots and acne scars. Yesterday's mascara gave her raccoon eyes, but she didn't seem to care.

"No. I was waiting for my partners to become available." The sarcasm in his voice was thick. "He just got back." Mark gestured toward Gavin.

"And where the hell were you?" Randi shifted her gun to point at Gavin.

"Easy there, sister. I was out getting food." He looked briefly at Mark. When Randi turned her attention to the

Walmart bags abandoned on the floor by the entrance, Gavin flipped his hand near his temple quickly, in a gesture that expressed his opinion of the woman.

Mark shrugged. That was what happened when things got out of control, and that was on him. He was the only one who knew the entire plan, although Gavin seemed to have a good idea where everything was headed. They should've done better work securing a safer location to hold the girl. The houseboat was convenient but had proven to be a huge mistake, one from which they couldn't step back.

Randi focused on him again. "Well, I'm available now. What the heck are you still waiting for? Make that call. I want my money."

Without notice, Gavin leaped and grabbed Randi's forearms, holding them in a vise, his knuckles white. She was no match for him; she was half his size, barely a hundred pounds. She whimpered, swore, and writhed for a while until she dropped the gun and Gavin's grip eased a bit. It bounced, clattering on the wooden floor, then settled behind the dirty laundry hamper.

"We got guns too, sister, and we know how to use them. How about we behave like civilized people instead of shooting each other?" Gavin jolted her to make his point, holding her in a tight grip with her back against his chest and her forearms locked in his strong hands.

Randi nodded, but her bloodshot eyes were shooting daggers of pure rage. She was dangerous, explosive, uncontrollable.

Mark picked up the gun and chuckled at the color of its handle. The lower end of the grip had rhinestones on it, but it was a nine-millimeter handgun, nevertheless, and a good one, a Smith & Wesson M&P9 Shield. Those went for at least three hundred on the street, five hundred if new. With that kind of bling on it, probably six. Maybe the junkie wasn't that desperate after all; only smart, fearless, and greedy.

He shoved the gun into his other pocket and went into the living room, and took a seat at the small table where his laptop was running. Then he looked at Gavin, who wasn't letting Randi out of his grip.

Feeling her way with her hands, Paige came out of the bathroom and stopped, unsure where to go. Shifting her weight from one foot to the other, she waited, trembling hands feeling the air around her, tears soaking the beige scarf.

Gavin let Randi go with a shove and grabbed Paige's arm firmly. The girl shrieked. "What the hell? Why is she free?" Dragging her along, he found a roll of duct tape in a kitchen drawer and taped the girl's mouth shut. Then he wrapped some tape around her wrists with harsh, angry gestures. Mark pushed him aside, inserting himself between him and the girl.

"Enough already. She's not going anywhere," he hissed in Gavin's ear. "There's no need for that."

His partner let go of the girl's arm with a glare and an oath. Mark clasped her bound hands and led her back to the room where she'd been held. He helped her sit on the mattress. She winced when he tried to push her down and resisted, muffled words coming through the duct tape.

"Please, I'll be good, I promise."

"It's better if you sleep," he whispered. "It will be over soon."

Then he left, closing the door behind him but leaving the light on.

Randi and Gavin were sizing each other up in the living room, staring at each other like two mad alley cats before a fight to the death, one with rage, the other with unspeakable contempt. Mark hoped he could control them just long enough to finish the job. Then maybe Aquila would let him leave and consider his debt squared away.

"All right, let's make the call."

16

RANSOM

Twenty-five hours missing

Tess paced the Walsh residence living room like a caged animal. The sun was about to set, the perfectly blue sky already tinted with hues of yellow and purple, but she didn't notice it beyond measuring the passing of time in many different ways. It was almost eight, and the dreaded twenty-four-hour milestone was a thing of the past. Why weren't they calling? Waiting for the phone to ring wasn't something she'd been accustomed to, mainly because she never had to do that before. The types of unsubs she'd chased weren't willing to return their victims, their intentions almost always lethal.

She wanted to be out there, interviewing the school's former janitor, revisiting the theater, and walking in the unsub's footsteps, timing how long it had taken him to enter the building, to reach Miriam, to subdue her, and to leave.

Instead, she had to let Patto do all that because she was stuck waiting by the phone. The first contact with the kidnappers could give her what she needed to start building a profile. Was the unsub team financially motivated? Or were they paid by Mitchell in an attempt to control the prosecutor assigned to his RICO case? Before she could answer that question, there was no profile, the difference between ransom kidnappings and organized crime significant and complex.

Ransom kidnappers were in it for themselves, and all they wanted was money; if things went smoothly, the chances of recovering Paige unharmed were sizeable. Two challenges faced the resolution of such a case: the execution of a safe ransom drop and victim recovery and the team dynamics, which carried explosive risk, internal frictions within the team or individual greed combined with simple math that could potentially motivate one team member to eliminate another just to increase their own take. Add fear and stress as one would add gunpowder and gasoline to a well-stoked fire, and things could go sideways quickly. That particular factor made the first twenty-four hours critical in any abduction; after that, each hour increased the risk that the kidnapping could turn into a homicide case.

Tess walked over to the kitchen sink and turned on the faucet. Tearing a section of paper towel from a roll, she moistened it and wiped her face, willing the tiredness away from her eyes, her lined forehead, her tense jaw. Then she stopped behind Donovan, looking at his screen. He was accessing video surveillance feeds from the area where the unsub had abandoned the Subaru and disappeared, most likely in another vehicle. Tapped into stoplight cameras, ATMs, and any street-installed cameras he could access, he was looking for the vehicle the unsub took from the parking lot where he changed cars.

"Anything?" she asked, although she already knew the answer. If he'd found anything, he would've told her.

"I know for sure they didn't leave the parking lot on foot. No pedestrian traffic on that street for thirty-seven minutes after we lose the Subaru here, two blocks west of the parking lot."

"He did his homework," Tess growled. "He probably has all the blind spots in the city mapped."

"Seems that way," Donovan replied, then stretched his back without standing from his chair. He intertwined his fingers and stretched his arms above his head until his joints cracked, and he let out a satisfied breath. "Now I'm pairing vehicles I see leaving the blind spot with the ones that enter it. The one we'll see leaving, without any record of entering a few minutes earlier, that's our unsub. Then we'll grab—"

The mobile phone connected to one of the tracking briefcases rang loudly, sending a rush through Tess's blood. "Mrs. Walsh?" she called loudly.

Miriam rushed to the table, barefoot, wearing jeans and a light blue shirt. The white bathrobe was gone, but her hair was disheveled, and the shirt wrinkled. She'd been lying down. Max still wore the same clothes as the night before, but the tie was gone, and the shirt wasn't tucked in. His eyes had dark circles underneath.

Miriam's chest heaved with shallow, fast breaths. She stopped in front of the tracing briefcases, her eyes fixed on Tess.

"Let it ring twice, not more," Tess spoke quickly while grabbing a headset and keeping one of the ear cups over her right ear. "Don't refuse any demands, and ask to speak with Paige. Keep him talking as much as you can."

Miriam nodded. Her lips trembled, and her hand shook badly as she picked up the phone. She almost dropped it when the cable connecting it to the call tracing equipment got tangled in the briefcase handle. She gasped but recovered it before it hit the table and swiped to accept the call.

"Yes?" Her voice quivered.

"We have your daughter. If you want to see her again, have one million dollars in nonsequential, unmarked, twenty-dollar bills ready in one hour, and wait for my call." There was a short silence, but Miriam was too stunned to say anything. "The Broward County district attorney has sucked the life out of hundreds of innocent people. He deserves to pay." The voice was electronic, artificial, and lacked any intonation. Most likely, it came from one of the text-to-speech applications that littered the internet and made kidnapping investigations increasingly difficult. There was no background noise of any kind; the unsub must've connected the call directly to the app and entered what he wanted to say as text on a screen.

Miriam's eyes widened in panic. "But I don't—"

Tess slashed through the air with her hand, urging her to stop arguing with the unsub, then nodded and gestured with her hand, to signal her to agree to whatever the voice said. Then she gestured some more, reminding her to keep the unsub talking.

"Yes, yes, I'll get the money. Can I speak to my—"

"No trackers, no GPS, or the girl dies." The call ended.

Donovan shook his head, defeated. "It was a VoIP call, bouncing around the world from server to server."

Miriam broke in bitter sobs. "No... my baby." She pushed Max away and bent down, her hands pressed against her chest. Her husband wrapped his arms around her shoulders and gently held her as she heaved.

"Mrs. Walsh, I'm afraid we must stay focused," Tess said, her voice as soothing as she could manage, but undertones of urgency still seeped through. They only had one hour and were not prepared.

She looked at Tess through a veil of tears. "We don't have that kind of money lying around. It's late... I can't go to the bank—"

"We could call some people," Max offered, but his voice didn't sound convinced.

Tess frowned, thinking of what that implied. More people knowing about Paige being gone. More risk the media would find out. "I'd rather we didn't, not at this time. The note they left advised specifically against drawing attention and media involvement."

Miriam lowered her eyes, shaking her head bitterly. "Then, how are we going to do this?"

"Let me work something out," Tess replied, clenching her teeth at the thought of calling Pearson. Tension twisted her gut into a painful knot. What if he couldn't pull it off?

She called him twice, both times the call ending in his voicemail after a long string of rings. Under the Walshes' alarmed stares, she typed a text message instead, advising him of the situation and asking for help.

Then she held her breath, trying to hide her fears. What if he didn't reply, or worse, if he had no answer? When the message chime finally went off, she was startled, although she'd been staring at the screen for minutes in a row.

The message was simple and to the point, in typical Pearson style.

Courier on his way. Send updates.

She turned her phone briefly toward the Walshes. "We're good."

Miriam sighed and laughed between tears, then reached out over the table and squeezed Tess's hands. "Thank you. I'll pay it back, all of it, I promise." Tess nodded, unable to say a word, the woman's gratitude tugging at the strings of her heart. The victims she was used to dealing with were cold and pale and emotionless by the time Tess met them, more often than not lying on the medical examiner's stainless steel exam tables. Witnessing Miriam's turmoil so up-close did things to her she wasn't ready for, stirring questions in her mind she'd thought she'd already answered a long time ago about having a child, a family of her own.

Max had disappeared into the bedroom and returned a minute later wearing a fresh shirt and jeans and holding a pair of clean socks in his hand. He pulled a chair from the table and sat, then slipped on his socks and stood. "What do I do, Agent Winnett? How do I handle this?"

"You don't," she replied calmly. "I will."

"No, no," Miriam reacted, her voice filled with worry. "If they see you're not me, if they find out you're a cop, they'll—" she covered her mouth with her hand, stifling a sob. "They'll kill her."

"They won't know it's not you," Tess replied calmly. "Donovan will go back to the theater and borrow some props."

"I will?" he asked, frowning at Tess. "What exactly will I be bringing?"

She ignored his question and texted the theater manager. As soon as the phone chimed with his reply, she looked at him. "A wig that matches Miriam's hair and clothing that matches her style. She's a size four; I'm an eight, her clothes won't fit me."

"How the heck do you expect me to do this kind of stuff? I don't know anything about—"

"It's hair and clothing, D. The wig should be red and long and wavy. The clothes should be black and modern, with zippers and accessories and stuff." She smiled awkwardly, seeing how Miriam was staring at her. "The manager met Miriam last night; he'll know what he needs to give you."

"*I should go,*" Miriam said, "*I'm her mother. It's me they want.*"

Tess bit her lip, thinking how to best convince her. She was sure a good part of Miriam's drive to make the drop was driven by her need to see Paige as soon as possible, to hold her, to be reunited with the daughter she missed dearly. But that fragile emotional state had no place in a cold and dangerous business transaction. "That's not going to work, Mrs. Walsh. You've never done this before, and it's risky. Things could go wrong, and we could end up giving them another hostage instead of getting Paige."

Tears rolled down Miriam's face, but she remained strong, her eyes firmly looking at Tess. "I'm not scared. I want to do this."

"Honey, please listen to Agent Winnett," Max said, speaking softly, but his voice was fraught with tension. "She knows better what to do if things don't work out as expected."

She turned to face him, enraged. "You're saying I'm too weak to hold it together?"

"He's saying you probably never had to shoot a man," Tess intervened.

The doorbell echoed strangely just as Donovan was getting ready to head out. Hand on her weapon, Tess looked at the visitor before opening the door. Through the beveled glass, she could see a junior agent from the regional office carrying two medium-sized duffel bags.

She opened the door, and he stepped inside only enough to drop the bags in the entryway, then he greeted Tess with one quick nod and disappeared.

Donovan left a short moment later, then Tess locked the door and returned to the dining room, where her presence interrupted a low-voiced argument between the Walshes.

"What's going on?" Tess asked, after looking at Miriam, then at Max. They both seemed adamant about something, still retaining a bit of the anger stirred up by their earlier argument.

"Ah, I just wish people would trust that I can do whatever I set my mind to do," Miriam said, her voice cutting, loaded with frustration.

Max breathed loudly and looked sideways before replying. "It's not about you—"

"It's not about either of you," Tess intervened. "It's the best way to handle a dangerous situation." They didn't seem convinced. "I've spent twelve years chasing perps with a gun in my hand, catching killers, reading their facial expressions during interviews, knowing when they lie and when they tell the truth. That's my skill set. Yours is architecture," she nodded toward Max, "and yours is pharmacy management. And being a mother." She paused for a bit, while an unexpected knot in her throat choked her. "I can't compete with you at being a mother; I wouldn't even think of trying. So, when the time comes, I'll take a step back and let you take back your daughter." She looked at Miriam with urgency in her eyes. "We're not there yet. The tricky part is just starting."

Her words had the effect of a cold shower. They took their seats quietly, without saying anything else. Tess welcomed the respite. It gave her time to think of something that had been troubling her since she'd listened to the ransom call.

She'd assumed that the unsubs were either after the money or after the DA. She had not anticipated the scenario in which the unsubs were after the DA and after money, payback for what seemed to be some damage he'd caused the unsub in the past. Maybe he'd wrongfully convicted someone or prosecuted someone with too much grit.

Either way, whatever profile elements she thought she had were falling apart, and a new fact emerged, troublesome and deadly.

The unsub's motivation was personal.

17

LOCKER

Thirty-six hours missing

The rising sun lit the sky with bright, optimistic morning hues, the beautiful new day a stark contrast with the raw emotions brought by the second dawn since Paige had been taken. After last night's frenzy to prepare the ransom drop and be ready for the second call, nothing had happened. No calls, no text messages, nothing but unbearable silence.

For endless hours.

The night before, Miriam and Max had watched her prepare for the ransom drop with Donovan's help. They'd exchanged few words among them, spending most of the time huddled together, holding hands and staying out of the way. The couple looked at them with concern, second-guessing every decision they made and every detail they planned for. The tiny GPS transmitters Donovan slipped inside the duffel bag handles were a source of dispute; Miriam worried the unsub might find them and retaliate. The same with the microphone Tess had affixed to her chest.

She had every right to be worried. Tess wouldn't openly admit, but she was increasingly concerned. A vengeful, greedy unsub would've called within the hour to give them little time to prepare backup teams and get organized. A vengeful unsub who only wanted the DA punished could've potentially toyed with the parents about the ransom, having no intention to release Paige; the girl might've already been dead. A third scenario out of the many that swirled inside Tess's mind was that something happened to throw them off somehow, a scenario that carried immense risk for the little girl's safety.

Twelve incredibly long hours had passed, and very little progress had been made. Donovan had tracked the car the unsub had picked up from the parking lot where he'd abandoned the Subaru. It was a dead end; a beat-up minivan with fake dealer plates that had probably been already abandoned again, who knows where. A BOLO was put on it the moment Donovan had identified it, but nothing so far.

None of the street cameras caught it at a good enough angle to capture a clean shot of the driver's face. Hours and hours of sifting through street videos awaited, with low chances of a positive ID.

Special Agent Patto had called in the results of his interview with the former janitor; it was another dead end. Friday afternoon, the man had attended a wedding and had over a hundred witnesses to vouch for him, on top of countless videos and photos.

They had nothing except a phone that wouldn't ring and the district attorney himself.

Why did the unsub call the mother when he wanted to punish the father? Why not call the DA directly? Or had he? If that was the case, why wasn't the DA keeping her apprised?

After she'd dozed off at the dining table with her head nested on her folded arms, Tess had reviewed the RICO case one last time before starting the excruciating task of reviewing all the cases Joyce had prosecuted and won. There were hundreds of such cases, and any of the defendants could've been the unsub they were looking for. Before diving in, she tasked

Donovan with weeding out the ones that didn't fit: defendants who were still locked up, defendants who had since died, although there was a small risk their surviving family members might've taken on a vengeance crusade in their name, defendants who had since admitted their guilt, and defendants who had served little or no time. The resulting pile lined up for the gruesome task of manual review had 322 cases. Any of those defendants could've been the unsub who was holding Paige hostage.

While Donovan sifted through the case files organizing them by length of sentence and number of appeals, Tess had worn a hole in the floor, pacing it from the dining table where the phones were connected to the tracking briefcases to the back door leading to the patio, and back. When the call came in, she was about to go outside for a breath of fresh air.

She rushed to the phone, just as Miriam was about to snatch it from the charger. "Remember, let it ring twice, and agree with whatever he wants." She put the headset at her ear.

"Yes," Miriam said, her voice choked, raspy.

"Good morning, I hope," a woman said. "Do you have any news? It's Mrs. Langhorne."

Tess muttered an oath and slid her hand across her neck in a gesture telling Miriam to end the call.

"Nothing so far, and I need to get off the phone in case someone calls."

"Oh, so sorry—," Langhorne started to say, but Miriam had already ended the call. She turned toward Tess, her eyes brimming with tears.

"How much longer do we wait? Huh?" She paced back and forth, only two steps in each direction, frantic. "I—I just can't take it anymore, do you—"

The phone rang again, sending a rush of adrenaline through Tess's body. "Let it ring twice," she started, but Miriam took the call after the first ring.

"Yes," she said while Tess scrambled to get the headset on.

The artificial voice said, "Drive to the Miami International Airport, north terminal, just you, no cops, no feds. Open locker number thirty-four and find a new phone in there. Leave yours in the locker, and follow the instructions you receive by text. You have forty minutes."

Tess set a timer on her phone.

"When can I—" The call ended before Miriam could finish her question.

"Time to roll." Tess dropped the headset on the table. Grabbing the clothing and wig Donovan had brought from the theater the night before, she rushed into the bathroom to change.

She was going to wear black, tight-fitting denim and a black Chanel jacket, probably fake, with a lot of metallic fasteners and zippers, on top of her own shirt. The theater clothes smelled of stale air and moldy, dusty backstage wardrobes, of other people's dry sweat. The wig was a good, snug fit, and Tess didn't waste too much time arranging the red hair locks in Miriam's style; she just put a ball cap on and wide, fashionable shades she'd borrowed from her. She tucked her Sig under her belt and slid on a pair of Miriam's boots that were a bit too large.

She got out of the bathroom and extended her hand toward Max. "I'll need your keys." He seemed confused. "They took the Subaru. What would your wife drive?"

"Ah, yes." He took the keys from his pocket and handed them to her.

As she turned to leave, Miriam clasped her forearm with both her hands. "Please bring my baby home," she pleaded, her voice a tear-filled whisper.

Tess looked straight at her, then reached out and squeezed her frozen hand. "I'll get her back. I won't stop until I do." Then she grabbed the duffel bags and rushed outside.

She climbed into the blue BMW after she'd thrown the duffel bags onto the back seat. If she was going to make the deadline, she had to floor it all the way.

The streets were mostly clear until she reached the interstate. After taking the ramp, she had to weave her way through the relatively light Sunday morning traffic. She'd considered notifying local law enforcement about her vehicle to avoid being stopped for speeding, but had chosen not to. The people who had taken Paige seemed savvy enough to have a police radio to monitor or even a cop on their side. She couldn't risk it.

Her timer showed a little over two minutes left when she pulled over in front of the terminal. There was no time to find parking. She left the car in front of the entrance but took the keys, grabbed the duffel bags, and ran toward the main building, ignoring the parking enforcement officer who was shouting after her. Once inside, she stopped, frantically looking for the lockers.

Only forty-nine seconds remained on her timer when she located them, tucked against a wall and painted metallic blue, organized in four rows with automated payment machines at the center, equipped to take credit cards and cash. She found locker 34 and tried to open it, but it was locked. With only seconds to spare, she dropped the duffel bags at her feet and pulled at it as hard as she could, then checked Miriam's phone for a message.

There was none.

Out of options, she looked around for anyone who didn't belong, who looked as if they were lingering, waiting for something. Out of the countless people passing by none stood out.

A second after the timer ran out, a text message chimed on Miriam's phone.

The locker code is 341.

She entered it, and the locker opened. Inside, she found a burner phone and a security screening wand. That spelled trouble. She had a weapon under her belt, and a mic taped to her chest. Crouching by the bags, she unzipped one of them and discreetly dropped her Sig in it under cover of her flashy black jacket.

The burner rang with a loud and antiquated ring tone she vaguely recognized. She hesitated for a moment, worried the unsub might realize her voice wasn't Miriam's.

"Yes," she said, imitating Miriam as best as she could.

"Leave your phone in the locker. Take only this one with you." The robotic voice paused for a beat. "Put the call on speaker. Run the wand thoroughly over your body, slowly. I am watching you."

It was too soon to ask any questions. She looked around but still couldn't see anyone. The unsub was probably watching through a video camera. Picking up the wand, she ran it over her legs, then her upper body, where it beeped almost constantly because of the zippers and buckles that adorned the jacket.

"Take that thing off and put it in the locker, then run the wand again."

They were watching her. The thought of it sent a shiver down her spine. Carefully avoiding coming too close to the mic she was wearing, she ran the wand over her body, her arms, around her head. Then she waited while the open call remained deathly quiet. Had the unsub noticed it wasn't Miriam he was speaking to?

The artificial voice returned. "Leave the wand and the jacket inside the locker room. Take the money and exit the terminal, then flag the third cab you see passing by. You have three minutes to get outside." The call ended before she could say anything.

She followed the instructions to the letter and barely made it to the curb in the three minutes they'd given her. The third cab she saw didn't stop; it already had a fare. But the next one did. Refusing the driver's help with the bags, she threw them on the back seat by her side and slammed the door.

"Where to?" the cabbie asked.

"I don't know," she replied, keeping her voice low in case they were listening. The flip phone could've been bugged. "Just drive."

They had been driving for a few minutes when the next call came.

"Return to the airport and put the money in locker forty-five. Use the same code, then leave. You have six minutes. We'll be watching." She checked the time on the flip phone but didn't dare set a timer on her own in case she was closely monitored.

"How about Paige?" she asked, but they'd hung up already. "Take me back to the airport, please, as quickly as you can," she told the driver. He threw her a surprised glance in the rearview mirror, then took the first left turn. Ignoring that, she unzipped the duffel bag and retrieved her gun, slowly, hiding her moves from the driver and whoever else might've been watching.

By now, Donovan was ready to assist with tracking the unsub the moment he'd touch the money. Even if they weren't going to let Paige go, Tess would still find them. That poor little girl, she must've been scared out of her mind. She hoped, against all the grim FBI statistics, that she was unharmed and still alive; she couldn't bring herself to accept the idea of another outcome. As the overweight cabbie approached the terminal, she closed her eyes for a moment and saw herself with her Sig in hand, squeezing the trigger and firing bullet after bullet into the unsub's chest.

Locker 45 was empty, the door slightly open. She shoved the bags inside with some difficulty, then forced the door closed and locked it. Then she left, carefully noticing every little detail of what she saw, every passenger, every behavior that didn't fit or object that didn't belong. Nothing caught her attention.

A few minutes later, she drove away in the BMW that somehow had not been towed yet, after giving the parking officer a lengthy explanation instead of showing her credentials. It was safer that way.

Making sure she wasn't followed, she entered a Walmart store and bought a quick change of clothes; this time, she was a flashy tourist with dubious fashion sense, wearing a long, gathered skirt with a colorful flower pattern and a red, striped top, a straw hat, and a pair of cheap, green sunglasses with wide lenses that smelled of heated plastic. She packed the wig and everything she'd worn before in a flashy backpack and added earbuds to her attire. A bright red lipstick completed her shopping list and her new appearance.

Abandoning the BMW in the store parking lot, she called an Uber and returned to the airport, backpack casually on her shoulder. There, she waited at a safe distance, killing time at a distant coffee shop with a direct line of sight to the lockers.

Locker 45 was still closed.

No one had come to take the money.

18

BLOOD

"Why the hell is it taking so long?" Randi snapped, propping her hands on her hips. She'd stopped squarely in front of Mark and stared at him as if he were somehow to blame. "If you think you can pull a fast one on me, you're dead wrong, buddy." She drew closer and sucked her teeth, inches away from his face. He could smell her acrid breath and cheap perfume, mixed with body odor; it had been a while since she'd taken a shower.

"You're starting to piss me off, woman," he hissed. "Shut your trap already." He pushed her aside and looked at his phone for the tenth time in just as many minutes. Gavin had been gone a while, longer than he'd anticipated. Something was wrong. Sliding the phone in his pocket, he went into the girl's room, with Randi on his trail. Nothing could keep that woman away; she was like a flea on a dog, itching badly, annoying, kindling a desire to waste her blood on the stained living room carpet.

Paige was lying on her side, weeping quietly, her blindfold sodden. The sound of his footfalls probably scared her because she started trembling. She'd peeled off the duct tape covering her mouth, but he didn't mind; she'd been quiet and hadn't caused them any trouble.

He pulled a candy bar out of his pocket and tore off the wrapping. "Here, I brought you something." He tried to put the candy bar in her hand. When his hand touched hers, she startled and wormed away on the mattress until she reached the wall. "I won't hurt you, I promise," he whispered. "It's just food, that's all. A Snickers bar." Hesitantly, she reached out timidly with her hands, still bound together with duct tape.

Randi scoffed loudly and slapped her hands against her thighs in frustration. "Unbelievable. What are you going to do next, read her a bedtime story?"

He stood and reached her in two heavy steps. He grabbed her arm and dragged her out of the room. "Mind your own damn business." He let her go and closed the door to the girl's room, not before seeing she was eating her candy bar. Then he shoved Randi into the living room. "I could kill you right now," he said, glaring at her and grinding his teeth, wondering what was keeping him from doing it. "I don't believe your homies exist." He touched her dirty cheek with two fingers, sliding them down toward her neck in an unspoken warning.

She didn't flinch. "Wanna see for yourself, asshole?" She grabbed his hand and dragged him to the open window. There, she put two fingers in her mouth and whistled. A bald, brawny man, a neckless Goliath covered in pale prison ink who was standing a few yards away, abandoned his fishing rod on the dock and looked their way. He reminded him of the men he'd met in the prison shower, the gangbangers who believed he'd be more compliant without teeth. The tattooed hunk recognized Randi and waved at her. She waved back.

"There, happy now?" she asked, her face scrunched in angry contempt. "You think you can take my man Joe and his friends with your scrawny little twigs?" She pinched his bicep with a derisive cackle. "Go for it, then. Show me what you got."

It took all his willpower to not wring her neck.

He was still struggling to breathe normally when Gavin walked through the door empty-handed. He looked shaken, not his normal, reassured self. Something had gone wrong.

"Where's the money?" Randi asked, rushing toward him. She grabbed his arm and shook it. "Where?"

He didn't acknowledge her in any way. Looking straight at Mark, he said, "They took us for fools, bro. They sent a fed." He drew air with a quick, loud sound, as if he'd been holding his breath for a while. "I left the money there. I didn't touch it."

Blood drained from Mark's face. He knew going after the ransom was a bad move. "Are you sure?"

"Hey, what do you mean, you left it there? Where's my bloody money?" Randi shouted, grabbing Gavin by the lapels. She was several inches shorter than him but didn't seem to care. He swatted her away with one swift shove that landed her on the floor, cursing mouthfuls.

"Of course, I'm sure. It's the same fed that came to the theater earlier. I was just a few feet away from her." He took out his phone and brought up the video recording from the camera he'd placed at the airport. Navigating through the lengthy video with his finger, he froze it on a screen that showed the woman when she'd reached locker 34 and had looked straight into the camera without knowing. "That's not the kid's mother."

In the blurry video, the woman's hair matched Miriam's, and so did her clothes, but she seemed shorter and not as skinny.

Gavin searched through the videos on the laptop while Mark watched a section of the airport recording. Pulling up a video from the theater, Gavin said, "See this broad? That's the fed I saw the other night."

Mark stared at the phone's screen, speechless, unable to think. Gavin misread that as doubt and snatched the phone out of his hand.

"Here, I'll show you." He located another section of the airport video he wanted Mark to watch. "Take a look at this, then you tell me if you think I should've taken the money."

Randi picked herself up from the floor and inserted herself between the two men, staring at the same screen. Mark watched the grainy video, waiting to see what was happening that had Gavin so spooked. As far as he could tell, the fed was following Gavin's instructions. She'd taken the flip phone, had read the text, but then she crouched on the floor and did something to one of the duffel bags.

"She had a gun, man. See here?" He froze the playback to the moment where the woman let the weapon fall into a duffel bag. For a split second, the gun came into sight, just as she'd let it drop.

Mark stared at Gavin with an intensity his partner understood, seeing how spooked he was. If they'd somehow screwed this job for Aquila, their bodies would never be found. The Big Man might've known that was going to happen, and that's why they weren't supposed to take the ransom; Aquila always knew everything, planned everything. Any moment now, Mr. Erwin would call with—

"Do you know what happens to people who stand between me and my money?" Randi grabbed Gavin's sleeve. "They die." Her voice was a low, menacing hiss.

He pulled himself free from her grasp. "Screw you, bitch. What was I gonna do, come back home with the feds in tow?"

Randi's brow scrunched as she scowled at him, then at Mark. "If this is some scheme to screw with me, you're fish food, I swear."

Visibly irritated, probably even more than Mark was, Gavin raised his arms in the air. "You junkie moron! Give this bitch a fix because her brain stopped working," he quipped, looking Mark's way, his attempt at humor falling on deaf ears. Then he stared straight at Randi. "Do you think I would've come back here, if I had the money, to put up with a scourge like you?"

Instead of angering her, Gavin's words must've rung true with her because her scowl disappeared, replaced by a glint of determination in her bloodshot eyes. Quick as lightning, she pulled a small switchblade from her purse and rushed toward the back room. Before Mark could stop her, she released the spring, the blade echoing strangely in the house, then she slashed the girl's arm.

Paige shrieked and started crying, loud, pained sobs. Blindly kicking the air around her, she took her bound hands to the scarf wrapped around her head, desperately trying to remove it.

Leaning on the girl's body to hold her in place and tearing a piece of the girl's shirt, Randi soaked some blood into it, just as Mark grabbed her and lifted her in the air by her throat.

"I don't care about Joe or any other loser muscle you'll set on me," Mark growled in her ear as she was choking, gasping for air. Once in the living room, he threw her on the floor, knocking the air out of her lungs. She gasped, still holding on to the bloodied piece of white fabric. "I'm not in the business of hurting kids, you hear me?" Still on the floor and out of breath, Randi nodded while her eyes shot poisonous arrows. "Come near that kid again, and I will end you where you breathe."

He shot Gavin a look; he was staring at the woman writhing on the floor, the expression in his eyes one of curiosity and something else, equally bothersome, as if he'd found Randi's actions commendable, rational under the circumstances. As if he respected her.

Shrugging off his renewed concerns about Gavin, he went back into the girl's room with a first aid kit he took from the bathroom. There was some gauze in there, old and yellowed, but it was going to be good enough.

Paige sobbed bitterly. The cut ran along her forearm from under the elbow almost to the wrist, missing all the major vessels but bleeding profusely. Hands still bound, she'd tried to feel her wound with her face, smudging blood all over her clothes, her lips, her hair.

When he touched her, she shrieked.

"Shut that kid up already," Randi's commanding voice came from the living room.

She was right; that's how they ended up with the pest in the first place, voices carrying clearly over the water. Still, he ignored her and focused on the girl. "Shh," he whispered. "I'm going to tie this up, and it won't bleed anymore." Frowning, he stared at the bleeding gash, wondering what he could do. Paige needed stiches but that wasn't an option.

When he returned into the living room, Randi was sitting at the small table, wearing blue nitrile gloves, and passed him a pair before handing him an envelope. The look in her eyes was pure, distilled hatred, homicidal, not something Mark had seen since he'd left the joint. "Have this sent to the kid's mother. That'll change her mind about screwing with my money."

The blood-stained piece of fabric was folded inside the envelope, together with a handwritten note that read, "This is what happens when you can't follow simple instructions. Next time I'll send body parts."

19

EXPERTISE

Thirty-nine hours missing

Nothing happened for one incredibly long hour. Tess watched locker 45 every few moments, in passing, while shifting her gaze between the arrivals and departures schedule displayed on a big monitor to her right and the security gates at her left. Agent Patto continued to read his newspaper, seemingly indifferent to the constant flow of passengers around him.

One more glance at the large, digital clock affixed to the terminal wall, and she got up, frustration suffocating her. She thought she had a chance to find that little girl, to end her captivity. Walking briskly in a flurry of colorful, silky fabric that swirled around her legs, she left the terminal and climbed into the first cab available. Thirty minutes later, she returned to the Walsh residence, driving Max's Beemer.

The door opened before she had the chance to touch the handle. Max, pale and disheveled, with a haunted look in his eyes, invited her inside.

"Agent Donovan told us," he said, wringing his hands. "What happened?"

She looked at Miriam, who stood by the table, weeping softly. "I don't know yet. No one came to take the money. No one called either."

"What happens next?" Max asked.

She wished she had more answers. "We wait. I left the money there; maybe someone will come by and pick it up. We have an agent watching."

"What if they take the money?" Miriam asked. Her voice was brittle and faint. "How will I get my daughter?"

Tess frowned. She knew about the tracking devices in the bag handles, and she'd just told her about Patto. "We'll track the bags and locate the place where they keep her. As soon as we know that, we'll—"

"You'll do what? Shoot your way into the place they hold my daughter? Risk killing her?" Miriam gasped, covering her mouth with her hand. "Oh, God," she whispered.

Tess touched the woman's shoulder, but she withdrew as if the contact burned her skin. "Please, try to understand. All we need is a location. Once we have that, we'll get her." She said the words but struggled with everything that was happening. How could she build a profile without any information? She had no evidence except some videos demonstrating how the unsub had waltzed into that theater and taken the girl without hesitation. No forensics because the Subaru had been wiped clean of prints. The lab was still picking it apart, but she wasn't holding her breath. The call couldn't be traced, the voice was synthetic, the place the unsub had chosen for the drop only substantiating his professionalism in executing the crime. He wasn't making any mistakes.

Miriam turned her back, refusing to listen, and Tess didn't blame her. Somewhere, a little girl was going through hell while she struggled to find her footing, to know which way to look. Was the answer buried in one of the 322 case files DA

Joyce had prosecuted in his entire career? Was the unsub an ex-con he'd put away?

She walked over to Donovan. He'd loosened his tie and removed his jacket. His sleeves were rolled up, and his hair was tousled from the many times he'd run his fingers through it, while seated in front of the computer he hadn't left for almost a day and a half.

"How are we doing on the list of ex-cons?"

He rubbed his forehead with his fingers for a brief moment. "Are we considering those who have since moved out of state?"

"Let's stay at state level for now," she replied, wondering if she wasn't making a mistake. "Let's focus on those who were released in the past three—no, twelve months. I don't believe this unsub would've waited more to exact his revenge. Prioritize them by length of time served." If she could only reach out to the DA without fear of screwing things up. Her gut kept telling her she should pursue the RICO case, despite the ransom demand. Allan Curtis Mitchell could've orchestrated such a precise attack. He was a mobster with access to power, money, and professional hitters with nothing to lose. Regardless, she sat by Donovan's side, reviewing case file after case file. There was no getting near Mitchell.

It was about one in the afternoon when the doorbell rang. Tess pulled her weapon and approached the door, tiptoeing until she could see through the beveled glass a young man, wearing a shirt and ball cap with the 60 Minute Courier logo, a black, tilted ellipse with the number 60 embroidered in bright red. She tucked the gun at her belt and opened the door.

"Mrs. Miriam Walsh?" he asked, chewing gum with his mouth wide open. His head wobbled as if he were one of those dashboard hula girls. From up close, Tess could hear the music blaring in his earbuds.

"I'm Mrs. Walsh," Miriam said, approaching quickly. The man placed an envelope in her hand and extended a digital scanner she signed with her fingernail.

Tess slipped on a glove, then took the envelope from her. There was no sender, and the side of the flap had been stained with something that could've been blood. Frowning, she took the envelope to the dining table and said, "trash bag."

Donovan stood and followed Max's instructions, then returned with a new bag he laid flat on the table.

She set the envelope on the plastic, carefully detaching the flap with the tip of her gloved finger. Then she removed the contents and cringed. The blood-stained fabric felt moist to the touch through the blue nitrile glove.

"Oh, no," Miriam sobbed, clasping her hands over her mouth. Max rushed to hold her. "They killed my baby."

"No, they haven't," Tess replied, grinding her teeth. If she only got her hands on the scum who'd done that. "This was just a warning." She pushed the letter toward her, over the plastic-covered surface of the table, but gestured to stop her when she was about to pick it up.

Then she turned to Donovan. "We need DNA on this blood, and Patto should retrieve the money and the phone from the airport. Oh, and that metal detector wand they had me use might have a serial number we could trace." Donovan nodded and started typing, while she returned to Miriam's side.

Without touching it, Miriam read the letter, sniffling, wiping her tears with trembling fingers. Then, without warning, she pounced on Tess before Max could hold her back.

"What are you doing to save my baby?" she shouted, sobbing uncontrollably with her mouth wide open. Tess stood calmly, not backing away, ready to help Max hold her if he needed it. "Do you have any idea what you're doing? Have you ever worked kidnappings?"

She looked briefly at Max. His eyes were haunted, sad, welling up.

"No, this is my first ransom kidnapping," she replied, instilling confidence and reassurance in her voice. "But I know my job, and I—"

"You don't know shit!" she yelled, the profanity unexpected, sounding foreign to the classy, educated woman that Miriam was, and hence even more powerful. "My baby could be dead for all I know, and it's because of you." She choked and coughed, the inability to continue yelling at Tess enraging her. "What kind of kidnappings have you worked? What other kinds are there?" she asked when she could speak again.

She looked at Max again, briefly, a warning of what was to come. He closed his eyes, bracing himself.

"I only worked serial killer kidnapping cases," she said, her voice a hushed whisper, as if lowering her voice would make the words go unnoticed.

She gasped and stared at Tess, her mouth agape, speechless. Slowly, she seemed to gather her thoughts, struggling to understand. "Why on earth would the DA assign you, out of all people, to work this case?" Her voice had dropped to a choked murmur. A tremor ran through her body. "Does a serial killer have my little girl? Oh, God…" She dropped to her knees, sobbing heavily and gasping for air, her wails heart-wrenching. "No, please, tell me that's not true." Max crouched behind her and wrapped his arms around her.

"It isn't true," Tess replied, feeling the threat of her own tears squeezing her throat like cold, iron fingers. What the woman was going through was unimaginable. "We have absolutely no information that points to your daughter's kidnapper being a serial killer."

From where she'd dropped on the floor, her legs folded underneath her and leaning against Max's chest, she looked at Tess as if she'd seen a stranger.

"Give me your phone?" Miriam asked Max, then dialed a number and put the phone on speaker.

"Hello," a man replied, and Tess recognized DA Joyce's voice.

She held on to Max's arm and stood. "Darrel, it's me, Miriam."

Tess heard Darrel's breath on the open call. "Any news?"

"No. Just one question." Her voice was low and menacing, the tears now gone, replaced by the powerful grit she'd admired about Miriam on so many occasions. "Why did you assign this Agent Winnett to find your daughter?" Raw anger and disappointment tinted her voice, but there was something else too, something Tess couldn't name, the admirable courage of a mother fighting for her child. "She's your daughter too, Darrel. Don't you want her back?" As she asked the question, she choked, unable to fully articulate the words.

"Of course, I want her back," Joyce replied. "What kind of question is that?"

"Then explain to me why, out of an entire federal building full of agents, you picked one who's never worked a kidnapping before. Do you know her specialty?" She paused for a beat, but Joyce probably knew better than to take the bait. "Serial killers, Darrel," she spat the words as if they burned her lips as they came out. "Why did you bring a serial killer expert to screw up our daughter's case?"

"I'm sure she's not screwing it up, Miriam. She knows what she's doing."

"You don't know anything," she shouted. "If you'd cared, you could've called and asked already." Tess caught the quick, apologetic glimpse Max threw her. "She botched the ransom drop today and didn't bring my baby back to me." The last few words ended in tears, but she drew breath sharply and continued, "So, tell me, you couldn't find anyone else to look for your daughter?"

"Am I on speaker, Mir?"

Hearing Darrel use the shortened name for his ex-wife, Max let go of her shoulders and took a step back. The Walsh family had some strange dynamics going on, undercurrents of issues Tess didn't yet grasp.

"Yes, you're on speaker, and she can hear you. But never mind her; I want to know. Why her? Is she someone you're screwing?"

Tess's eyebrows shot up. She didn't see that coming. Visibly embarrassed, Max glanced at her briefly then stared at the floor, flushed.

"Miriam, get a hold of yourself," Joyce replied coldly. "I'm only going to say this once, so pay attention and don't ever question my motives again. I asked for her because Winnett is the best there is in the entire field office. Quantico's Behavioral Analysis Unit is holding a spot for her, but she prefers to stay here and work alone for some reason. I don't care that her expertise is serial killers." He paused for a brief moment. "I asked for her because I trust her to do the right thing. She always does."

Silence took over the room. Miriam seemed at a loss for words, and Max continued to avoid looking at Tess. Donovan glanced at her for a moment, then lowered his eyes to the computer screen.

"When it comes to my daughter," Darrel added, "I only want the best. What happened between you and me is history, and it doesn't matter one bit when it comes to Paige. Is that clear?" He waited for a moment, but Miriam didn't say a word. "All right, then, call me if you have any news. Good night, Miriam." Three beeps and the line went dead.

The awkward silence continued to linger, but Tess wasn't paying attention. Something DA Joyce had said brought back memories.

20

WARNING

Three years ago

"Agent Winnett, did you read my client her rights before questioning her?" The defense attorney for Nichole Cobbins looked awkward in his Armani suit, the culprit being his impressive potbelly. He had a round face and eyes that fired darts dipped in poison whenever he was interviewing a witness from the prosecutor's list but otherwise turned gentle and watery as if he was about to share into the tear-shedding often done by defense witnesses while on the stand. Coincidentally, his name was Aaron Feely.

"At the time I asked the first few questions, Mrs. Cobbins was not a suspect."

"So, you admit you did not Mirandize her?"

"Miranda warning applies to suspects in custody," Tess smiled sweetly, "as I'm sure you're aware." That set Feely's face on fire. Blotches of red and purple appeared within seconds, while his forehead beaded with sweat. "Again, at the time, Mrs. Cobbins was not in custody, nor was she considered a suspect."

"Why were you questioning her then?"

Tess's smile vanished. "At that point, I suspected she was her husband's victim, not accomplice, forced to provide—"

"A victim, indeed," Feely interrupted, turning toward the jury and making a demonstrative gesture with his hands. "The wife of a serial killer who had tortured and killed twenty-seven women has been nothing more than another one of his victims."

"Objection," DA Joyce said, standing up. "Opposing counsel is testifying."

"Withdrawn," Feely quickly conceded. His last remark would be stricken from the record, but the jurors had heard it, and the seed of doubt had been planted in their minds. "No more questions for this witness." Panting from the effort to stand and speak at the same time, Feely returned to his seat.

Tess stepped down from the stand, feeling good about herself and how she'd fielded Feely's questions. The case had been a particularly challenging one. When suspected, Larry Cobbins had been provided alibis by his wife, Nichole. For a few excruciating weeks, Tess had been chasing ghosts all over Miami, looking for a man she didn't know she'd already found.

Larry Cobbins matched to the letter the profile she'd built, based on victimology, forensics, and modus operandi. He was disorganized, his abductions were rash and violent, his signature speaking of a sadistic rapist and killer who took pleasure in torturing women for days before killing them by drowning them in tap water, most likely by forcibly submerging their heads into a tub.

Cobbins had been unable to hold on to a job for more than a few weeks and worked occasionally unloading cargo at PortMiami or some truck terminal, his strong muscles and large frame helping him land such work almost effortlessly. But Tess had suspected he rounded up his income with money and valuables taken from the women he kidnapped. Several of the victims' cars were never recovered, and Tess believed they'd been traded to shady garages to be sold for parts or taken out of the country.

At least three more victims had died because Nichole Cobbins had lied to Tess when asked about her husband's whereabouts the night one of the women disappeared. She vouched for him without batting an eyelash, and, because of her lie, Cobbins was able to continue raping and killing. But Tess had her eyes on him and sensed the wife was lying; sadly, that wasn't enough for a judge to issue a warrant.

Despite Nichole's repeated statements vouching for him, Tess decided to break into the Cobbins' Glades ranch and see for herself if Larry Cobbins was really at home every night, soon after another woman had gone missing in what she'd determined was the unsub's comfort zone.

She knocked on the door first, and Nichole answered, a little flustered. She answered Tess's questions a little too quickly, often looking over her shoulder and noticeably eager to see Tess gone. She said Larry was home but was sleeping after being sick with food poisoning, and she didn't want to wake him. Then, Nichole tried to close the door, but Tess's foot was holding it open. She pushed her way in and drew her weapon, then started searching the house.

Turned out Larry was there after all, and so was the woman he'd recently abducted, screaming under the blade of his knife. There was a cup of coffee placed on a small table by an armchair, a few feet away from where he was busying himself with that poor woman. It was still warm. The cup had traces of lipstick on it. Nichole liked to watch.

When Larry Cobbins turned and charged with a knife in his hand, two bullets to the chest in rapid sequence did away with him in less than a second. Bile rising in her throat, she cuffed the screaming and kicking Nichole and threw her in the back of her black, unmarked Suburban. She deserved to rot in jail.

Nichole Cobbins was not a victim. But, in all fairness, having been more preoccupied with tending to the victim until the ambulance arrived, Tess hadn't read Nichole her Miranda rights; the closest she'd come to it was when she'd told the woman to shut the heck up.

Tess breathed; good thing she was off the stand. Some things were better left unsaid.

She remained in the courtroom for the remainder of the session, eager to hear the victim's testimony. After the poor woman described how Nichole liked to sip her coffee and watch her husband torture and rape her, whatever points Feely had scored earlier with the jurors had been erased.

As soon as the judge's gavel fell, Tess rushed out of the courtroom, eager to grab some lunch and head back to the office. She didn't walk far before DA Joyce grabbed her arm and stopped her.

"Special Agent Winnett, hold on for just a moment."

Frowning, she turned to face him. His face was tense, vertical lines flanking his mouth, his brow furrowed, his jaws clenched. She glared at his hand where it squeezed her arm, and he promptly released it. "What can I do for you, Mr. Joyce?" *Her voice was cold, uninviting, yet professional. Nothing good could come out of antagonizing the district attorney.*

"You might be proud of yourself, Agent Winnett, and we might win this case, but make no mistake: we came close to having this case thrown out of court." *He spoke in a low voice, with his back turned to the hordes of people walking past them on their way to lunch.*

Tess's heart sank. "What do you mean?"

"I'm tired of fearing the cross with you on the stand. You have zero respect for procedure and you couldn't care less for the people whose lives you put in danger, as long as you get your man." *He spat the words in a tight cadence she'd seen him use only with the most hostile of witnesses.* "You always have to do the right thing by your standards, isn't that right, Agent Winnett? Is that what makes you tick? Running your own show?"

She wasn't going to let him trample all over her. "No, Mr. Joyce, catching serial killers is what makes me tick. Speaking for the victims. If that means I always do the right thing by my standards, then yes, I guess I do."

"How about following the rules?" He drew his face closer to hers. She could smell the aftershave still lingering on his face and the faint scent of deodorant. Uncomfortable, she pulled back until she hit the wall behind her. He closed the distance between them before continuing. "Smarter, more experienced people than you deemed it necessary to investigate crimes a certain way. Yet you always forge your own path. You kill the suspects if you have the slightest reason to, taking the role of judge and executioner, and always leave it up to us to clean up your messes."

Tess thrust her chin forward. She was getting angry; he had no right to come at her the way he did. Power freak. "Sir, let me remind you I've been cleared in every shooting I have been involved in. My case clearing rate is the best—"

He scowled at her. "I don't want to hear it! We have rules for a reason. The law is not here to serve your whim or your record-breaking ambition, SA Winnett, are we clear?"

She bit her lip to remain silent, the best course of action when attorneys were involved, especially prosecutors. There was nothing she could say to win him over, not now, when he was fuming, irrationally angry over something that, to her, seemed inconsequential. She didn't lower her gaze, though; she stared right at him, telling him she wasn't intimidated nor apologetic.

Drawing closer, he hissed in her ear, "If I ever need a reckless, out-of-the-box thinker, a gun-wielding maniac who could chase down a perp and rescue a girl without any respect for anyone else's rights or well-being, I'll know who to call, and I'll call you the best there is." His rapid-fire words registered acutely on her brain, unexpected and confusing at the same time. Was he appreciative of her methods? Or not? "Until then," he continued, "don't let me catch you again interrogating suspects without Mirandizing them or entering premises without probable cause." He pulled slightly back and spoke almost normally. The crowd walking through the *corridor had cleared almost entirely.* "She could've walked, do you realize that? After helping her husband kill twenty-seven women that we know of?" *He paused for a beat, staring at her intently.* "I don't know about you, but I don't want that weighing on my conscience."

Still frowning, Tess nodded. She didn't trust herself to speak, her throat parchment dry and constricted, her mid buzzing with everything he'd said.

"This is your final warning, Agent Winnett," *he added, lowering his voice again but keeping his distance. He pressed his lips together and nodded once, then walked away with a brisk gait.*

Three years ago, DA Joyce had said, *I'll call you the best there is.*

While on the phone with his ex-wife, he'd just called her that.

He was sending her a message.

21

PRINTER

"Good morning, and happy Monday to you," Donovan greeted DA Joyce's stunning assistant in a cheerful voice. The name tag on her desk read Solange Jandreau. After everything settled down, he had to come up with a reason to stop by the DA's office several more times, enough to work up the nerve and ask the beautiful Solange out on a date.

She seemed a little confused, but he held up his ID badge that hung from a lanyard in green and orange, bearing the logo of the Miami Hurricanes football team. "I'll pretend I'm not offended you forgot my name," he quipped, smiling widely. "Bennie, from IT."

Solange smiled while her cheeks tinged with blush. "Oh, I'm so sorry. I thought you were one of the young attorneys from Dade County."

Unfazed, he pointed at his formal business attire and scoffed. "Yeah, right? Because they have us wearing suits when crawling under people's desks to pull cables and hook up the internet. Makes tons of sense," he added sarcastically, lowering his voice in a conspirative manner. The woman still smiled but was starting to lose her patience, as illustrated by the rhythmic tapping of her pen against a file folder. "Just a quick job today, replacing Mr. Joyce's toner." He was holding the toner, still sealed inside its original box, on top of a clipboard with a work order bearing the insignia of the state attorney's office in blue and gold.

"I'll buzz you in," the woman said, picking up the phone. She pressed a button and announced, "I have IT here to change your toner." There was a short pause, then she hung up and invited him to proceed with a hand gesture.

District Attorney Joyce was seated behind a desk covered in case files, some open and peppered with color-coded tags and sticky notes. He'd taken off his jacket and hung it on the back of one of the visitor chairs positioned in front of his desk. He looked distraught, black circles under his eyes underlining his tormented stare. Within a split second after Donovan entered, he focused. Whatever glimpse Donovan had caught of his internal turmoil was gone, replaced by a cold and distant professional demeanor. Yet beads of sweat formed at the roots of the district attorney's salt-and-pepper hair as if someone had turned up the thermostat in his office by some twenty degrees. The DA was afraid of something; even Donovan could tell, even if he wasn't a field agent.

"Good morning," Donovan said politely. "I'm here to service your LaserJet printer."

Joyce stared at Donovan inquisitively, frowning slightly. Donovan remained unfazed, giving the office a quick look. Taking a small device from his pocket, he slid it under his phone and pretended to be texting for a few seconds while slowly moving around the room under Joyce's perplexed stare.

The red LED on the device lit up twice, both times when he was facing the DA's desk. The office was bugged; that was certain. Maybe his computer was monitored too, or perhaps one of the bugs was on his person, but Donovan knew he couldn't come any closer without raising suspicions. From that distance, he couldn't be sure if the bug was audio only or video with sound; all he'd been able to determine was that the bugs existed and were operational.

Instead, he located the printer, placed conveniently on a small desk in the corner, by the bookcase. Unsealing the toner and removing it from its packaging, he threw the DA a quick glance and said, "I'll be out of your hair in no time, sir."

Joyce seemed frozen in his seat, elbows on the desk, leaning forward, with a puzzled expression on his face at first, replaced by one of hopeful understanding. "Take your time," he eventually said. "I need this printer to work."

"Understood," Donovan replied casually. Whistling quietly to himself, he inserted the new toner into the empty slot and closed the printer cover. Then, getting Joyce's attention but keeping his back turned toward the location of the bugs he'd detected, he discreetly planted a bug under the desk, pretending to inspect the printer's cables. Joyce nodded discreetly.

Satisfied, he put the old toner into the box and dropped it in the wastebasket underneath the printer desk. Pushing a few buttons, he watched calmly as a test page was being printed, then threw that in the same wastebasket, and said, "All done. I'll need you to sign here for me." He put the clipboard on the desk in front of Joyce.

"They have us do forms for IT supplies now?" Donovan muttered, then grabbed a pen, getting ready to sign.

Donovan chuckled. "Yes, they do, as if we didn't have enough paperwork on our hands." Another chuckle. "They want to be sure we don't take the toners home to sell them on eBay or something."

He tapped with his finger on the page, right where he'd filled up a few words in his scratchy handwriting.

HP LaserJet Pro M15w toner replacement serial #GT-UR-MSG-TW.

Joyce frowned, seeming confused. He'd never before been asked to sign such a form because Donovan had designed it himself that morning and had printed it on Max Walsh's color printer, a decoy meant for whoever was watching Joyce. In the serial number he'd scribbled on the form, he'd embedded an abbreviated notice to Joyce from Tess. Read carefully, the serial number meant, "Got your message—Tess Winnett."

Donovan took out his own pen and underlined the printer's serial number on the work order. "Here is fine, sir."

Joyce's pen hovered in midair above the form as realization washed over his face. He scribbled his name on the form, then handed Donovan the clipboard, a hint of a smile tugging at the corner of his lips. "Thanks. Are you sure it will work?"

"It has to," Donovan replied calmly with a light shrug. The DA must've been asking about Tess the only way he could if he knew he was being watched. "This brand of printer never quits."

22

MITCHELL

Darrel Joyce waited for the phone to ring for a few long minutes, the tension in his chest increasing, his breaths fast and shallow. But the black burner phone remained quiet. He'd found the phone in his own kitchen, the morning after Paige went missing when he received one call. There was no telling if the men who had Paige had witnessed his exchange with the so-called IT guy.

He didn't recognize the young man who had changed the toner in his printer and had managed to pass on Winnett's message, although he knew most of the FBI agents in the regional office. The man wasn't from the Broward County Judicial Complex IT staff; as the most senior employee, he knew all of them. A federal agent or not, Winnett had sent that man. That meant she was already aware the kidnappers were after him and was playing her cards accordingly.

Strange how life worked, humbling him into needing the very person whose methods he'd despised and often criticized from way up on his high horse. But when his own daughter had been taken, his perspective suddenly changed, and the woman he'd chastised numerous times for her methods had become his only hope to see Paige again. He'd looked upon her passionate approach to her investigations with contempt, fearing she'd damage his career if left unchecked, bursting through doors without probable cause. But Winnett had that passion for all the victims in the cases she worked, not just the ones she knew personally. That made him, Florida District Attorney Darrel Joyce, a man with double standards.

That was an understatement.

In instances where threats or violence targeted prosecutors or judges, the law was clear. His obligation was to report the threat so that an independent prosecutor could investigate the kidnapping and take over his caseload. The risk, unacceptable for Joyce, was the life of his daughter. Once her life lost the bargaining chip value it held, she'd become nothing but a liability, someone who'd seen their faces and heard their voices, someone who could pick them out in a police lineup. They'd dispose of her and just disappear so that he, and everyone else in the DA's office, would learn the lesson.

Had he been asked a week ago what he'd demand of his employees to do in such a situation, his answer would've come quickly. "Abide by the law. No one in my office is above it."

He'd done the exact opposite of that.

If he got caught complying with his daughter's kidnappers' requests instead of reporting them, if somehow the news of her abduction leaked to the media, he risked everything he'd worked for his entire life, who he was, his entire future. They'd revoke his license to practice law; he'd be disbarred, and that was only the beginning. He'd be charged with official misconduct and risk serving time behind bars, although there were mitigating circumstances to consider. It all depended on the judge who'd take the bench. Had he made that particular judge an enemy during who knows what trial? Would that judge also be a man of double standards, eager to advance his career and preach from high moral grounds when someone else's kid was involved?

He'd be finished, either way. He'd probably have to take on landscaping to earn a living; no one else would hire him.

Still, the thought of reporting Paige's abduction had not crossed his mind, not even for a second. Her life was more precious than anything he had worked for, than his own life. And maybe Winnett, that reckless, gun-wielding profiler, that out-of-the-box thinker with little respect for procedure, could work some magic and find his little girl. Bring her home safe.

That was his only hope.

Until then, he had to act like nothing was out of the ordinary. Most of all, he couldn't let his rage influence his decisions; he had to stay calm and wait for the phone to ring while no one could find out what was going on.

He pulled a tissue from the box of Kleenex in his top drawer, only this time he wasn't suffering from allergies. He wiped the sweat off his forehead, then threw the tissue in the wastebasket, and checked the flip phone once again, for the fifth time since the unknown man had left his office. It was fully charged and turned on, just like the kidnappers had demanded, but no calls and no messages. Not yet.

Letting a long breath out of his lungs, he stood and walked over to the filing cabinet. Case files were organized not alphabetically but in order of priority. A top-drawer case was one of high importance, like a multiple homicide or a human trafficking case. A bottom-drawer case usually held drug-related crimes and burglaries, all aggravated enough to warrant his personal involvement. Otherwise, the lesser-charge cases landed in similar filing cabinets that adorned the office of one of the over two hundred prosecutors who worked for him.

He pulled open the first drawer and extracted a case file so thick he could barely grab it with one hand. The cover had a series of labels and stamps, giving key information about the case, such as case number and defendant name. It was the only

RICO case he was prosecuting at the time, the defendant none other than Allan Curtis Mitchell, the only one of his defendants who could've had the stones to take his daughter. Inside those neatly organized pages, there was the key to what those people were after.

He carried the case file to his desk and set it down, then cleared his desk of any other open files, stacking them neatly in the corner. Sol would archive those later after he'd left for the day.

He needed a fresh perspective; until Paige was taken, his priority was getting a conviction. Now, he needed to be one step ahead of the kidnappers, to anticipate what Mitchell wanted and how to negotiate his daughter's release. Clearing his mind of everything he thought he knew about that case, he started reading the documents, taking occasional notes on his personal notepad.

Mitchell had been the bane of his professional existence, and the charges he'd finally been able to bring against him had taken almost ten years of surveillance, undercover work, plea deals, and evidence collecting minutiae. Mitchell's crime organization dated back forty years, when he, at the time only nineteen, had sold his first packet of white powder at the corner of a downtown street. Soon after that, he'd realized there was more money to be made if other people spent their time under the hot Florida sun, peddling product at street corners and risking arrest, while he was out on the Atlantic with his thirty-six foot, four-engine speedboat, fishing. Or, occasionally, hauling suitcases full of cash straight to Grand Bahama.

Within the first decade of activity, Mitchell had grown his reign over the land to include all the southeastern states and had diversified into racketeering, human trafficking, and anything else he could think of to make more money. For him, it was never enough; having grown up on the streets of the city, raised by a mother who'd been homeless half the time, the other half turning tricks for cheap behind gas stations, and living in weekly rates motels. Occasionally, he'd been pounded on by a junkie father, for a reason or not. Mitchell had witnessed early on the pull drugs had on his parents; they would've done anything to get more. Sold their souls, everything they owned, even him. One day, a bulky, sleazy-looking man stuck a wad of cash in his mother's hand at the corner of Seventh and Tenth in Overtown, then grabbed his hand and dragged him away. He screamed and kicked while the man loaded him into this Escalade, begged his mother to intervene, but the bitch was busy counting her new money. He was seventeen at the time. A week later, she was dead from an overdose, not even two hundred feet from where she'd sold him.

Three years later, the bulky man who'd laid hands on him worked for Mitchell and had no idea who he was, in fact, working for. Mitchell had reserved for him a special kind of punishment, one that took the patience of a spider waiting for its prey. As far as Darrel knew, he was the only man in Mitchell's organization to serve any time; he got caught dealing after an anonymous call gave him up. He was sentenced and locked up in the state penitentiary. There, rumor had it, Mitchell arranged him to be beaten and raped every night. Just like he'd been. When the man died, he had no idea who'd killed him and why. Allan Mitchell wasn't about ego; he was about power and money.

Other than that particular man, no other member of Mitchell's organization had served time, although Darrel suspected his tentacles reached behind bars somehow. He made sure bail was posted for anyone indicted, earning him a hero's reputation among his people. But soon enough, accidents happened or people disappeared. The lore going around was that Mitchell always took care of his own and took them to Canada or the Bahamas in his own boat. Many cop hours had been wasted trying to catch Mitchell hauling anyone out of the country. Whenever boarded by the Coast Guard, the only thing that was found on Mitchell's boat was fish, and even for that, he had a valid license. The truth Darrel suspected, albeit without any evidentiary support, was that he killed anyone who risked bringing his organization down.

Until now.

Everything changed when Mitchell's own son, Edward, was charged with racketeering. When it came to his own flesh and blood, Mitchell, just like Darrel, had double standards. That case file was also top-drawer in DA Joyce's filing cabinet, but it had earned a lengthy continuance due to special circumstances.

Two witnesses had come forward, willing to testify against Edward Mitchell; the entire case was built on their statements. The first witness, Tara Henson, was a coffee shop owner who could barely make ends meet. At twenty-nine years of age, the brave woman had refused to pay Ed Mitchell for protection and instead had called the DA's office, offering to testify. After her coffee shop had been set on fire, she thought she had nothing left to lose. She did... A drive-by shooting took her out two days before she was due in court.

The second witness, Jonas Ingram, stopped paying for protection after having paid for many years. His restaurant met a similar fate as Tara's coffee shop. Heartbroken after having lost his wife to cancer earlier that year and then his business, Jonas made his mission in life to bring Edward Mitchell's criminal organization down. Another drive-by shooting put four bullets in his body and claimed the lives of two innocent bystanders.

Only Jonas Ingram had survived the attack. His commitment to bringing down the criminal organizations that had ruined his life was rekindled by the paralysis that now confined him to a wheelchair after one of the bullets had severed his spinal cord. He picked Allan Mitchell's face from a photo array as the man he'd seen that night in the back seat of the black SUV that had crippled him for life.

Darrel still wondered if Jonas had indeed seen Allan Mitchell in that SUV. It was usually reckless for someone like the calculated crime boss to let himself be seen in the vehicle involved in a shooting, in the execution of a witness, no less. Perhaps Mitchell felt strongly against the people who were willing to put his son behind bars for life and wanted to see them taken out firsthand. Or perhaps Jonas Ingram was making that up, knowing his testimony would carry a lot of weight due to his personal history and desperate to make the mobster pay. If that was the case, Darrel didn't want to know; he was willing to look the other way and not question Jonas about it because he too was itching to see Mitchell locked up.

It had to be Mitchell who took his daughter. It matched his style and the lengths he'd go to protect the empire he'd built and his own family. He probably wanted the surviving witness, Jonas Ingram, killed.

Darrel picked up the phone and dialed the extension for the detective on his staff, a former Miami PD lieutenant by the name of Johnnie Lowe. Darrel had recruited Lowe because he was not only bright but devious enough in his investigations to uncover things that others couldn't find. He lied with talent and creativity; he was a natural. He was street savvy and had successfully completed several undercover missions into the organized crime that marred Southern Florida.

"Yes, boss," Lowe said.

"About the witnesses in the Mitchell case. How reliable were they?"

"Want me to dig up whatever dirt I can find on our little birdies?"

"Every last speck of it. Whatever's there, I don't want the defense attorney to surprise us with it. And believe me, they'll try their best."

"Got it, boss." He ended the call, leaving heavy silence to settle in Darrel's office.

When the flip phone rang, Darrel was almost halfway through reviewing the RICO case. Jumpy, he dropped his pen and swore under his breath, then took the call on speaker. "Hello."

"What did we talk about?" It was the same artificial, flat voice he'd heard before. "What was that printer nonsense? Do you think I'm stupid?"

A jolt of fear lit Darrel's gut on fire. "I have to keep appearances. That's what you told me to do." He paused for a moment, waiting for the caller's reaction. None came. "I can't act crazy all of a sudden. IT is in and out of here like they own the equipment." He couldn't help adding a tinge of sarcasm to his voice. "You've been watching me a long time. You must've seen IT come in here before," he bluffed. Then he stopped talking and waited.

"Whatever." The robotic voice lacked any intonation, but Darrel could still read the caller's state of mind by the words he chose. "Don't screw this up, because I swear to you, you'll never see her again."

"Understood." He drew breath sharply and added, "I heard you want ransom too?"

"Yes, and you're going to pay it with a smile or else we double it. Is that clear?"

"Crystal," he replied quickly. That was strange. Mitchell would've not made such a move for money, and none of his people would've gone rogue unless they were suicidal.

"Make no mistake," the robot added, and Darrel could've sworn he sensed a threatening tone in the flat, automated voice. "You're recorded everywhere. Your home, your office, your car. If any of the cameras go dark or silent, we'll send you a finger."

"No need for that," he blurted, springing from his chair although he had nowhere to go. "Please, I'll do whatever you want."

"That's the spirit that will get your kid back home in one piece."

"When will I know what you want? I've been waiting for—"

"When we're good and ready."

Silence returned to Darrel's office and found him biting on his clenched fist to contain the scream that burned his chest, demanding to come out. He wanted to smash things, to roar so loudly the entire building would know his rage. Instead, he sat on his chair and resumed studying the Mitchell case file while his rage, turned inward, brought the sting of tears to his eyes.

23

MOVE

Mark disconnected the phone from the laptop after ending the call with the DA and scowled at Randi. She'd stood by his side the entire time, hands propped on her hips, tapping impatiently with the heel of her shoe against the floor. As if she were the boss of him, instead of the slimy, crawling parasite she really was.

"What the hell was that about?" she asked. "Who was that?"

"The girl's father," he replied dryly.

"And why didn't you ask him for the ransom money?"

"Because." He slammed the lid on his laptop and stood, towering over her with his fists clenched, but his unspoken threat had no effect. The bitch was nothing if not brazen. Disgusting too. Her breath smelled bad, as usual, not that it was much of a nuisance when her stink competed with Gavin's dirty socks and beat-up footwear, and the musty odor of the carpets.

It was Gavin's turn to fix some food, and he was taking his sweet time opening a few cans of tuna to eat with crackers. What on earth could take him so damn long? He looked toward the kitchen, but he wasn't there. Frowning, Mark started looking for him.

The light was off in the bathroom; Gavin wasn't there. Next, Mark rushed to the back room, where they held Paige. He could hear whimpers coming from in there, faint and breathy as if she was struggling to draw air.

He opened the door silently and found Gavin standing by the kid's mattress, his hand on his crotch. He was licking his lips, staring at the girl intently, as if in a trance. Without saying a word, Mark grabbed Gavin by the throat and shoved him out of the girl's room. The man didn't fight him back; only gasped for air and groaned.

Mark shoved him all the way to the living room, where he slammed him against the wall with a loud thud. "Nothing makes me want to throw up more than a sick bastard who looks at kids like that," he growled, close to Gavin's stubbly face. "Remember why we're doing this, and don't screw it up. I can always make a call, you know, and solve your damn problem." He let Gavin go, but the man stood there, leaning against the wall, staring at Mark with fearful rage in his eyes.

"It won't happen again," he muttered, staring at the floor. "I wasn't going to touch her."

Mark's lip curled in disgust. "Get out of my sight." Gavin faltered toward the kitchen. A moment later, loud thuds marked each tuna can he was placing on the table. "And wash your damn hands."

"Ooh," Randi said, leaning against Mark's arm as if they were old friends. Mark pulled away. "You impress me. But that doesn't explain why I don't have my money yet. What the heck are you still waiting for?"

"Yeah, Mark, what *are* we waiting for?" Gavin said, abandoning his tuna cans and approaching the two. "They'll clear up that image enough to make my mug recognizable, then what? What do you think will happen? Do you think I can just go back to work next week?"

"I want my money now," Randi said, raising her voice and poking Mark in the chest with a long, acrylic fingernail. "Not later. Now."

A loud wail came from the girl's room. Mark rushed over to her while Randi shouted behind him, "Seriously? Shut that kid up. You can hear her all the way from the Keys."

Ignoring the irritating pest, he entered the room and looked at Paige. Her face was flushed and covered in sweat. She still lay curled on her left side, like she had been since Randi had sliced her right arm. The wound dressing he'd improvised was stained with dried blood and a yellowish discharge.

He touched her forehead, and she shrieked. "Shh, it's okay," he whispered, covering her mouth quickly with his hand. "What's wrong?" She was burning up with fever.

"It hurts," she said, lifting her arm a few inches in the air. Her body shook in bursts of tremors, a sign her fever was still climbing. "Get me a thermometer," he ordered Randi. The woman followed him everywhere he went, stuck on him like the leech that she was.

"Where do you think I can find a thermometer in this pigsty? And why are you whispering?"

"Bathroom, dipstick. Go."

Mark rummaged through what was left in the first aid kit. Just some more Band-Aids, small scissors, peroxide, antiseptic powder, tape. He took the scissors and cut Paige's dressing off, gently removing it where it had stuck to the edges of her wound. She whimpered at times but lay still, her entire body shaking.

The cut was red and swollen; it was infected and still wide open. Mark touched it with the back of his hand; it was burning hot. "Okay," he whispered. "I'll just wash this with a little water, then it will be super-duper fine," he explained, then turned to Randi, who'd just returned with a thermometer. "Towel."

He put the thermometer in the girl's mouth, then waited for the beep. The display read 103.1. She needed antibiotics, but he had nowhere to get those from, not unless he was willing to beat the streets scouting for some contraband tetracycline.

He folded the towel Randi had snatched from the bathroom and put it under the girl's arm. She cried when he poured peroxide over the wound and it sizzled, but he did it again, then sprinkled some antiseptic powder in the gash and closed it as best as he could with some butterfly Band-Aids, then applied some tape. There was no gauze left, but he improvised, tearing off his sleeve and cutting through the seam until he could wrap it around the girl's arm.

He left her with a candy bar and a bottle of water, then headed for the living room. "We need to move out of here," he announced.

"You need to stop stalling and get me my money!" Randi shouted in his face.

"We'll make another ransom call after we move," he replied calmly. She wasn't calling the shots; he was.

"And this time, they won't send that fed?" Gavin asked derisively.

"I don't think they will," Mark replied coldly. He was supposed to be on his side, but he was more and more inclined to side with the parasite. "I believe they learned their lesson."

Gavin paced the room angrily. The air smelled of canned tuna from the open cans he'd abandoned on the table, a couple of flies already buzzing around them. "You know what I believe?" he asked, shooting him a quick glance as if to see if he could afford to defy him so soon after he'd banged him against the wall. "I believe you're not thinking of the ransom as much as you should. I don't think you have it figured out. How will we take the money? How will you give the kid back when everything is over?"

Mark stared at Gavin, his lips pressed together in a fine line. Was he serious, bringing that up in front of the junkie? "That's not your concern."

"Yeah, but it's mine," Randi snapped. "I'm making it mine. I wasted enough time with you losers. How are you planning to give the kid back when you take the money? Because I'm thinking we shouldn't."

"Shouldn't what?"

"Give her back. Let them pay, and then we'll drown her." She bit the tip of her finger, studying him with inquisitive eyes. "Unless you're doing someone else's bidding and didn't bother to share that minor detail with your friends."

Mark ground his teeth. "Enough of this already. We have other things to consider. I warned you." He leaned over Randi until their eyes were inches apart. "You have no idea what you got yourself into." Her pupils dilated just a little bit. "And you," he said to Gavin, "you know better than this, so shut up and be patient. And stay the hell away from that girl."

"I do now," Randi replied. She was livid. "You've already been paid to take the girl, haven't you? You're screwing us both."

Mark took a deep breath of air. He'd thought he could control Gavin, and he could, but the both of them joining forces could prove tricky. They could turn against him on a dime, stab him in the back when he didn't see them coming. The only chance he had was to continue dangling the carrot in front of their faces. As long as they believed they still had a shot at landing that ransom, they would behave.

Gavin was a good actor and could convince anyone of everything, but Mark was the brains behind the operation and the connection with Aquila. The entire operation had been planned by him, alone, and Gavin knew that well. But Randi knew how to stoke Gavin's burning greed and didn't stop doing it, poking him and manipulating him like a masterful puppeteer. She was the one he needed to win over.

"Listen," he told Randi, "I could've already killed you, and by the time your good old friend Joe would've caught wind of it, we would've been long gone." He'd thought of that many times, wishing he could put some distance between him and the annoying little junkie even if that distance was vertical, but there was no way out. She texted Joe every hour or so. If he wasted her and left with Paige and Gavin, Joe would report them to the cops, and then Aquila would come after him. And from Aquila, there was no escape. He scared him ten times more than the cops did. "Just be patient for a little while longer; you'll get your money, both of you. We'll find a new place and move; we've been here too long and made too much noise. Not even your man Joe can stop the cops if they find us."

He hoped, against all reason, that the new place wouldn't come with Randi's personal bodyguard. Maybe he would get lucky, and the hulk preferred to stay behind and keep on fishing from the dock.

24

PROMISE

Sixty-three hours missing

Tess had managed to keep Donovan's incursion into DA Joyce's office a secret from Miriam and her husband. Rescuing Paige Joyce posed a high degree of operational sensitivity and risk, and the woman's raw emotional state was a threat to any such action. Tess had also kept to herself her belief that the people holding Miriam's daughter were less interested in money than in something else, most probably having to do with one of the cases the DA was prosecuting.

Since Donovan's return, they'd been sifting through his active cases. She'd abandoned the ex-con scenario the moment she'd understood the message Darrel Joyce was trying to convey. All those years ago, when he'd scolded her on the courthouse corridor, he'd said, *"If I ever need a reckless, out-of-the-box thinker, a gun-wielding maniac who could chase down a perp and rescue a girl without any respect for anyone else's rights or well-being, I'll know who to call, and I'll call you the best there is."* And yesterday afternoon, he'd called her exactly that, word for word, implicitly inviting her to break down doors and bring his girl back home, regardless of procedure or consequences.

She'd gambled everything on the idea that DA Joyce had carefully chosen his words when he'd spoken with Miriam. Therefore, she changed the direction she had started pursuing earlier in the investigation. If DA Joyce was the kidnappers' target, there was only one way to find out, and that was to bug his office discreetly, so that no one would know.

About half an hour after Donovan's return, a call received by DA Joyce in his office had caught her attention. Wearing an earbud connected to the monitoring app installed on their phones, both Tess and Donovan listened to the conversation between the DA and the text-to-speech processor the kidnappers used. It was the DA's question to them that brought answers to Tess's own question. He'd asked, "I heard you want a ransom too?"

They wanted something else more than ransom, before ransom. Something was worth more to the kidnappers than the million dollars they were trying to get in small, nonsequential bills.

The day before, Tess had gone out on a limb when she'd abandoned the ex-con route; at the time, there wasn't enough information to support that decision. Yet, her gut was telling her the unsub she was looking for wasn't someone from DA Joyce's past, regardless of what the first ransom caller had said. It had to be someone from his present, someone powerful enough to get something like that accomplished with the level of accuracy it had been executed, without hesitation. Only one case matched those parameters in Joyce's deck: Allan Curtis Mitchell's RICO charges.

Before immersing herself in reviewing the case file, Tess paused for a moment, reaching for the box of cold pizza on the table and grabbing a slice. She folded it in half and bit into it hungrily, her mouth instantly filled with the strong taste of mozzarella and pepperoni. The crust was just about perfectly crunchy, and she willed herself to chew it thoroughly instead of gulping it down like a starved wolf after a long winter.

She wiped her fingers on a napkin, then, unsatisfied because her fingers still felt greasy, washed her hands at the kitchen sink, then took a seat next to Donovan, ready to dive into the Mitchell case file. She leaned her forehead into her cold hands, feeling instant relief from the tension keeping her head in a vise.

When the phone rang, Tess jumped out of her skin. It was Miriam's phone they had retrieved from the airport locker box the night before and had been guarding ever since. After more than a day of waiting, pacing the floor, and sobbing, the heartbroken mother had finally given in and taken a sleeping pill. Still, before the phone could ring a second time, she rushed out of the bedroom, pale and unsure on her feet, with Max by her side.

"Remember, agree to anything—" Tess started to say, but Miriam waved her off with a hand gesture.

"Hello," she said, taking the call, her breath shuddering.

"Time for you to pay," the computerized voice said. Tess held one earbud at her ear and listened intently. Something was different. There was background noise this time, all sorts of sounds.

"Yes, I'll pay," Miriam said quickly, "just tell me what to do."

"Don't play any stupid games. Don't send a cop. Come yourself."

"Y—yes, I'll come myself, I swear."

It was the same robotic voice, but the word choices were different. Tess closed her eyes, listening, trying to visualize the unsub who was on the phone.

"Go to the International Mall, and take the money into the restroom by Camille La Vie. Be there at five today. Come alone, or you'll never see your kid again."

Tess took notes about the store name, the way the location had been identified.

Miriam choked and started sobbing. "Y—yes, I'll be there. Please, let me talk to my baby."

The robotic voice replied after a short delay, the lack of inflection making the words sound strange. "Ha, ha, what you want is irrelevant, biatch. If you don't like the terms, just say the word, and we'll send her body to you." Then the call ended, leaving Miriam sobbing heavily in Max's arms, seemingly unable to stand.

Tess wrote down the word biatch on her notepad. "The caller is a woman," she announced.

"Are you sure?" Max asked. "I thought you said—"

"It's a different caller than before. Women speak differently than men. They use longer phrases, more words to express the same concepts. It's in women's nature to be talkative. And the word choices also support the theory this unsub is a woman."

Miriam wiped her eyes and nose on a Domino's Pizza napkin. "What word choices?" she asked, her voice still choked with tears but starting to regain its strength, pulling from that inner reservoir of grit she had in apparently endless supply.

"Most men wouldn't know what Camille La Vie is or ever use the word biatch."

Donovan nodded, looking at Max. "True."

Max veered his eyes. "I thought it was an error, a typo the caller might've made when they used the text-to-speech software."

"It was initially an affectionate way some women addressed their friends, also women." Tess shrugged. It had never happened to her; no one had called her that, no one ever would.

The two men stared at each other.

"We have to get ready," Tess added. "In less than five hours, we have to be at the mall, ready for the exchange." She paused, looking at Miriam intently, unsure she was ready to hear what she had to say. "Until then, I believe there's information on this call that would help us locate the unsub."

"What information?" Donovan asked. "You mean, the background noise?"

"Exactly. It seems this unsub wasn't tech-savvy enough to connect the text-to-speech converter via cable; they used the phone's microphone instead, and it captured all sorts of things. Let's find out what else is making noise in the unsub's neighborhood."

"I'll remove the text, and then we'll listen," Donovan said, then started typing.

Miriam paced nervously for a few moments, biting her index finger, then stopped in front of Tess, who was leaning over Donovan's shoulder, watching him work on the call recording.

"Agent Winnett, how does one prepare for something like this?"

"First of all, you sleep. We have about four hours until we have to leave. Three of those hours, you can sleep. Now they've called and still want their money. That's the best news I've heard in a while," she smiled encouragingly, omitting to add she didn't understand their mixed strategy. It wasn't making any sense... was the unsub after money? Or after something to do with the DA's cases? It was obviously more than one person on the kidnappers' team, but could it be they were fragmented in their intent? Some were after the DA, while others after the ransom?

A hint of a smile tugged at her lips when she realized what she was witnessing. A divided team. Just like she'd anticipated. The unsub team had been tasked to kidnap the DA's daughter, but some of them saw an opportunity for a quick buck and took it. That scenario was a fit.

Miriam stomped her foot down, irritated with the answer. Max put his hands on her shoulders, pulling her gently into an embrace. She freed herself angrily. "Where's Darrel when we need him? Doesn't that man care about his daughter?" Then she walked into her bedroom and slammed the door behind her, not seeing the hurt in her husband's eyes.

"She's under a lot of stress," Tess said. "You both are. I'm sure she—"

"I was never the one, Agent Winnett," he said, speaking softly, his voice riddled with sad undertones. "It was always Darrel, even after she'd kicked him out, after she'd divorced him, after she called him all those names because he didn't come more often to spend time with Paige." He pressed his lips together for a moment, looking at the floor, then lifted his eyes at Tess. "Have you noticed how her entire face lights up when she speaks with him? When he's in the room?"

"I've also noticed how she's managing poorly a lot of unresolved anger for the man. Being cheated on, having your entire life ripped away from you in one moment, is not something too easy to overcome, no matter how strong she is."

He nodded, as if to thank her. "You're a profiler, Agent Winnett, right?"

"Yes," she replied, frowning slightly. She didn't want to be pulled in the middle of a marital crisis in full bloom.

"Do you think she'll ever love me like—" he cleared his throat quietly, "like she loves him?" He'd lowered his voice, but Donovan still threw him a quick, surprised glance.

"I believe she already does," Tess said. "She's a strong, independent woman who wouldn't tolerate anyone around her she didn't love. Can you imagine Miriam allowing someone she doesn't care about to develop a relationship like yours with Paige?" She shook her head. "Uh-uh, that would never happen."

"She's like my own daughter, you know?" Max said softly. "Please, Agent Winnett, bring our daughter back. She must be so scared, out there, all alone with those strangers." His eyes glinted with rage as he talked about the kidnappers, a rare sight for the kind, levelheaded architect.

Tess nodded and squeezed the man's hand. "I'll bring her back." She hesitated, thinking if she should share with Max a little more of what she knew, but decided not to. She just added simply, "I promise."

25

LEAVING

When Mark returned from his search for a new location, he found Gavin asleep in front of the TV. It wasn't even five in the afternoon yet, and his partner was already pickled, an empty bottle of whiskey in hand. He snored loudly with his mouth open and his head tilted to the side.

It had taken him a while to find a motel with room access directly from the parking lot, where they didn't ask too many questions and were willing to check Ulysses S. Grant's identification instead of his own. He'd stopped by a few streets he knew well downtown, where he'd asked some questions and scored himself four capsules of tetracycline for a twenty-dollar bill. Steep, but he wasn't willing to bargain; he was just desperate to get out of there before he gave in to the burning urge to fork out a hundred for a couple of grams of snow.

He'd made it back to the houseboat without giving into temptation, but shaking, as if resisting the urge had drained him of energy. Finding Gavin sleeping it off after he'd been gone less than two hours pissed him off to no end. He was supposed to monitor Joyce and tell him if the DA did anything out of the ordinary. He should've checked on what was happening at the theater, where Brassfield's security guys were still fiddling with that damn video, and he should've kept an eye on Randi.

Where the heck was Randi?

He shook Gavin, grabbing him by the arm. "Wake the hell up." Gavin sat crookedly, blinking fast and scrunching his face in the intense light. "Where's Randi?"

He looked around, then sprung to his feet, the empty bottle still in his hand. "Don't know, man. She was right here, drinking with me." Slack-jawed, he must've realized what he'd done because he turned to Mark with eyes dilated in fear. "I swear, brother, she was right here."

"Screw this, Gavin," Mark snapped. "I can't trust you worth a damn, can I?" He went quickly through the entire houseboat, checking every room. She was gone, but at least Paige was still there. Then he opened the window and looked for Joe. He wasn't fishing off the dock anymore; he was gone.

Feeling the blood draining from his face, he rushed to the laptop he'd left open because Gavin was supposed to monitor the DA on it. Shifting through the screens and checking the active apps, he found the text-to-speech app active; it had been recently used. The contents of the last dialogue were still there, and it wasn't anything he recognized.

"Aargh," he shouted, more enraged than he'd ever been, clenching his fists and trembling from the effort it took him to keep from pummeling Gavin to death. "Damn bitch, she crossed us. She's picking up the ransom money right now."

Gavin threw the bottle against the wall, where it broke with a loud noise. Glass shards clinked when they fell on the TV table, the rest spreading on the stained carpet silently.

Unable to breathe from the rage that suffocated him, he grabbed Gavin by the lapels and shoved him hard against the wall. The entire room shook, and an ashtray fell from the coffee table with a muted thump.

Still clasping a fistful of Gavin's sweaty, smelly shirt, Mark drew close to his face until he could see the sweat breaking at the roots of his oily hair. "What do you think she's gonna do, Gav? Bring it all here to share with us and stay friends?"

He let go of him, shaking his hand as if it were wet, as if to get rid of the soil he'd picked up on his skin by touching Gavin.

"I'll kill her," Gavin stated matter-of-factly. Then he opened a drawer in the kitchen and pulled out his gun. He checked the ammo, then racked it to put a bullet on the spout and shoved it at the back of his pants.

"You do that," Mark said, although he couldn't believe he'd said it. He'd never taken a life and, until Paige, had never harmed a human being, not physically anyway. Yet something strange was happening to him when he envisioned that double-crossing junkie shot in the head a couple of times, staining the asphalt somewhere. He was salivating as if he were thinking of a juicy burger or a mountain of cheese fries stacked high on his plate. If Randi were there right that moment, he'd pull the trigger himself and feel good about it.

Vengeance had to wait.

"We need to get out of here first." He sucked a long breath into his lungs and started moving quickly through the house, gathering everything he wanted to take with him: guns, ammo, some clothing, whatever money he still had left from the brick Mr. Erwin had paid in advance when he'd tasked him with taking Paige. "The bitch could call the cops with our location."

Gavin stood in the middle of the living room, frozen in place, his mouth agape. Mark snapped his fingers in front of his eyes, startling him out of the daze he was in. "Wake the hell up, and let's go. Bring the car around to the side. I'll grab the girl."

Taking a small water bottle from the fridge, he went into the back room. Paige whimpered, scared by his noisy footfalls, and pulled away from the edge of the mattress.

"Shh, you're okay," he whispered. "Here, take this. It's water. I have some pills for you to help with your arm." He put the water bottle in her hand, then put the pills in her mouth, one by one. He gave her two tetracycline and one of his sleeping pills to keep her quiet while they were on the move.

By the time Gavin returned with the car, she was out like a light.

Moving quickly and silently, the two men loaded everything they wanted to take with them into the car.

"What about the houseboat?" Gavin asked. "It's got fingerprints and DNA and shit. We should burn it."

"We'll come back tonight and take it out to the ocean and sink it. That way, we won't have the place swarming with cops." He couldn't help himself and poked Gavin's forehead with his finger in a derisive gesture. "What, you think if you burn it down, they won't have records of who leased the slip? You're not that bright, are you?"

"Ah, screw you," Gavin replied. "You would've been a gangbanger's bitch if it weren't for me." He pretended to think, then added, "No, wait, they were five, but I heard they didn't mind sharing."

Mark nodded. "Yeah, that's true, and that's why I took you in on this job because you and I go way back. But you have to stay smart, man, and think. Don't do anything stupid, okay? We're almost home free. Leave the thinking to me, all right?"

Gavin gawked at him, speechless. Mark went into the back room and scooped Paige in his arms, then took her to the car, shielding her from view with a blanket. Anyone watching could've picked up on the fact that the girl was blindfolded and wounded and consider those facts as worthy of a 911 call. She squirmed in his arms and cried softly. Then he set her down on the back seat of the minivan. She shifted and moaned, sleepy yet awake. Gavin followed, carrying a couple of liquor bottles, then took the passenger seat after putting the bottles on the backseat floor.

Although senseless, considering what was about to happen with the place, Mark locked the front door and climbed behind the wheel, after looking carefully around, to see if anyone had noticed them leaving. It was a sunny yet chilly Monday afternoon, and it was getting late. Not too many people were out at their boats, and it was a bit early for dusk anglers. It was all good.

He'd climbed behind the wheel and was about to turn the key in the ignition, when Mr. Erwin called. "We have instructions for you. Make the call today." Hearing his high-pitched voice turned his gut into a knot of fear and dread. Was he already aware of what had gone wrong? Of Randi and her crazy idea to snatch the money and run?

He listened to the instructions carefully, then he replied, "Consider it done."

Swallowing hard, his mouth suddenly dry, he started the engine and drove off silently for a minute or two. Then, glancing briefly at Gavin, he said, "We have to ditch this car."

26

DEMANDS

DA Joyce couldn't wait to be rid of the young assistant district attorney who used any opportunity to get what was known internally as face time with the boss. Darrel loved to see ambition in young attorneys and usually took great pleasure in teaching the ropes of his trade to the newest members of his team, but not today. He just wanted the man gone.

He stood and straightened his back, then propped his hands on his hips. With a frown he didn't even try to hide, he interrupted the prosecutor's verbal stream. "Anything urgent?" he'd asked, placing emphasis on the word urgent. The young prosecutor, bright and perceptive, stopped talking and thanked him quickly before leaving.

Finally, he was alone, although not quite. Countless cameras could've been trained on him at the time, and he didn't even know how many or where they were. He tried to focus on the RICO case, but his mind wasn't into it, overworked with anxiety and overcaffeinated. Rehearsing the various things he could say to the kidnappers, depending on what their demands would be, just as he usually rehearsed the nights before delivering closing arguments in his most significant cases, he'd worked himself into a state of upheaval.

Over the past few hours, since he'd received Tess Winnett's message, he'd been able to think of little else. What would she do? How would she go about catching the kidnappers and freeing his daughter? If he had a say in it, he preferred she killed them all; it would make things easier for everyone involved. He didn't care about double standards anymore.

Pacing restlessly in his office between the windows overlooking SE Sixth Street and the massive, solid walnut door, he kept wondering what Mitchell wanted. It had to do with the witness; that had to be it. How would he negotiate with the kidnappers if they demanded he kill the witness? There was no possible way to do that and still walk free. But could he take a life to save Paige?

He hoped he'd never find out the answer to that question.

He needed some space where he could walk and gather his thoughts. Usually, he did that on the long corridors of the courthouse, but now, he'd settle for an unused courtroom, where no one would disturb him. Where there weren't any cameras.

Loosening his tie, he pushed the door handle, yanking it open. Then, he froze in his tracks, remembering the flip phone they demanded he keep on him at all times. Was that phone bugged too? Probably.

He swung by his desk and grabbed the burner, wishing he could stomp on it viciously, smashing it into a thousand shards. Wishing his daughter was at home with Miriam, giving his ex-wife countless more reasons to yell at him.

Just thinking of Paige made him grind his teeth and curse under his breath. All those years he'd kept himself away from his daughter, thinking she was better off in the long term if she wasn't touched by the world of killers and rapists and traffickers he dealt with every day. Fearing a day like today would come and sacrificing his relationship with his daughter to prevent it. Yet he'd failed; the dreaded nightmare had turned into reality.

For everyone else out there, Paige was Max Walsh's child.

There was no photo of her in his wallet nor on his desk, not a single one in his entire home. He hadn't whispered a word about her at work when she'd been born. He hadn't fought for joint custody and skipped most of his scheduled visitation days. He'd managed to get the divorce case file sealed. Alimony payments were made through a shell company. And still, they knew.

How?

That didn't matter anymore. He had to get her back; whatever the heck they wanted, he'd find a way to make it happen.

He found an empty courtroom and, out of habit, sat at the prosecutor's table, staring into thin air, breathing slowly and deeply, willing his mind to quiet and start working the way it did when he was at the top of his game.

What would Winnett do?

The sound of the burner phone ringing echoed strangely against the empty courtroom walls. "Damn," he muttered, wishing he'd stayed put in his office. Winnett had put her own bug in his office for that exact reason; to hear what they demanded of him. But no, he had to stroll away and do something stupid like being five stories and a long corridor away from his office. Out of options, he took the call.

"Yes." His voice sounded strangled. He cleared his throat quietly.

"We want Jason Ingram alive," the artificial voice announced.

He stayed silent, waiting for the caller to continue, but there was only silence on the open line.

"How will I get my daughter back?" he eventually asked.

"After we get the witness."

He pressed his lips together and looked at the scratched surface of the table. That was a tall order. At least they didn't want Ingram killed; they probably wanted to kill him themselves, to be sure he was really gone this time. "This will take some time," he said, starting to say the things he'd rehearsed for hours. "He's in US Marshals' custody; he's a protected witness."

"You don't have time," the artificial voice said. "They're moving him from lockup tomorrow at three P.M. to an unknown location. Grab him and deliver him behind the old Sears store, in the parking lot." How did they know when the witness was being moved? Joyce himself had not been informed, and Ingram was his witness.

He knew where that was. Even during the day, that parking lot was deserted, and there were no cameras in use. "Okay, but I want to speak with my daughter."

The call ended abruptly, leaving Darrel fuming. It took every ounce of willpower he had to not tear that phone to pieces. He remembered his office was bugged, and that meant he could still speak to the kidnappers. He could still make them hear what he had to say.

He rushed through the empty corridor and stopped briefly in front of the elevators. He pushed the call button a few times, but none came. Unwilling to wait any longer, he took the stairs, climbing the steps two at a time until he reached his level. From there, in a few large steps, he reached his office, passing by Sol without acknowledging her.

"Are you okay?" he heard her ask, but waved her off with a hand gesture before the door closed behind him. She'd probably never seen him running like a madman through the hallways.

Once in the relative privacy of his own office, he stopped in front of his desk and put his hands on the gleaming surface, leaning against it as if he was going to speak with someone sitting in his chair.

Keeping his voice low, he said, "Listen to me and listen good. If you so much as touch a hair on my girl's head, if you harm her in any way, I'll do nothing else with the rest of my life except hunt you down and make you pay for it. One scream at a time... that's how you'll pay for it, you hear me?" He paused, wondering if they'd heard him, waiting for the phone to ring, but there was only silence and his rage, both thick, all-consuming. "I'll get you your witness, but you better have my little girl, do you understand?" Livid, he slammed his hands against the surface of his desk, then started pacing the room angrily, struggling to breathe.

If nothing else, now Winnett knew they'd called and that they wanted a witness. There was no way he could communicate the rest of their demands to her.

Moments later, the flip phone rang. Holding his breath, Darrel took the call on speaker. "Yes," he replied, his voice cold, menacing.

"Daddy?" Paige cried, sounding distant as if someone else held the phone close to her mouth.

"Paige? Baby, I'm here—" He heard a loud blow, then a shriek, then his daughter sobbing hard. "You son of a bitch—"

"Remember who calls the shots here, asshole," the artificial voice said. "I won't remind you again."

27

BREAKING NEWS

Sixty-seven hours missing

Shadows were growing longer on the Walsh patio as the sun descended toward the horizon line. Soon, Tess would have to prep Miriam for the ransom drop, although she still believed an untrained civilian had no business engaging in a hostage recovery.

Some things still tugged at her gut since the day before when the DA's unexpected statement had thrown her into a frenzy of preparations. Who was that teacher who had so conveniently identified the man in the theater pickup video, the driver of the Subaru, as the school's former janitor? All he'd done was waste their time and send them on a fool's errand. As a profiler, she recognized a known behavior, returning to the scene of the crime, as one that raised a red flag; however, the story the man had told about leaving his phone could've been true.

It was a potential lead she needed to follow up on. After all, the man who'd assaulted Miriam knew his way well around the theater. He seemed at ease among the teachers and parents. He almost... belonged.

Two teachers were called back to the theater when Brassfield had been summoned by the first responders to the 911 call: Mrs. Langhorne and Mr. Mowrey, the science teacher. Tess had a hundred witnesses, but couldn't question any of them, because the kidnapping was kept under strict wraps. But she could still ask Mrs. Langhorne and Mr. Mowrey a few more questions. So far, they'd kept their mouths shut.

Lastly, Donovan had watched endless hours of phone videos collected by Mrs. Langhorne from all the attending parents and teachers, hoping they could catch a better view of the unsub's face. He'd caught a few frames where the man's face was partly visible, albeit shrouded in darkness and hard to distinguish under his hoodie. It was time for Tess to watch some of those videos herself, to see what else caught her eye. Maybe it was something in the people's movement in the audience. Perhaps someone wasn't paying as much attention to the stage and was looking at something else, seeming distracted or nervous, or something. Anything.

She needed to catch a break.

"You ready with the ransom call?" she asked, keeping her voice low so as to not wake Miriam, although she didn't believe the woman was sleeping. There was an unrelenting fire fueling Miriam's endless energy, the love for her daughter, the absolute determination to do anything she could to bring her home.

"I need a few more minutes."

Hiding her frustration from Donovan, who didn't deserve the sting of it, she pulled up some videos sent by Mrs. Langhorne. The sunlight coming through the back door hit the screen of her laptop, making it almost impossible to discern anything on the poorly taken videos.

Grabbing her laptop, she walked toward the bedrooms and sat on the floor, unwilling to enter any of the other rooms without permission. But the hallway was dark enough to give her what she needed.

She started watching, keeping the sound barely audible. She knew the time code when the man had approached Miriam and when they left the auditorium, so she went quickly through the shaking, poorly taken videos, looking to catch a better glimpse of who the mysterious man might've been.

About eight videos later, she'd gained nothing. She'd just wasted more time, and Paige didn't have any time to waste. Starting a new playback, she was getting ready to fast forward to where Paige was sprinkling breadcrumbs through the forest, but that particular video didn't start when the curtain rose. It started a little later; maybe that parent had been held up in traffic. The play had already begun, and the stage performers were Paige and her leading man—a boy about her age—and an adult wearing the woodcutter's costume and a mask.

Why was there an adult on the stage? It was supposed to be a children's play.

"I'm ready," Donovan announced.

She got up from the floor, struggling a little; her body craved a shower and at least twelve hours of sleep. Donovan handed her an earbud she slid into her ear, then said, "Punch it."

The sound quality was unexpectedly good. She could hear water sloshing against a dock, gulls calling, distant, unintelligible conversation, a dog barking, and a bell or a chime of some sort.

"I know that sound," Donovan said. He listened to that section of the recording several times more, with his eyes closed. "I know where this is; I keep my boat there. It's Palm Harbor Marina."

"Are you sure?" Tess asked, a wave of excitement washing over her. "It's not Miami Beach Marina or some other place?"

He hesitated long enough to seed the doubt in her mind. "I don't think so. I recognize the buoy bell." He lowered his gaze for a moment. "But I can't be sure Miami Beach Marina doesn't have one just like it. I don't spend much time over there; too rich for my taste."

"How big is Palm Harbor Marina?"

"Five docks, each about fifty wet slips, about sixty percent of those we'd find at their docks if we went there now."

"And they're all taken?" Tess knew very little about boating life.

"There's a year-long waiting list for a slip."

She checked the time. "Do you think you can get us the names of those who rent slips over there?" Maybe there was a name on that list that meant something, that could narrow down the search through over a hundred boats. While they'd bang on cabin doors, the kidnappers could spook, and Paige's life could be in even more danger than it already was.

He looked around him as if to check if anyone could overhear their conversation. "Legally?" he whispered. "It would take a while."

Tess looked him straight in the eye. "In this case, I don't care. As far as I know, we never had this conversation."

"Fair enough," he replied. He typed fast, his fingers dancing above the keyboard.

Wringing her hands, Tess returned to her laptop. She watched the video again, noting the woodcutter's appearance on the stage, the time codes when he was visible. Then she fast-forwarded to the end of the play, where the man appeared again. He was there all right, in plain sight, on the stage, playing his part.

Only he'd been gone from the stage between 5:53 and 6:40. Per the security videos she'd seen at the theater, Miriam had been assaulted and dragged into the closet at 6:27. The woodworker had not been on the stage at that time. His final scene had started at 6:41 and lasted until 6:48. Then the masked woodworker took a curtain call with all the children at precisely 6:51.

An unsub who knew precisely what he was doing and had planned this well in advance could've made it happen, even if that meant he'd had only a few minutes between his public appearances and the details of the abduction: Miriam's extraction from the auditorium, her assault, bringing the Subaru to the front to pick up Paige. It was tight, with zero room for error, but not impossible.

Feeling a sense of excitement in her gut, she dialed Mrs. Langhorne's number and stepped out on the patio.

"Mrs. Langhorne, this is Special Agent Winnett with the FBI." The woman acknowledged her weakly, her voice sounding strangled, fearful. "Do you have a moment?"

"Y—yes, I do."

"First of all, thank you for obtaining those videos from the parents; that was immensely helpful."

"Absolutely. It was the least I could do."

"I noticed an adult male playing the woodcutter character in the play, the father."

"Yes, Mr. Brannan, our PE teacher."

"Why was the part given to an adult?"

"Well, some of the parents had an issue with a child playing the part of someone who sells their children for money. They didn't want their children to identify with such a situation and to understand that it was an option." She sighed from the bottom of her lungs. "Parents these days, they're ridiculous sometimes. But we had no choice but to cast an adult, and Mr. Brannan offered."

He did, didn't he? Tess thought. *Interesting.* "Between the opening scene and the ending, where was Mr. Brannan?"

"Oh, he was there, backstage."

"You sure about that?"

"I'm positive," she replied, not a trace of hesitation in her voice.

That simple word burned her lead to ashes. "Do you think you could give me his phone number? I'm not sure I have it. I have yours and Mr. Mowrey's, but not his."

"Sure," she replied, then read the number slowly as if Tess hadn't graduated second grade yet and couldn't take notes any faster. "But you might not find him; he's on vacation as of today."

"Did he call in?"

"Oh, no, he had travel arrangements and all, a Mediterranean cruise." Excitement bubbled in her voice. "He booked his vacation time a couple of months ago. I believe he left immediately after the play, or maybe on Sunday?" She paused for a moment. "You know, teachers don't normally get vacation requests approved during the school year; we have an entire summer to do whatever we want, right?"

"What happened?"

"The principal granted him an exception. The cruise tickets were on sale, and he's an amazing teacher. We want him to stay with us."

"All right, Mrs. Langhorne, thank you."

"Um, you think you could put in a good word for me with the parents? You know, like, tell them I helped?"

"I'll see what I can do," Tess replied and ended the call. She wasn't going to say a word; through her preposterous carelessness, Langhorne had facilitated Paige's kidnapping.

She pulled the sliding door open and entered the living room. Miriam was up, wearing jeans and a light jacket, and sneakers instead of her usual heels.

"I'm ready to go," she said, clasping her hands together. Max watched from a distance, leaning against the wall, a wounded soldier who could barely stand the general's decision to bench him.

"We're going to have you wear a wire," Tess said, "and we'll be seconds away from you at all times. Please take your jacket off."

"I don't want a wire," she replied. "What if they catch me?" Her green eyes were intense, authoritative, demanding. She wasn't going to budge, and Tess didn't insist; after all, the moment she was on her own, she could rip that wire off her body and throw it in the nearest trash can. Some battles just couldn't be won.

"All right," she conceded. Miriam's shoulders relaxed a little. "Follow our instructions to the letter. I'll be there with you myself, staying out of sight, but you won't be in harm's way if you do as I tell you." She nodded and licked her pale, chapped lips. Surprisingly, she hadn't put on makeup and didn't seem to care about her appearance anymore. "Stay in public areas, the more crowded, the better. Ask them to tell you where Paige is; get a precise address or clear instructions. Try to hold on to the money until you do; that's your bargaining chip." Miriam swallowed hard and nodded again. "Good, then we're set. Make sure you have your phone with you and a spare in your car." She gave her a burner phone from the kit she carried after saving her own number in it. "Call me if you need me. This is in case they take your phone. Hide it somewhere."

She crouched down and slid the small flip phone in her shoe, under her arch.

"Smart," Tess said with a smile. "I wouldn't've thought to put it there. I'll remember that when I do body searches on suspects."

"I have high arches," she replied. "I've been wearing heels all my life." She breathed loudly, forcing the air into her lungs, probably to build up courage. "Let's go, please. I can't wait anymore."

"Hey, Winnett?" Donovan called from the front door, his voice riddled with undertones of alarm. "We're screwed. TV crews are on the front lawn."

28

SUBPOENA

It was getting too hot in DA Joyce's office. It must've been the sun, still strong before setting, bringing enough heat through the thermopane windows to make him sweat profusely. He loosened his tie another inch and walked over to the thermostat. It showed seventy-two degrees, but he doubted that was true. He lowered the setting to sixty-seven and stood directly under a vent until he felt better.

There, under the cooling jet of air, he gathered his thoughts and started to build a strategy. How could he deliver the witness to the kidnappers? It wasn't as if he'd be able to saunter into lockup and say, "I'll take Ingram with me." Not even the powerful state district attorney could pull that one off, not with a witness in US Marshals' protection.

For a moment, he wondered if he would've done it. If all the doors were open, if he could just grab Ingram out of protective custody and walk away unscathed, would he have done it? Would he place his daughter's life above everyone else's?

"In a heartbeat," he whispered to himself. Ashamed, he lowered his head, feeling the cutting air freeze the sweat on his nape. No life was above his daughter's, not even his own, and let all those who'd judge go screw themselves. This was war.

Breathing deeply, he walked over to his desk and sat, his favorite writing implement in hand, ready to write names on a list. Names and court dates, scribbled the way he always did, using a 0.5 mechanical pencil on a small, ruled notepad, the perfect size to write instructions for Sol and then tear off the page to hand them over.

Then he buzzed her in.

She entered quickly, without knocking, and stopped sharply in front of his desk. "Whoa, it's freezing in here." She ran her hands over her arms. "Are you okay?"

Her question shot a pang of fear through his gut. Of course, she'd notice something was wrong with him, but the people listening to every word he was saying could panic and do something rash if he didn't play his cards right.

In his entire career, he'd never been seen so disheveled, his tie loosened, hanging crookedly over a shirt covered in sweat stains. "I'm okay, Sol, just this damn migraine killing me," he replied calmly, closing his eyes as he would've instinctively done if a migraine had been the culprit. But he welcomed the private darkness behind the closed eyelids, the possibility to hide his lie better from a bright, perceptive woman who knew him well. Who cared.

"What can I get you?" she offered. "I have Motrin if you'd like, or you could do the unfathomable and go home early. You don't have any court appearances or appointments left for today."

He opened his eyes and looked at her intently, searching her eyes for clues she might've been aware of what was going on. "No, I still have plenty to do."

"Then, how about I get you a fresh shirt and tie?" She smiled, her incredibly white teeth sparkling against her deep red lip gloss. "You know, just in case someone stops by."

He frowned, surprised and humbled. "You have clean shirts for me? And ties?"

"I kept a few back when I picked up your laundry," she replied, tilting her head just a touch. "You know, over time."

He smiled for a brief moment before the tension wiped out that tiny gesture of gratitude from his thin, tense lips. "I'll take you up on that, but first, get subpoenas issued for these witnesses, please. The first one needs to be marked urgent and delivered tonight or first thing tomorrow morning."

She took the page he'd torn from his small notepad and read it, her thin, perfectly manicured finger stopping on each name as she went through the list. Then the same finger returned to the first name on the list and tapped it twice, the paper rustling in the tense silence.

"Defense is going to balk at this one," she said. He held his breath, silently willing her to not read names. She never did; she liked numbers better. "This special agent—why her? She wasn't the arresting—"

"I'm calling her to give expert testimony on serial offender investigative procedure. The defense can go ahead and ask for a continuance."

"Do we have a home address on file for her?"

"Have it delivered to her boss, SAC Pearson at the regional office. He'll know where to find her on such short notice."

She frowned and leaned a little closer over the desk, studying him, probably noticing all the things that were wrong with him. "Really, are you okay?"

"Yeah," he sighed, then ran his hand over his crew-cut hair, the calming gesture failing to bring the much-needed relief. "I'm falling behind with these cases," he gestured at the pile stacked on the edge of his desk. "I might pull one of the ADAs to assist. By the way, when's the next court date for the Allan case?"

The same index finger touched her lips for a brief second. "Um, this coming Wednesday, the day after tomorrow."

He stood, arranging his shirt collar and tightening his tie as if he wasn't going to get changed out of those clothes soon. "Okay, then, we need to scramble. We're not even close to being ready."

29

MONEY DROP

Seventy-one hours missing

Tess rushed to the window and looked outside. One after another, news vans marked with colorful, recognizable TV channel logos were pulling onto the street. "Oh, crap," she whispered, then looked at Donovan. "How the hell did they find out?"

Miriam rushed to the window and pulled the curtains shut, then grabbed the TV remote with trembling hands and dropped it, sending it clattering on the gleaming hardwood floor. It slid under the sofa. Max was quick to retrieve it and turn the TV on just in time to catch the news announcer saying, "Paige Joyce, the daughter of pharmacy owner Miriam Joyce and District Attorney Darrel Joyce, is rumored to have been kidnapped and held for ransom."

"Oh, no," Miriam gasped, staring wide-eyed at the screen. "What are they going to do to my baby?" Max wrapped his arms around her thin shoulders, and she didn't reject him. "How can we tell them we didn't do this?" He had no answers for her. Burrowing her face at his chest, she wept heavily, her shoulders heaving with every breath.

"It's going to be okay," Max whispered, "you'll see. They'll take the money, and you'll bring her back home to us. Come on, chin up," he said, lifting her chin gently and placing a soft kiss on her trembling lips. "You have to go."

Tess watched their moment, unsettled. Max seemed like the ideal husband, always there, gentle and supportive, but he was unexpectedly calm under the circumstances as if he'd been expecting the media to show up on his lawn. As if he thought that was a good thing.

But there was no time to call him on it, not before the ransom drop anyway. Checking the backyard quickly, she noticed a narrow gate connecting their yard with the neighbors' yard behind theirs. "What's that for?" she pointed at the gate.

"Their kids always throw their toys over the fence, and we didn't mind it. We're friends."

"Friends enough to cut through their yard for the ransom drop?"

He nodded vigorously. "Absolutely."

Maybe they stood a chance to handle the ransom drop and Paige's rescue before the unsubs learned about the media issue. The note they'd put in Miriam's pocket advised specifically against drawing attention to Paige's kidnapping or getting the media involved. Things could turn ugly if they found out too early.

She stopped, frozen in place by the incongruity of her own thoughts. Too early? For what? She'd just heard DA Joyce speaking about a witness he wanted; she didn't have specifics, just what she'd heard the DA say, then the heart-wrenching call where they put Paige on the phone. Whatever the ransom drop was about, it was just a ruse, some diversion meant to hide their real agenda, a witness in some case, most likely the RICO case brought against Allan Mitchell.

There wasn't a chance in hell they'd get Paige after the money drop.

Tess wished she had made time to study that RICO file cover to cover; she didn't have all the details, but she remembered the prosecution's case was built around the testimony of one surviving witness, a man by the name of Jonas Ingram. That's where her research had stopped, her time split between ransom calls and botched drops and leads she'd chased that didn't pan out.

Did they want that witness, Ingram? Then, what was the deal with the ransom? How did it make sense to send the girl's parents in two different directions? Or was the unsub team fractured, like she'd seen happen so many times before? A million dollars was enough bait to turn even the straightest, most honorable of kidnappers into a backstabbing traitor who'd sell their own mother.

If the unsub team was fractured, how could she pit them against each other if she didn't have direct access to the one unsub who picked up the cash? The answer was simple. They had to capture the unsub at the drop; there was no other way. Capture him or her, then lean on them until they spilled everything they knew. That part, the interrogation, she had that covered; she could get anyone to talk. As for the capture, Miriam would throw a fit if she knew what she was planning. The poor woman expected her daughter to be released tonight; Tess now realized that wasn't going to happen, not until the witness issue was handled, whatever that was.

They had to catch the unsub that was going to pick up the money. Paige's life depended on it.

She turned to Miriam and found her standing by the back door, pale and determined, the two duffel bags at her feet. "Ready?" Tess asked, although the answer was right under her eyes.

"As I'll ever be." The reply came in a tense, breathy voice.

"Tell Patto to pull the car around and pick us up on the street behind us," she told Donovan.

He made the call to Patto while Tess checked her weapon.

"N—no, please," Miriam whispered, staring at her gun. "Promise me you won't interfere. It's my baby's life we're talking about."

Tess stared at her for a brief moment. "It's just force of habit before going out in the field. Nothing to worry about." She was a big fan of telling the truth, but this wasn't the time for full transparency. The woman was already a ball of taut, frayed nerves.

"D, why don't you go out there and speak with the media?"

His eyebrows popped. "Me? Are you kidding?"

"Tell them they can't be on the lawn because, legally, that's trespassing. Tell them that we'll let them know as soon as we hear anything." He still stared at her incredulously. "Sheesh, Donovan, just distract them until we leave."

"I can help with that," Max offered. "I'll say all that."

"And not a word more, all right?" Tess added and waited for Max to acknowledge. He nodded, but his gaze shifted sideways as if he was hiding something. As if he was planning what he was about to say, something entirely different from what she had in mind.

As much as she would've wanted to persuade Max Walsh into toeing the line, she was running out of time.

She opened the back door and exited, ready to pull back inside if she saw any reporters. There were none. She beckoned Miriam to follow her, and they rushed over to the fence. Tess opened the gate and let Miriam go first while she closed the gate behind her. Then she took the lead again, making sure no reporters were waiting for them in the street.

Patto stopped his SUV at the curb, and Miriam took the back seat. Tess climbed in the front.

"Final check," Tess said. "You have both phones?"

"Yes." Miriam's voice was strong and firm yet understandably tense.

Patto peeled from the curb and took the shortest way to the interstate.

"Tell me again, what are you supposed to do?"

Miriam inhaled sharply. "Wait for them to make contact. Try to get the location where they keep my baby girl or information on how I'll get her back. Keep tears in check," she added with a quick, sad smile. "Don't pay them until I know about Paige, or at least try not to pay them."

"Yes, try," Tess repeated. *You won't succeed,* she thought, *but I could be wrong.* "Just be safe."

They drove in silence the short time it took them to reach the mall. Patto stopped by the entrance closest to the rendezvous point, and Miriam climbed out of the SUV, carrying the two bags. Tess watched her enter the mall, then turned to Patto and said, "Drop me at the next entrance. Then park the car and go in after her. Stay out of sight."

"You got it." Patto was a man of few words and excellent reliability, although he refused to wear something less conspicuous than his usual dark suit, white shirt, and Ray-Ban sunglasses. The man looked, walked, and talked like the lead character from Men in Black, minus the humor.

Tess climbed out of the SUV at the next entrance and made her way toward the Camille La Vie store, carrying an oversized shopping bag she'd borrowed from Miriam, filled with crumpled gift-wrapping tissue. She walked with a determined stride and a tourist's smile on her face, dressed in jeans and a loud shirt at least two numbers too large, borrowed from Max's closet.

The mall was filled with shoppers, mostly tourists, but a few locals too. She could tell them apart effortlessly. Fragments of lively chatter and merchant calls, background music from a radio station playing hit songs, and the mouthwatering smells coming from the food court reminded her of the many months that had passed since she'd taken an afternoon off for herself to just hang out. Among people, looking at nice things, maybe even buying something.

There was never enough time.

She located the women's restroom entrance just as Miriam stepped inside, tentative, a little shaky. Tess found a good vantage point in front of Churro Mania, a sweets shop selling scrumptious desserts and hot chocolate. She bought a couple of churros and started eating one as slowly as she could, although it was melt-in-your-mouth delicious.

Then she saw the unsub, approaching stealthily from the entrance, almost touching the wall. She was a young, bleached blonde in dire need of personal hygiene and a clean wardrobe. She looked like a junkie and moved like one, although she was visibly trying to go unnoticed.

At first, Tess had been sure the bleached blonde was the unsub; on second thought, she didn't know what to believe. The woman didn't fit the profile one iota. Junkies weren't organized or disciplined enough to execute the bold plan she'd seen carried out to perfection when Paige had been taken. Still, she pushed the comm button and said, "Got possible unsub pussyfooting by the wall, blonde female in jeans and denim jacket."

"Copy that; I have her," Patto confirmed.

The woman went straight for the restroom without checking her surroundings. She wasn't a professional like Allan Mitchell would hire. Tess waited, unsure if she was really the unsub or just someone who'd happened to stroll by needing the restroom at the wrong time.

Then she heard a scream and a long wail and saw the woman bolting out of the restroom with the two duffel bags in her arms. She was running faster than Tess would've anticipated, seeing how thin she was.

"Unsub's fleeing," Tess said in the comm.

"Copy, I got her."

"I'm right behind you." Tess rushed into the restroom.

Miriam was on the floor struggling to get up, her nose bleeding profusely. "She took the money, and I asked about Paige like you said, and she—just punched me." She sobbed hard, a trembling heap on the white marble floor.

Tess gave her a hand and pulled her up to her feet. "Listen, I have to run and catch that woman. It's our only chance to get Paige. Stay here and wait for me, all right?" Miriam nodded.

Running as fast as she could, she left the restroom, making for the exit. Once in the parking lot, she stopped for a moment, searching for Patto. She saw him a good distance away, heading toward the streets where the traffic was heavy and rushed.

With long, cadenced strides, she ran as fast as she could, her heart pumping fast in her chest, her lungs burning. She pushed harder and ran faster, gaining on Patto and the blonde. Weighed down by the money bags and cutting her way through pedestrian traffic, the woman was losing ground, but not fast enough. Soon, she'd make it to the street where she could easily disappear into the heavy traffic.

She wasn't going to reach her in time.

Patto must've had the same thought because he stopped and pulled out his weapon. "Stop, or I'll shoot," he shouted.

The woman faltered as if considering if she should stop but kept on running.

Just as a breathless and bleeding Miriam caught up with her, Tess pressed the comm button and said, "Don't shoot. She's the only one who knows where Paige is."

"Copy that," came Patto's reply, then a gunshot reverberated in the evening air.

"No," Miriam screamed, then watched the scene with both hands clasping her open mouth.

Shot in the leg while running, the woman fell to the ground and rolled into the street, in the path of a speeding bus. Moments later, twenty-dollar bills were flying through the air, settling quietly on the asphalt like tree leaves in the fall, only to be whirled up in the air again by whooshing traffic.

30

PANIC

The sky was starting to show the colors of dawn toward the beach, but the Atlantic coast was miles away from the cheap motel Mark was so desperate to leave.

"Why the hell are we running again, man?" Gavin asked, rubbing his sweaty forehead with chubby fingers. By looking at him and considering the empty bottle that had rolled under his bed, he was battling a huge hangover. "Where would we go this time, huh?"

Mark shot him an angry glare as he collected the items scattered through the room. "Away from here. That's where we're going." He closed the zipper on a large duffel bag he'd filled with clothes before leaving the houseboat, then dropped it at Gavin's feet in an unspoken invitation to take it to the car. "Have you seen how that guy was staring?"

"Who? The weirdo in one-oh-nine?" Gavin asked, scratching his belly through the thinning fabric of his dirty wifebeater. "He was just some sorry dude, man. He didn't mean anything."

"Will you bet your life he isn't going to call anyone? I won't bet mine, in case you're wondering." Gavin might've seemed like the perfect solution for his dilemma at some point, but he was more and more of a deadweight now. Every little thing he had to do, he had to explain and then argue over until he wanted to strangle him with his own hands. He'd become a liability, a man who couldn't be trusted, with the few exceptions when he could be anyone and do anything, for short periods, before slipping into a drunken, argumentative stupor.

Gavin took the bags to the car, then drove it back to their room and stopped it close to the door.

"How about my money, man?" he whispered. The light in the room next door came on, and the occupant started moving about, his footfalls noisy through the paper-thin walls.

Mark stared at the window, wondering if their neighbor was about to pull the curtains and peek outside. He waited for a while, but he only heard a toilet flushing, then the water running at the kitchenette sink. Relieved, he went inside their room and scooped Paige off the couch where she'd spent the night. Her skin burned in contact with his hand. Her fever had dropped after the pills, but since last night it was climbing steadily. She shifted in her sleep, whimpering.

He took her outside and laid her on the backseat of the minivan, then slid the door closed, not minding the noise it made. Now anyone who looked would've seen two guys leaving a motel room, and soon they'd be out of there anyway.

He climbed behind the wheel and waited impatiently for Gavin to take another leak and get in the passenger seat. Then he drove off, staying at the speed limit, not really knowing where he was going. Once he got a new car, he'd find another no-tell motel where he could send Gavin to pay for a room in cash, then lay low until the job was done.

"Have you seen what happened with Randi, man? They fucking killed her," Gavin said for the fifteenth time since they'd watched the news on television. "That's what cops do, bro."

"It was an accident, didn't you see?" The man was nothing if not dense as a brick wall. "She got hit by a bus, Gav. After she'd been paid."

"What are you saying? That they're willing to pay again?"

"Damn right, they are." He wasn't going to tell him what else he thought. That sooner rather than later, Aquila would come after them with a vengeance for screwing up his plans and collecting the ransom when they should've just followed a set of simple instructions. For getting a stranger, a loose-mouthed junkie no less, involved in the operation without his say-so. For pasting Paige's name and the DA's all over the television, internet, and social media, completely screwing up Aquila's plans. How would the DA be allowed anywhere near that witness, now that everyone knew his daughter had been nabbed?

He weighed his options for a long moment, driving aimlessly through the sleeping streets of the city. Soon, Mr. Erwin would call and that wasn't a call he was looking forward to. Or maybe he won't call anymore; Mark would just not wake up tomorrow morning or be shot while waiting for the traffic light to turn green at the following street corner. Still, he couldn't decide in Aquila's place how to proceed; he had to wait for instructions.

But what would he say about Randi and the ransom she'd collected? How would he explain that away when he'd been paid generously by Mr. Erwin to get a specific job done? No matter how he twisted his mind, he couldn't come up with a decent excuse he could hope to offer Mr. Erwin while begging him to not take his miserable life.

Maybe he would just tell him the truth, about how Randi had been blackmailing him, and how he thought he had things under control. The truth was so twisted and screwed up, Mr. Erwin might actually believe it.

For now, he'd keep on going. He needed a new car, but he had to steal one; there was no other way. He'd only had this one prepared at that parking lot downtown; he hadn't anticipated he'd need more than one. But now that the cops had Randi, they'd find out she lived in a houseboat, and they'd stumble across her friend Joe, who knew what car they were driving.

He'd be more than thrilled to offer his help, quick to rat on him for a few bucks. Gavin would've turned on him too, if he'd seen the announcement Mark had caught on TV while he was in the john, taking a dump.

Two hundred and fifty thousand dollars for any information about Paige. That guy in 109 might've watched the news last night. Not then, when he was visibly drunk, but when he'd wake up this morning, he might realize two men looking like Mark and Gavin had no business traveling with a sleeping child, and he'd pick up the phone and make that call. It was like a free lottery ticket, right? Maybe he'd win a quarter mil. Yes, that piece of crap Max Walsh had placed a bounty on their heads, and now the entire state of Florida was out hunting for them.

How long before Gavin learned about the bounty? And what would he do?

"How did you meet the Big Man?" Mark asked casually. He'd never met Aquila himself, but the day Gavin had saved his life in the joint, he used his name freely, like someone who knew him personally and was comfortable throwing his name around.

"I never met him," Gavin replied with a morose grimace on his face. "Why d'you ask?"

"You used his name to get those guys to back off."

"Ah, that," Gavin looked at him briefly before staring at the empty road ahead. "A skinny guy with a screechy voice told me to bail you out and use that name."

That had to be Mr. Erwin.

"Paid me to, is more like it," Gavin added, laughing. "The skinny dude was powerful in there; no one dared cross him. Sometimes I miss the joint, man. Life was easier. Made more sense."

Gavin was an idiot. Hands down. Why not go bitch slap a cop and make your dreams come true? Mark thought. Mr. Erwin probably didn't remember Gavin after all those years. But why did he save him? What made him, Mark Crane, worth saving? What was he to Aquila to warrant the money he'd spent on him all those years? It couldn't've been about the girl; she wasn't even born when he'd done his time.

On a whim, he took a right turn and headed into a shopping center parking lot. First, he circled around, looking at how the surveillance cameras were placed and where he could grab a car without being seen.

When a silver Toyota Sienna pulled into the parking lot, Mark followed it from a distance, hoping it would stop at a distance from the cameras. It stopped right between the posts; he'd show on both cameras, but he'd keep his head down, and so would Gavin.

"Get ready," he said, and Gavin nodded. "I need her out of it, but alive," he added, talking about the minivan's driver.

He pulled up at the back of the silver minivan, blocking it. Then Gavin hopped out, keeping his head lowered and his ball cap on, and asked the woman, "'Scuse me, where's that Lowe's store? Wasn't it supposed to be here?"

A little frightened at first, the woman turned her head to look behind her, where Lowe's was. Gavin pounced. He hit her in the back of her head, and she fell into his arms, dropping the car keys on the ground. Gavin dragged her to the Honda minivan and put her inside, while Mark moved Paige to the Toyota, then moved their luggage.

Picking up the Toyota's keys from the ground, Mark climbed behind the wheel and pulled out of the parking slot.

Gavin parked the green Honda in the same spot, then closed the door and joined him in the Toyota.

The entire thing had taken them less than one minute.

Maybe the woman would wake up and raise hell, and cops would see them on video, but for a while, at least, they were okay, far from being out of the woods yet, far from knowing what would happen to him if the DA failed to deliver the witness Aquila wanted. It didn't matter whose fault it was; Aquila didn't seem like a man who'd bother to ask.

He recalled something his cellmate once told him when he was struggling with detox. He'd said, "When you're going through hell, keep going."

31

AFTERMATH

Eighty-two hours missing

It had been the night from hell. The third night in a row when Tess didn't get much sleep, but this time, it had been particularly challenging. It felt as if the entire world conspired to throw as many curveballs as possible. Anything that could've gone wrong did precisely that as if an unseen master puppeteer pulled all the strings that would end Paige's young life despite Tess's best efforts.

Patto... What a mess. As soon as her initial consternation after seeing the woman run over by the bus dissipated, she'd called for police support and rushed over to Patto, who stood frozen with the gun in his hand. She disarmed him effortlessly, ejected the bullet from the barrel, then slipped the weapon into her pocket. He was still staring at the body bleeding on the asphalt, too shocked to realize what was going on around him.

She grabbed his arm, squeezing it hard, and looked straight into his vacant eyes. "What the hell were you thinking?" Her voice was loaded with undertones of rage and desperation. "I specifically told you not to take that shot." He stood silently, not moving a muscle, not acknowledging he'd heard her. "You never shoot a fleeing suspect in the back, not unless they're about to put lives in danger." He must've known that; every law enforcement officer and FBI agent abided by that rule. "She was our only chance to find that girl."

Appearing out of nowhere, out of breath and disheveled, Miriam pounced and started pummeling Patto with her tiny fists, sobbing. "You killed my baby," she cried, hitting him wherever she could. He stood and took it, staring into the distance, not raising a finger to defend himself. "You son of a bitch," Miriam shouted, then gasped for air and choked. She coughed, then pounded on him some more. "You killed her!" The last word ended in a wail that had her bending over as if she couldn't stand straight anymore when her pain was too much to bear.

Tess grabbed Miriam's arms from behind, pulling her away. Where the hell were those cops when she needed them? The scene was an out-of-control mess. The bus driver had fainted by the right front wheel of his vehicle, while frenzied crowds were scrambling to grab as much cash as they could, trampling over people who were picking money off the ground, not caring if they stepped into the victim's blood as they grabbed another twenty. While she had to fight Miriam, whose despair-fueled rage was stoking her physical strength.

Holding Miriam's arms tightly from behind, she said, "I understand how you must feel, but I'll have to handcuff you unless you settle down. You shouldn't be here anyway. You were supposed to wait inside."

Thankfully, the cops took just a few minutes to arrive. She would've normally advised the local LEOs about the ransom drop, but this case required a different approach, and she'd bent procedure to the breaking point. She'd advised them of some FBI action in the general area of the mall, without telling them what the action was or the exact location, and had requested units on standby in case she needed them. She'd say that she feared too many police cars would scare the unsub away and jeopardize the drop.

Working quickly and effectively, the cops blocked traffic, pushed the crowds away, and started taking statements. One of them offered to take Miriam off her hands, but she declined, asking the officer to locate and retrieve Patto's Suburban instead.

The coroner's van pulled up at the scene, driving over the curb, with Doc Rizza himself showing up despite the late hour. She was still holding Miriam when he approached. The woman was almost limp in her grip, her head hanging low, her face shielded by loose strands of her long hair.

"I heard you got into some unexpected trouble," he said, running his hand through his tousled tufts of hair. He wore a wrinkled Hawaiian shirt and was putting on a fresh lab coat over it. "What happened?"

"You'll find a GSW in her left leg; that's from SA Patto's service weapon. She fell into oncoming traffic."

Doc Rizza crouched with difficulty by the body, his girth and age both getting in his way, then put one knee on the asphalt for support. With gloved hands, he examined the woman's head quickly, then stood with a groan and peeled off his blood-stained gloves. "Multiple compound skull fractures, some depressed, and that's only what I've noticed in the first five seconds. She didn't stand a chance," he said with sadness in his voice. "People never win when they go against busses."

"He killed her," Miriam cried, lifting her head and looking at the medical examiner.

"I need her identified as soon as possible, Doc," Tess pleaded.

"Uh-huh, say no more," he mumbled, seemingly relieved he didn't have to reply to Miriam's comment. Opening his kit, he extracted a mobile fingerprint scanner. Then he crouched by the body and, after putting on fresh gloves, he scanned the victim's index print. A few seconds passed, then a beep got their attention.

"Randi Rowland, twenty-six. She's local; born in Miami-Dade." He stood and held the scanner briefly in front of Tess's eyes. "A long rap sheet for drug-related offenses, mostly minor. No current address."

Two cops walked over to them, and one said, "We have SA Patto's vehicle pulled here, ma'am." She looked where the man was pointing and hesitated for a moment, inclined to let them take Miriam to Patto's SUV.

Instead, she released her grip on the woman's arms and said, "Mrs. Walsh, let's go to the car. You'll be able to wait there until I wrap up here, and we can go home."

Miriam turned to face Tess and reached for her arm with trembling fingers. "My baby is dead... they'll kill her," she stated, too drained to sob anymore. Her tear-streaked face was immobile, her swollen eyes despairing yet immensely tired.

A flash of light almost blinded Tess for a brief moment, followed by others. Frowning, she squinted under the continued flashes and saw a bunch of reporters standing only a few yards away. They had crossed through the landscaping and climbed over the hedges. A couple of uniformed deputies struggled to keep them at bay, while one shouted, "I need some yellow tape over here."

The media had arrived.

Lowering her head, she rushed Miriam to Patto's SUV and loaded her in the back. The SUV had deeply tinted windows, meant to give the woman some privacy, even if the reporters had powerful lenses.

About twenty minutes later, after Doc Rizza had loaded Randi into his van and the local deputies assured her they had the situation under control, she grabbed Patto and took him aside, out of everyone's earshot.

"Patto, listen to me." He didn't seem to have heard her. She shook him until he made good, solid eye contact showing a flicker of comprehension. "I'll take you home. I have your weapon. Nothing will happen until tomorrow, so get some sleep. Put your thoughts in order. Tomorrow, first thing, you don't talk with anyone before you get a lawyer, is that clear?" He'd disregarded her order and had pulled that trigger, but he'd meant well; she was sure about that. From where he'd fired the shot, he couldn't've appreciated correctly how close Randi was to the road or seen the incoming bus.

All that had happened last night.

By the time she'd persuaded Miriam to lie down, it was almost two A.M., and she couldn't walk straight anymore. Tess caught a few hours of shuteye on the Walshes' sofa while Donovan dozed with his head resting on his folded arms at the table.

She woke up to the chime of a new, incoming message from SAC Pearson. Leaning against the armrest, she looked at the screen, squinting under the piercing rays of the rising sun.

Winnett, are you in control of your case? Phones are ringing off the hook.

She read the message twice, struggling with sleep-blurred vision, not understanding clearly what he meant. Then she noticed the link that had been sent with it. She clicked it while anxiety twisted her gut into a knot. He knew about what had happened at the mall; she'd informed him personally the night before. This had to be something else.

The Web page opened a video taken from the local TV news channel. It was filmed while she and Miriam had left for the ransom drop, and Max had spoken with the press on his front lawn. The video showed Max standing calmly in front of the cameras, pleading with the public to share anything they might know about Paige's whereabouts. Then he'd paused for a brief moment and offered a reward for any information leading to the safe return of his stepdaughter, in the amount of a quarter-million dollars. The reporters had fallen silent for the briefest of moments, then had clamored until the video ended with a screen showing Paige's photo and providing the local FBI hotline as a contact number.

He hadn't stuttered nor paused to find his words or fight off tears. It was a planned speech, well-rehearsed and perfectly delivered with the ideal mix of emotions, his charismatic eyes vibrating with just the right amount of sadness and hope.

"Son of a bitch," she muttered as she sprung off the sofa and found her shoes. Then she rushed to the master bedroom and pounded on the door. "Mr. Walsh, I need to speak with you right now." She waited a few seconds, then banged again, this time louder. "Mr. Walsh?"

Miriam opened the door, wrapping the sash of her bathrobe around her thin body. "What is it?" Worried, she rushed into the living room, where she stopped, confused, worried.

Then Max appeared, and Tess turned to him like a harpy. "It was you, wasn't it? You called them!" she shouted, pointing at the front door, beyond which several TV news vans still lingered.

He held her gaze without flinching. "What if it was me? You aren't doing much to get our daughter back, now are you?"

She slapped her forehead in a gesture of deep frustration, turning on her heels away from him. She couldn't bear the sight of him. The presumptuous little prick! She would've loved to land her fist right in the middle of that arrogant smirk of his.

"You've done what?" Miriam charged. In front of her unleashed rage, he withdrew and lowered his gaze. "You called them? You? When you knew they said no press?" She wasn't crying, her dry eyes throwing daggers of rage. "Get out of this house."

Taken aback, he opened his mouth to say something, raising his hands in a pacifying gesture.

"Right now!" Miriam snapped. "Out!"

Tess wondered what was worse, to keep them cooped up together, a barrel of gunpowder with a short fuse that could be lit anytime, by anything, or have that loose cannon out there, unsupervised. She touched Miriam's elbow; the woman pulled away as if she'd stepped on a poisonous snake.

"What?"

"I don't believe it's the smart thing to do, considering what he's done." Tess had no problem speaking of Max as if he weren't in the room. "Maybe it's better you keep an eye on him here until this is over."

Miriam breathed, forcing air into her lungs, then exhaling loudly, a sigh loaded with anger and disappointment and the markings of a broken marriage soon to follow. "I understand. But how will this end? Do we even have the slightest chance to get her back? We just killed one of them for crying out loud and failed to pay the ransom twice!"

"Yes, yes, I know all that, but we have leads now. That woman's name, and soon we'll have her associates. And there's something else," she said, biting her lip and hoping she was doing the right thing. "They might be after your ex-husband. We believe they might want something from him, not just the ransom money."

"What?" she asked. Her eyebrows shot up, crinkling her smooth forehead with the lines of disbelief.

"I told you they were hiding something," Max said. "Didn't I tell you? It's always about the famous Darrel Joyce, isn't it?"

Without a word, she slapped him hard across the face. "You've lost the right to speak in this house."

"Miriam, please," he pleaded, but she'd turned her back to him.

The doorbell rang, but Tess ignored it, thinking it was one of the reporters. Donovan opened the door, though, after looking at the visitor's ID through the glass.

Miriam had grabbed her hands and was squeezing them with frozen fingers. "You're saying there's still hope? My baby could still be alive?"

"Yes, that's exactly what I'm saying." Tess didn't expect the hug she received and endured it, although she was quite uncomfortable. "We need to have a strategy in place, what to say if the kidnappers call about last night's snafu."

"Winnett," Donovan called with a somber tone. He stood a few feet away, holding a folded piece of paper, a welcome opportunity to step away from the Walshes. The static between them loaded the air with crackling electricity.

"What is it?" she asked, reaching for the paper.

"You're due in court in an hour," he announced with an unusual frown on his face. Few things made the analyst frown if they weren't broken databases or malfunctioning computers.

She unfolded the subpoena, thinking she needed to call the prosecutor and advise she couldn't appear. But then she saw the prosecutor's name: Darrel Joyce. "Okay," she muttered, putting the subpoena in her pocket.

"There's something else too," Donovan said, leading the way to his laptop. A video taken by one of the spectators at the theater was ready to be played back. He pressed a button, and the video started to run, showing the children walking through the woods, sprinkling confetti breadcrumbs. "Here," he said, tapping with the finger on the screen. The woman he was pointing at was sitting on the front row, and her head was visible throughout the video. "She doesn't move from there until they drop the curtain."

"Wait, isn't that Mrs. Langhorne?" Tess asked, recognizing the woman's hair and feeling a surge of rage rushing through her veins, setting her blood on fire. "I'll charge her with obstruction; I swear I will." She took out her phone and dialed Langhorne's number, not giving a crap it wasn't even seven A.M. yet. "Good morning," Tess said coldly when the woman picked up the call. "You said the PE teacher was backstage the entire time when he wasn't performing on the stage. Is that correct?"

"Yes, yes, he was," she replied quickly, sounding quite sure of herself, albeit a bit worried.

"Where were you during this time?"

"I was in my seat the entire time." At least that was the truth.

"Then, how could you know that this, um, Michael Brennan, was backstage?"

A quick, derisive cackle. "Where else could he be?"

Tess ended the call without saying another word, her jaws clenched so hard they hurt. "I want to put her through hell for what that little girl is enduring right now, you hear me?" she said quietly, through grinding teeth, looking at Donovan.

"Yes, I hear you making threats against a civilian, and I'll never admit I heard a word," he said, touching her forearm gently. "We'll get Paige back. Tell me what you need."

"I need this PE teacher's address, his full background, bank statements, the works. He was there, and he could've pulled it off. If it weren't for Langhorne's word—" She paused midphrase for a moment then added, "Run Langhorne too. Maybe she'd been paid to provide fake alibis."

She grabbed an apple from a fruit basket on the table and headed for the door. Miriam rushed to catch up with her. "You're leaving?"

"Only for a little while. I'm due in court."

32

WITNESS

"All rise," the county clerk called, then waited with a critical eye for everyone in the audience to stand. Tess was already in the courtroom; they'd allowed her to enter because hers was the first testimony of the day.

DA Joyce was already seated at the prosecutor's table, shuffling through his papers, and the defense was also present. She'd tried to make eye contact with Joyce earlier, but he acted as if he didn't know her. Keeping her distance, Tess waited impatiently for the session to start, wondering what she was doing there. Joyce knew she was busy trying to find his daughter; if he'd called her, it had to be necessary.

"The court is now in session, the Honorable Justice Pelaratti presiding."

The jurors entered through a side door in a single file and took their seats. They seemed worn out, disinterested, or maybe just tired. One yawned and lazily covered her mouth toward the tail end of the yawn.

The judge walked into the courtroom quickly, his back a little hunched, although he was about sixty years old and well built. "Please be seated," he said, and everyone complied. "Calling the case of the People of the State of Florida versus Emanuel Casado, trial part seventeen." His Italian accent was faint but recognizable. His voice was a deep baritone, reminding Tess of a pasta place downtown where all the waiters were first-generation Italian immigrants who liked to sing an old canzonetta at closing time. She always lingered when she ate there, their performances entertaining and memorable.

The defendant, seated at the defense table, lifted his head aggressively, his chin thrust forward, when the judge spoke his name. That wasn't the first time he was seated in the defendant's chair; he should've grown used to it.

"The prosecution may call their first witness for the day," the judge announced.

DA Joyce sprung to his feet. "Thank you, Your Honor." He looked at his papers briefly, then said, "The People call Therese Winnett."

She almost didn't recognize her own given name; it had been years since she'd shortened it to Tess and scowled at anyone who didn't respect her wishes. She stood and approached the stand, where the clerk instructed her to hold one hand in the air and answer the following question.

"Do you affirm that the testimony you are about to give will be the truth, the whole truth, and nothing but the truth?"

"I do." Her voice sounded strong, echoing in the almost empty courtroom. Probably the public and the media had grown bored with the many trial parts that were involved in putting a serial rapist behind bars and had stopped showing up. All for the better.

"Please state your first and last names," the clerk said.

"Therese Winnett."

"You may be seated," he instructed, then sat behind his desk.

"What is your occupation?" DA Joyce asked, still avoiding eye contact.

"I am a special agent with the Federal Bureau of Investigation." She'd testified many times before; she knew the best answers in court were the short, concise ones.

"What is your area of expertise?"

"I'm a behavioral analyst."

"In your professional capacity with the FBI, have you been involved in investigating serial rape offenders?"

"I have led investigations in over twenty such cases, yes."

"What is the most commonly encountered misconception the public has about sexual assault in general?" Joyce looked straight at her, nodding slightly as if to encourage her to speak her mind.

"Objection, Your Honor. Relevance." The defense attorney was a sharply dressed woman in her forties, her brown hair gathered in an off-putting bun. If it weren't for her hairdo, she would've been attractive. She remained standing, waiting for a ruling.

"Goes with the defense strategy to put the victim on trial, Your Honor," Joyce replied.

"I'll allow it, but make it quick." Then Pelaratti turned to her and made an inviting hand gesture. "The witness may answer."

The jurors watched the exchange, moving their heads as if watching a tennis match from courtside seats.

"There are two misconceptions, actually. The first one is that the victim somehow deserved what happened to her, either through provocative behavior, attire, or a promiscuous lifestyle. The second is that rape is only about sex."

Joyce walked to his desk and picked up a few sheets of paper. He dropped one on the defense desk, then took one to the bench and handed it to the judge. "Prosecution's exhibit fourteen, an article extracted from Psychology Today and authored by the witness, titled 'It's Never Only about Sex.'" He handed her a photocopy of the magazine page, with a section highlighted and a few words scribbled in his handwriting on the side. She squinted, trying to read.

Ingram witness in RICO case at three P.M. today when leaving WITSEC lockup. Meet behind Sears to deliver. Advise.

She understood why he'd called her to testify; he had no other way to give her the message.

"Would you please read the highlighted paragraph?" Joyce asked.

She looked toward the bench for a brief moment and locked eyes with Judge Pelaratti, who was staring inquisitively at her and the sheet of paper she was holding. From his vantage point, he could see her copy of the article, unlike his, had scribbled notes on the side but couldn't read them. She held her breath, hoping he wouldn't snatch the piece of paper out of her hands. But he sat there, staring at her with an indiscernible look in his eyes, waiting.

She cleared her throat and started reading. "The serial sexual offender has a psychological need to have absolute dominance, power, and control over his victims. Any opposition from their victims often fuels their determination and arousal, leading to a more satisfying release. While physical characteristics often play a role in the assailant's choice of victims, ultimately their motivation, while being fueled by lust, is essentially driven by the urge to control and, in extreme cases that devolve into serial homicide, to torture and even kill their victims as the ultimate form of power."

"Objection, Your Honor," the defense attorney stood with a look of stunned disbelief on her face. "The prejudice brought to my client by the reading of this paragraph is incalculable. My client has been charged with one count of aggravated sexual assault and one charge of aggravated battery. From there to—"

Pelaratti stopped her verbal attack with a gesture of his hand, then looked at Joyce. "I'd like to know why you thought it necessary to bring this witness to the stand today, Mr. Joyce."

"Your Honor, Emanuel Casado has been tried on another occasion for the same charges and found guilty. Before that, he was charged two other times, but the charges were dropped on technicalities. He's a repeat offender with a discernible pattern, and I believe there's value in exposing to the jury what experts believe that behavioral pattern actually means."

"Your Honor," the defense attorney called, raising her voice and her arms in the air in a gesture of dismay.

"I'll allow it, but get to the point. I won't tolerate it much longer. Drive it home, Mr. Joyce, or let it go."

"Thank you, Your Honor." He looked straight at Tess and asked, "In your professional opinion, what does the future hold for individuals with such motivations?"

He wasn't asking about Emanuel Casado; for the aggravated rapist sitting at the defense table cracking his knuckles, the future was crystal clear, and Joyce didn't need her to get a conviction; she'd read the file. He was asking about his daughter and about the RICO witness. She replied, "Individuals who display such elevated levels of aggression in pursuing their criminal goals inevitably end up behind bars or on death row. Some don't even survive being taken down." She chose her words carefully to respond to the real question Joyce was asking. "Law enforcement has a vast array of means at their disposal to map their whereabouts, establish victimology, and locate them with accuracy. In cases like these, the success rate is close to one hundred percent."

"Thank you, Special Agent Winnett," Joyce said, a brief smile appearing on his lips. "No more questions for this witness, Your Honor."

"Cross?" Pelaratti asked.

"Not at this time," the defense attorney replied, probably eager to see her gone from the courtroom.

"You may step down," Judge Pelaratti said, looking at her with that same long, inquisitive gaze.

She walked out of there briskly, still afraid the judge might call her back and snatch the sheet of paper she'd been holding tightly in her sweaty hand. Once at her car, she breathed with ease and read the message once more.

She had less than six hours to find Paige, before DA Joyce had to deliver the witness. Biting her lip, she wrote SAC Pearson a message.

I'm going to need some help.

33

LIES

Darrel waited until the judge left the courtroom before he breathed deeply, filling his lungs with air, then slowly letting that air out in a soft, calming sigh. He gathered his things and threw everything in his briefcase, then left the courtroom, among the last people to do so.

He'd counted on the defense to file for a continuance because he needed to clear his calendar for the day, and they didn't disappoint, giving him the time to figure out what he was going to do about Ingram. Everything was in Winnett's hands; perhaps she would find a solution that didn't put his little girl's life at risk.

But how would Winnett go after organized crime in less than five hours? How could she possibly plan to get his daughter back when the kidnappers were connected with the most significant crime organization in the southeast? And how was that dead junkie involved in all that? Mitchell wouldn't have trusted that woman with cleaning his toilets... she must've been a decoy, offering him plausible deniability. The man was nothing if not brilliant, and that was the challenge Winnett was facing. Yet her message had been clear. She had a way to get there and had almost a one hundred percent degree of confidence she'd apprehend the people who took Paige. Or kill them.

On his way to the elevators, he stopped by the restroom, eager to throw some cold water on his face and refocus. Endless nights of tossing and turning since Paige had been kidnapped were taking a toll, slowing his thought processes and slathering a thick layer of mental fog over his brain.

He entered the restroom and looked around; no one else was in there. Relaxing a little more, he put the briefcase on the countertop and turned on the faucet, letting the water run for a few seconds to get cold. Then he scooped some in his hands and washed his face, relishing the sensation, feeling the tension in his muscles melt and vanish with every splash of liquid.

Pulling a few towels from the dispenser, he tapped his face and his eyes, then opened his eyes and looked in the mirror. Behind him, Judge Pelaratti was staring at him through the mirror with an unforgiving, piercing gaze.

"Care to explain what kind of screwed-up stunt you just pulled in my courtroom?" His voice, low and menacing, was loaded with promises of a problematic future if he failed to put his concerns at ease.

Darrel's breath caught.

Everyone knew his daughter had been kidnapped; the entire morning he'd avoided people who wanted to express support, concern, or just a sickening curiosity and thirst for drama for someone else's pain. Probably his honor knew about it too and was waiting for him to fulfill his legal obligation and report the issue. He wasn't going to cut him any slack; the last time they spoke, Pelaratti had hung up on him, frustrated that Darrel didn't give him enough undivided attention for his endless rants about a privacy initiative. If anyone knew how to carry a grudge, it was Pelaratti, famous in all the southern districts for how easily he bristled and how vengefully he sought the blood of those who didn't show him the respect he thought he deserved.

Calmly, although adrenaline rushed through his body, driving his heart to beat faster and faster, he threw the towels into the trash can and turned around, pasting a polite smile on his lips. "Ah, Judge, I didn't hear you come in." He leaned casually against the countertop and waited, but the judge was staring at him, expecting an answer. "I'm not sure what you mean."

"That's how you're going to play this? Insulting my intelligence?" he shouted, his face coloring slightly with the deep, red shades of hypertension.

A clerk opened the door, saw them, then quickly disappeared.

"Nothing could be further from the truth. I thought Agent Winnett could bring a little perspective—"

"Shut up," he snapped. "You know better than this. We're not in chambers with defense counsel present. We will *not* discuss the case."

Darrel frowned, not sure how he could tread the water around the big shark to survive and reach the shore. He shrugged and raised his hands a few inches in a gesture of confusion. "Then, I don't understand—"

Judge Pelaratti shook his head slowly. Disbelief washed over his face, quickly replaced by disappointment. "I thought we had built enough of a professional relationship to justify your trust in me." He paused for a beat, but Darrel waited, not sure what he could say. "I heard your daughter was kidnapped."

"Ah, that," he replied, feigning surprise, then looked at the floor for a moment, allowing the judge to see how upset he was. "Yes, that's true. I'm hoping they'll get her back soon."

"Is it about the Casado case?"

Darrel looked straight at him. "Absolutely not."

"Any other case then?"

Hesitating for a split second, he veered his eyes sideways briefly. "No, that's not what they're after. I'm not involved."

"That's why you didn't report it, as is your sworn obligation?"

Darrel nodded, holding the judge's direct gaze steadily, while beads of sweat were breaking at the roots of his hair. "It has nothing to do with me."

"What do they want?" Pelaratti broke eye contact and clenched his hands together, rubbing them slowly as if getting ready for a fight.

"My ex-wife owns a pharmacy. They're after drug money. They asked for a million dollars. She paid the ransom, but then things went south, and I don't know—"

"I saw that too on the morning news. Some junkie was creamed, and the streets were papered with your cash, right?" He sounded heartless, the way he'd put it. Maybe he was a vicious, ambitious, vengeful son of a bitch, just like the courthouse rumors maintained.

Darrel scoffed. "Her money, not mine. I work for a government paycheck; I don't have that kind of money."

"So, why are you here today? You should take some time off and be with your family."

"It's better if I work." A crooked grin stretched his lips for a brief moment. "Believe me, my ex and I can't be in the same room without things going sideways fast." He breathed in and pressed his lips together in a gesture of regret. "I left my wife many years ago, soon after Paige was born. I was putting in eighty-hour weeks back then, ambitious, seeking a path for myself, and I forged that path. The tradeoff was my daughter. We're, um, not close. She was raised by my wife's second husband."

"That's pretty cold, even for you, Counselor," Pelaratti said, tilting his head as if considering a disturbing thought. "So, today's last-minute stunt with the witness was—?" The last words trailed off.

"Completely unrelated." The answer came with ease, lies pouring out of his mouth faster and more convincingly as time passed by.

He didn't know if the kidnappers were listening to his conversation. Was his clothing bugged? Maybe his briefcase? Were they listening through the phone he was supposed to carry with him at all times? Some apps turned any phone into a surveillance device. Or had they settled for planting cameras only in his office?

He couldn't be sure.

Even if he could've been certain no one was listening to him, he couldn't trust Pelaratti with his situation; Paige's life depended on his ability to deliver that witness, to remain the prosecutor on Mitchell's case.

As if reading his mind, Pelaratti asked, "You'd tell me if you were in any kind of trouble?"

"Yes, sir, I would," he replied without hesitation. That particular lie he'd rehearsed a lot.

"Then pay attention to what I'm about to say because I'm only going to say this once." He paused and paced slowly toward the door, as if he'd changed his mind and was leaving, but then returned and stopped squarely in front of Darrel. "Do you know what my name means in Italian?"

Darrel shook his head, surprised. "No, sir."

"It means the one who skins rats. I have no idea which one of my ancestors did what to earn this name, but it's in my blood and I won't hesitate to skin the rat that shows up in my courtroom and screws with me. Is that clear?"

Darrel's blood turned to ice. "Crystal."

"This is your one and only warning, Counselor, and I'll deny this conversation ever took place." Without another word, he opened the door and walked out. The door whooshed closed behind him, leaving Darrel panting, sweating, a nervous wreck leaning against the counter and staring in the mirror at a stranger's reflection.

Slowly, his pulse returned to normal as he played back the conversation in his mind. Had he said anything that could've rattled the kidnappers? Absolutely nothing. Had he given Pelaratti any reason to take action concerning Paige's kidnapping? None, but he'd been expecting the dreaded call from the state attorney general's office ever since he'd seen the news. Just like he'd explained Pelaratti off, he'd do it with the state attorney general if the call ever came. He only hoped he'd have better success with him than he'd had with the judge.

Leaving the restroom and heading toward his office, he looked at the people around him, wondering how many had seen the news or were nothing but spies working with the kidnappers, following his every move.

There was no way he could know.

34

HOUSEBOAT

Weaving through the leftovers of the morning rush-hour traffic, Tess had left the courthouse in the rearview mirror a while ago. In a few more minutes, she'd reach the Walsh residence, where the mercurial and highly emotional mother and the silent yet treacherous stepfather would burn who knows how much more time with useless arguments. She couldn't begin to understand what they were going through, but they should've understood by now that the time she spent holding their hands was less time spent looking for their daughter's kidnappers.

There should be laws preventing parents from being involved with their kidnapped child's case. All right, perhaps that was a bit harsh, maybe not laws, but at least procedures. If this had been a typical case, she would've asked a junior agent to keep them company and answer all their questions while she focused on the essential parts of tracking down the unsub. But she'd been handcuffed by the kidnappers' demands when they limited the number of agents involved in the case at only one. Donovan, she'd slipped him through the cracks, and, so far, no one had picked up on him. He looked younger than his age and had kept his head down, rarely leaving the Walsh living room.

Unsettling questions swirled through her mind. If the kidnappers wanted the witness in the RICO case, what had been the deal with the ransom? It had been set up twice by two different unsubs, a male and a female. Could the female caller have been Randi, the bleached blonde who died at the mall? Yes, the choice of vocabulary was a match with her shady background.

Then, what had happened with the ransom, and why was a ransom even considered? To keep the mother busy, certain her daughter's case was being investigated and managed, while the DA could get their witness for them? Was the ransom demand meant to deceive anyone who would've looked at Joyce as the target, allowing him to continue prosecuting the case, but under the unsub's terms? If yes, then who were the people who had called or come after the ransom? Were they also the people holding Paige, or only tight-lipped, overpaid gofers who were sent on errands?

She hadn't yet made it off the interstate when Donovan's call interrupted her musings.

"Hey, Winnett, you're going to want to hear this." The excitement in his voice was contagious. She needed good news. "The PE teacher, Michael Brennan, lives on a houseboat in Palm Harbor Marina."

She smiled widely and turned on her siren and flashers. "Meet me there. You always wanted to make field agent, right?"

"Right. Want me to call HRT?"

"Let's have the Hostage Rescue Team on standby." In the background, she heard him close his laptop and pull the zipper on its bag. "Bring me the clothes I was wearing yesterday. The colorful, touristy stuff."

"You mean that awful skirt and red top and hat?"

She chuckled, invigorated. She finally got to bust open a door and hoped to find Paige behind it. "I'm dressed for court, dummy, in a suit and heels. I can't even walk on a dock without losing a heel between those boards."

"Copy that," he replied. Tess could hear the tension in his voice despite her lame attempt at self-directed humor. "Meet you upfront."

"Oh, and Donovan? Don't say a word to the Walshes. Paige might not be there anymore. I don't want to get their hopes up."

"Understood." He ended the call, leaving her to the intermittent sound of the sirens she used only when she needed to clear heavy traffic out of her way.

Almost thirty minutes later, she pulled into the Palm Harbor Marina parking lot by Donovan's car. He handed her a large paper bag with the clothing she'd requested, then leaned against the hood of her Suburban, admiring the distant view of the ocean.

She changed quickly, eager to storm that houseboat and find Paige. Then she grabbed her gun in her hand and hid it in the oversized, pink purse that came with the outfit.

"Ready," she said, slamming the door of her SUV and locking it. "You stay behind at least fifty yards, okay?"

"Got it."

"Where's HRT?"

"In position, ready to roll in. They're a minute out."

"Good." She pasted a touristy, gullible smile on her face, walking quickly toward the fourth dock, where the PE teacher had leased his slip. Approaching as quickly as she could, she studied the thinning pedestrian traffic as she drew closer. A few anglers, loading mountains of hardware and huge coolers on their boats, about to leave the dock and spend the day out there in the sun, drinking, getting roasted, and pretending they were actually fishing. A young couple, who'd leased a boat for a deep-sea fishing experience and were waiting eagerly to start their trip. A man, whose bare back was covered in tattoos and red from sunburn, was sanding the side of his boat where he'd rammed it into the dock post, probably after one too many downed while out there fishing.

The houseboat came into sight. It was large and on two levels. Tess had expected just a pontoon with the sides walled up, barely able to keep rainwater out, but she found a full-blown house that was built on top of a large floating platform.

Tess stopped in front of the gangplank that connected the dock with the floating platform that served as the house's porch and called, "Ahoy!" much like a lost tourist would do, holding her straw hat in place with her hand. "Hello," she called again, louder. "We're supposed to leave in ten minutes. Can I come onboard?" No answer. Nothing moved on the houseboat, as far as she could see. The water reflected in some of the windows, blocking her view, but she pulled her weapon and abandoned the flashy, rhinestone-studded purse on the porch, then entered the house.

The first thing she noticed was the smell, a horrible mix of human filth, booze, and sweat. Flies were buzzing around leftover tuna in open cans. The TV was still on, but the sound was muted. She cleared the house room by room, ending with a tiny, windowless room, barely larger than the twin mattress on the floor.

She turned on the light and gasped. The mattress was stained with dried blood, enough of it to worry her. This must've been where the unsub had sliced Paige to get the blood sample they'd sent to Miriam by courier.

On the floor, in the far corner, a small pile of used gauze and surgical tape littered the dirty floor. Slipping a fresh glove, she picked up the gauze and studied it. Dry blood stains and yellowish blotches at the center of it. Tess laid the gauze on the mattress to ascertain the size and severity of the wound that had been wrapped with it. The dressing had been cut with scissors, probably from the small, first-aid kit she saw discarded on the floor, next to an open bottle of peroxide and a spent packet of antiseptic powder.

The girl's cut was a deep gash of at least eight inches in length that had become infected. The impossibly high stakes had just been raised.

Three more hours until Joyce had to deliver the witness, and she was too late to save Paige.

A chime on her phone advised her of a message from Pearson.

A man named Joe claims they're holding the girl on a houseboat in Palm Harbor Marina. Recording attached.

She listened intently, hoping the caller might've shared anything else of interest, but he just mentioned the houseboat, the fact that Randi had lived two boats down from it and that he wanted his reward. Too late for that, buddy; we already know all that. Well, almost, anyway. If none of her other, quicker plans panned out, she could interview Joe and see if he could earn that reward by providing valuable, actionable information.

She was about to leave the small, sad room where Paige had been held when a glimmer caught her eye. She crouched by the mattress and recovered a small, silver object. Then she smiled and closed her fingers around it.

It was a lion, the next charm on Paige's bracelet.

The charm told Tess that Paige was still fighting, was still aware, and hadn't been held anywhere else between being taken from the theater and being locked up in that awful place.

She left the houseboat and found Donovan at the edge of the dock. "Send HRT home, and call a crime scene unit to pick this place apart for fingerprints and evidence. They're gone."

"That's not why I'm here," he said, showing her his phone. She grabbed it with her left hand, squinting in the sunlight to make out what was on the screen.

"A couple of hours ago, two men carrying what appears to be a sleeping child stole this Toyota minivan from a Walmart parking lot, not far from here."

She frowned. A smart unsub like the one who'd orchestrated Paige Joyce's kidnapping would've not done that right under the cameras everyone knew the store had installed. Plenty of other places to steal cars from. "Weird," she said, thinking how best to spend the three short hours she had left before Joyce had to deliver the witness. What, if anything, made sense in this case?

"BOLO's out on the new vehicle," Donovan said. "I'll head back and start a trace via Real Time Crime cameras and all the street feeds. I'll find them. We're getting close."

"Not fast enough, D. The girl's wound is badly infected. She could get septicemia." Groaning with frustration, she grabbed the purse from the porch and followed Donovan to the entrance. "You do that, and I'll figure out how to steal a witness from the US Marshals."

"Are you seriously considering turning over a witness to a mobster?" Donovan stopped and stared at her in disbelief.

A chime from her phone got her attention. It was another message from Pearson.

It's done.

Two simple words that brought a hint of a smile to her eyes. "Well, maybe I won't have to."

35

News

Darrel Joyce paced through his office, too tense to do anything but stare at the clock on the wall, counting the minutes, wondering how he was going to deliver Ingram to the kidnappers. He'd passed on their demands to Agent Winnett, but hadn't heard a peep since, not from her, not from anyone. Except for a bitchy call from Miriam, who'd just finished tearing him a new one for keeping his distance during these trying times and choosing to be at work instead of at her whim, his phones had remained eerily silent. That silence had followed a wave of calls triggered by the breaking news of his daughter's kidnapping.

If nothing happened until, say, two P.M., would he drive to lockup and take the witness? He'd already answered that troublesome question; his daughter's life came above everyone else's, even his own. Assuming the US Marshals would just say, "Sure, Mr. District Attorney, take this witness and Godspeed," which would never happen, then what would he do? Would he deliver the witness by himself without Winnett's support to track the kidnappers and enforce an exchange—Paige for Ingram? If he drove by himself into that parking lot with Ingram in the car, anything could happen, from being gunned down, both of them, by men with machine guns, to being forced to relinquish the witness without getting Paige in return.

He stopped under the cooling stream of air coming from the ceiling vent and propped his hands on his thighs, staring at the floor, wondering what to do. He'd always been a man of action who took the lead and forged through, regardless of what life threw his way. That's how he'd grown to be the Broward County district attorney, with a promising future at state level and even beyond, by tackling challenges head-on, without hesitation, without the frozen claw of fear gripping his heart.

He'd never before been forced to choose between a loved one's life and someone else's. He'd never been in a position where his decision, unsupported by the law, would cost someone their life. That was a life-altering change.

Two knocks interrupted his grim thoughts. Sol popped her head in the door.

"Come in," he said, ambling toward his desk. He felt as if he were a hundred years old, bone tired.

"You should go home—" she started, but he glared at her, and she quickly clammed up.

"We have the Mitchell trial tomorrow," he said, surprising himself with how weary his voice sounded. "I can't go anywhere. I have to prepare." He paused for a beat, staring at the open file in front of him but not really seeing it. He looked at the clock again; it was still 1:15 P.M., like the last three times he'd checked.

She shifted her weight from one foot to the other, visibly uncomfortable. "Yeah, about that... I'm afraid I have some bad news. The witness in tomorrow's case, Jonas Ingram—"

He sprung to his feet, his heart thumping against his chest. "What about him?"

"He was shivved less than an hour ago."

"What? He was in protective custody for crying out loud."

"They got to him," Sol replied, tugging nervously at the edges of the bow that adorned the collar of her white silk blouse. "He's in intensive care. He's a tough cookie, that one, surviving so many attempts on his life. It's unbelievable."

He slowly sunk in his chair and buried his face in his trembling hands. "Without him, I have no case, and Mitchell walks."

She sighed. "I know, and I'm sorry. It's not like you don't need a break, right?" She waited, but he wasn't saying anything, too stunned to think straight. "Please let me know if there's anything I can do."

He didn't even notice when she disappeared, closing the door quietly behind her. His thoughts were racing, desperately swirling in his mind. They'll never believe he had nothing to do with the attack on Ingram's life. They'll think he's just lying, stalling, or refusing to comply, and they'll kill Paige.

Restless, he stood and started wearing a hole in the floor again, pacing back and forth anxiously. How would he argue in a court of law that he didn't have Ingram shivved? How would he persuade a jury? He'd create doubt, maybe point to the direction of a different potential perpetrator, one with a stronger motive, one who'd have better access.

"Call me," he said, speaking to the empty room in the hope the kidnappers were listening. "I need you to call me, damn it!" He paced some more, then returned to face his desk and stood in front of it, speaking clearly. "If you can hear me, call me. Did you have him shivved? Did you do this?" He clenched his fists and slammed them against the desk. "I want my daughter back! Call me, you son of a bitch, call me and tell me what to do now."

When the phone rang, he jumped out of his skin and scrambled to pick it up. "Yes."

"Did you arrange that?" the artificial voice read the words without any intonation.

"I swear I didn't, and you know it's true," he blurted, "because you had him stabbed, didn't you?" He waited for a long moment until the voice started reading words again.

"If you had the witness stabbed, if you think you're pulling a fast one, you'll be receiving your daughter's arm via courier tomorrow morning."

"No, no, please. I'll do whatever you want. I would've brought you Ingram, but now I can't. I'll do whatever you want, I swear, only don't hurt my baby." The last words ended in unexpected sobs. He'd never cried a tear in his entire adult life, and now he couldn't stop.

"Stand by for instructions."

"Please, let me speak to my—" Three beeps cut him off as the line went dead. "No," he wailed, holding his head in his hands, squeezing it hard as if to remove the pain locked in there.

Then, just as he was about to lose his mind, a thought appeared in his drained mind, drying his tears and bringing the light of hope with it.

What if it was Winnett who'd had the witness removed from the equation, for who knew what reason?

36

DOUBLE

Ninety hours missing

When Tess and Donovan returned to the Walsh residence, a few news vans still lingered on the street, their approach triggering the rather apathetic attention of several reporters. Camped out there in the street under the scorching sun, they'd probably had enough and wished they could go home already but couldn't. The hope they'd be among the first to report the safe return of the eight-year-old girl and the possibility of catching a tear-jerking moment on camera was enough to keep them there, sweaty and bored and tired.

As soon as she climbed out of the car, she held her hand in the air and said, "No comment," then rushed to the door. Before entering, she heard Miriam's raised voice, yelling at Max, calling him names in a slew of invectives she unloaded in rapid-fire speech, without pausing to draw breath.

Bracing herself, she entered the house, Donovan following and closing the door behind him quickly.

"You might want to keep this on the quiet side of things," Tess said coldly, gesturing toward the TV vans parked outside. "These people have powerful microphones, and I don't believe you'd like your tirade on the ten o'clock news."

Miriam stopped talking and stared at her, slack-jawed, stunned. Max stood by the back wall, leaning against it and looking at his feet with a miserable expression on his face. When he raised his eyes to look at Tess, she could see he'd been crying. His love for Paige seemed genuine, even if his actions had been uninspired and damaging.

"Don't you understand," he pleaded, now that Tess's arrival had silenced Miriam, "people might know where she is, and if there's money to be had, they might talk?"

Miriam turned to him, glaring. "Or they could kill my little girl, you son of a bitch. Paige is my baby, not yours! Mine. You should've asked," she added, ending in tears, her hands covering her face.

Slowly, Max approached her and folded her in his arms, and she didn't fight him back anymore. Burrowing her face at his chest, she wept, and his tears washed into her hair as he muttered in her ear, "We'll get her back, you'll see. I promise we will."

The phone rang, echoing strangely in the silent living room. Miriam pulled herself out of Max's embrace and rushed to the dining room table, where Donovan was already setting up the incoming call trace.

"Remember, keep him talking, agree, apologize, make promises," Tess blurted in a rush, while Miriam, already holding the phone with shaky fingers, was staring at her wide-eyed, nodding at every word she said.

"Hello," she said, her voice brittle, raspy.

"Scattering twenty-dollar bills on the highway doesn't equate to ransom payment," the impersonal voice said. "You killed one of us. Now the ransom is two million dollars, and it's your last chance. You have three hours."

"Yes, yes, I'll be ready, only please, let me speak to my little girl. I didn't—"

The call ended, and a moment of heavy, loaded silence ensued while Miriam stared at the phone in her hand as if it was about to explode. Gently, Donovan took it and placed it back in the cradle.

"Anything?" Tess whispered, looking at him. He just shook his head.

"How am I going to get two million dollars?" she asked, looking first at Tess, then at Max.

Max clasped his hands together. "Two hundred and fifty is all I have, and I can go to the bank—" but his wife wasn't listening anymore. She'd turned her back to him and had swiped the phone from the cradle, then she made a call.

"I don't care what you have to do," she said, the moment the other party picked up, "you just get me two million dollars. Mortgage your house, or I don't know, steal it, just bring my baby back. You're the almighty district attorney; just make it happen, or find people who can."

Tess looked briefly at Max, who'd lowered his head again.

"It's the third time she's called him today." Tess touched his arm in a gesture of encouragement, only hours after she would've gladly strangled him with her own hands.

Miriam ended her call and gave Donovan her phone. Approaching Tess with pleading eyes, she squeezed both her hands and whispered, "Please, help me. I'll pay everything back. I'll sell the drugstore, it doesn't matter, but I'll pay you back. Just let's finish this nightmare and bring Paige home. Please."

Tess nodded and pulled her hands from her grasp, and texted Pearson.

Ransom is 2mil now. Can you help?

A tense moment of silence, then a chime. Pearson had replied.

Stand by.

She looked at Miriam and nodded again. "I believe that's handled, but I—"

Miriam hugged her, whispering tearful words of gratitude. She pulled back, then looked Miriam in the eyes. "I need to work," she said gently. "Please, give us the time to do our jobs."

"Sure," she said quickly, walking backward, rushed to put some distance between them. "I'm sorry."

But Tess wasn't paying attention to her anymore. She was reviewing the scribbled notes she'd jotted down during the call. The unsub's word choices were indicative of a large, cultivated vocabulary. The typical organized crime gofer didn't use words such as *equate.*

So, then, who were these people?

First, violence against the little girl hadn't escalated, although she'd held her breath after the second botched attempt. Was that because they had paid the ransom after all? On the dreaded newscast that had covered Randi Rowland's death, the story had said, "She'd been killed during an apparently botched ransom payment for the release of Paige Joyce, the eight-year-old daughter of District Attorney Darrel Joyce, who was kidnapped last Friday." There had been no mention of the gunshot wound in her leg nor of the cops chasing her through the parking lot. Probably those details would surface before the end of the day when the media finished reviewing security footage and interviewing witnesses, but, until then, the unsubs might believe her death had been accidental.

Would they hurt Paige, as they'd promised? It was a strong possibility, but the biggest question remained: Why bother with ransom if what they wanted was Ingram? Maybe that's why they didn't hurt the girl or make more gruesome threats... because they had a different agenda, and the ransom was only keeping Miriam and her husband busy while the DA could do their bidding.

But what if there were tensions in the kidnappers' team? What if the initial assignment had been Ingram, but one or more unsubs had figured out there was money to be made?

She scratched the roots of her hair, thinking, staring into the distant landscape of the backyard palm trees against the blue sky. Which unsub would be crazy enough to go off script when working for someone like Mitchell? There wasn't a hole deep enough on the entire globe where Mitchell wouldn't find him and kill him, making an example out of him, if for nothing else, at least for disrespecting him.

It didn't fit. No matter how Tess looked at things, the picture wasn't clearly coming together. There were at least two men in the team; she'd seen them on the Walmart parking lot video. There used to be Randi, but she was now resting on Doc Rizza's stainless-steel table with a Y cut on her chest. Randi was a junkie, poorly educated; she'd dropped out of high school in her sophomore year. Yet one of the two men was using words like equate, and the other was a PE teacher who lived on a houseboat.

Graphology had determined that the note sent with Paige's blood was written by a woman. There was discernibly more violence in the ransom call Tess had ruled as having been made by a woman than in any of the other calls. The note mentioned body parts. The ransom call threatened to send a body. If she eliminated those two communications, she realized the other calls had been less threatening, as if the caller was distancing himself from the idea of hurting a child. His choice of words had been moderate and indirect, using phrases such as "she dies" in the initial note or "if you want to see your daughter again."

The mastermind behind the kidnapping was not a violent man, and that was great news for Paige. Randi had been the violent one, and the teacher was still an unknown.

"Oh, man," Donovan said, whispering. "We've been chasing our tails here," he said, and Tess rushed over to look at his screen. "See? This is Michael Brennan's school ID photo, and this is his driver's license." The two forms of identifications were displayed side by side on the screen. Then Donovan clicked his mouse, and a veteran's ID card was displayed instead of the school ID. Same name, Michael Brennan, but a different face.

"What?" Tess gasped. "Stolen identity? Then who is this guy?"

"We'll find out soon enough; they're still processing the houseboat, and I'm guessing they left a ton of fingerprints behind."

Tess frowned. "An unsub team so organized, so calculated, leaving fingerprints behind and letting themselves be captured on surveillance videos while stealing a car? What are we missing, D?"

"I don't know," he replied simply. "It's almost as if they grew tired of doing it right, or something changed."

That new piece of information was shedding some more light on the unsub team. One was intelligent, educated, calculated, organized. The other was someone using a stolen identity to work as a PE teacher; she was willing to bet good money against fallen palm tree leaves that man had done time and loved to be around children. A pedophile, maybe? Then Randi, a junkie with a violent streak. And a team dynamic in a continued state of flux, impossible to predict.

The answers were in the Mitchell RICO case and what the unsub would ask for next, now that the witness he'd wanted was off the table. Pearson had outdone himself, arranging the entire shivving behind bars legend for Ingram with such short notice. She'd held her breath for a while, fearing the kidnappers might retaliate and hurt Paige, but, as she'd anticipated, they'd probably been busy accusing one another.

"Could he be the guy who drove off with Paige in Miriam's Subaru?"

Donovan brought up on the screen a few other images taken from the surveillance video at the theater and studied them for a moment. "He could've been. You can't really tell from these images. The fog was thick that night, turning into water droplets on the windshield. He was smart enough not to use the wipers until he was out of camera range."

A loud chime emerged from Donovan's computer; it was a sound she recognized. She looked at Donovan.

"BOLO came back on the Toyota Sienna they stole at the Walmart store. It was found at a small gas station on the way out of town, due north. He stole a red Chevy Tahoe from there." He rubbed his hands together. "Small or not, it had cameras, and I have the feeds."

"Tell the local LEOs to send a crime scene unit and pick that minivan apart. I want every trace of evidence they can lift, any object, no matter how small."

Seeming a little surprised, Donovan turned his head to look at her. "Anything in particular they should be looking for?"

She smiled. "A unicorn."

37

LAST CHANCE

The Crusty Crab Motel was dirty and decrepit with grime and cigarette smoke. Everything smelled, even the walls. The bathroom reeked of cheap bleach someone had splashed in there, leaving streaks on the cracked tile floor. The bedsheets seemed clean, but Mark couldn't really tell; they stunk of chemicals so severely he could only assume.

Paige lay on one of the beds, moaning in her sleep. She was burning up with fever; last time he'd checked, her temperature had gone up to 104, and he was running out of options. Gavin couldn't be trusted to be alone with the girl, even if she was barely conscious, maybe even more so. Otherwise, he would've risked an incursion into downtown for some more antibiotics.

His partner was increasingly difficult; he'd moaned and griped for ten minutes just to cross the motel yard for some ice from the machine. Since he'd returned, he would not shut up about his money. He'd learned a lesson from Randi's move, but he'd learned the wrong one, growing suspicious of him, who didn't want the ransom in the first place. He wasn't going to kill Gavin for his share of the money; he just wasn't that kind of guy. Mark was only a man who seemed to always be in the wrong place at the wrong time, and if he needed anything, that was some voodoo to scare the bad luck away.

He packed some ice cubes in the towels he took from the bathroom and slid the packets under Paige's arms and around her neck, trying to bring her temperature down. The gash on her arm was swollen and had turned a dangerous color, a hue of deep red with purplish edges. She needed a hospital, and he couldn't take her to one. Not if he wanted to live.

Pressing his lips tightly together, he sat on the side of the bed and reset the thermometer.

"How are you going to get the money, man?" Gavin asked him for the tenth time in so many minutes. "We tried the airport lockbox, and they sent a fed. That bitch, Randi, tried the mall, and she ended up plastered on the asphalt. I don't want to be next, if you catch my drift."

Mark wasn't paying attention to Gavin's insistences; he didn't have everything figured out and had more pressing concerns than his partner's never-ending greed. But Gavin's patience must've been running thin; he walked toward Mark with a heavy, determined gait, every footfall a thump against the floor, and grabbed his arm. "Hey, I want my money," he said.

Mark stood and pushed him away. "And you'll get it in due time. I'm right here, not going anywhere. I won't stiff you, I swear."

Gavin stared at him for a long moment as if trying to determine whether Mark could be trusted, then lowered his gaze. "All right, my man, but we have to think of something. How will we get the money, huh? They'll send cops every time. Maybe if we make the meetup happen on the water, then we'd see them coming. What do you think? We could borrow that sweet, thirty-two-foot center console from old Dan; he'd give it to us. That baby does sixty knots."

The water meetup wasn't a half-bad idea, but Mark's focus was on a small display that read 104.6. He grabbed the ice bucket and gave it to Gavin. "Get me some more." His eyes landed on the empty, plastic-lined wastebasket. He gave that to Gavin. "Fill this up instead."

"You crazy? The entire joint doesn't have this much ice."

The phone rang loudly, the dreaded burner that only meant one thing: Mr. Erwin was calling. He cleared his throat and flipped it open, putting it on speaker. "Yes."

"You failed me," Mr. Erwin stated matter-of-factly. "I'm sorry I didn't let you die in prison, but that can be easily rectified."

A chill traveled down his spine, sending ice through his blood. "I—I can explain. We—I didn't do anything wrong."

"No? Then what am I hearing on the TV about this junkie who was gunned down after picking up a one-million-dollar ransom? After I had specifically told you no media and no ransom?"

He gasped, thinking of what he could say to explain, to make Mr. Erwin understand the bind he found himself in. There were no words, nothing he could say to exculpate himself. Nothing, because ever since he'd been tasked to take Paige Joyce, he couldn't handle the job by himself and had to let an unauthorized stranger in on the deal. The rest was the fruit of the poisonous tree.

"I'll do anything," he blurted instead. "Just tell me what you want me to tell the DA to do, and he'll do it. I promise you that."

"And you'll deliver this time?" Mr. Erwin's high-pitched voice was devoid of any emotion, cold, factual. Deathly.

"I swear," Mark said. "I swear it on my life."

There was a moment of silence, then the request came. "Tell him to drop all charges. The court date is tomorrow. Make it happen."

He couldn't even begin to comprehend the logic in that. The DA could drop charges tomorrow and refile them next week. That much he knew from the law books he'd studied while doing his time. He knew better than to open his mouth.

As if reading his mind, Mr. Erwin added, "Tell your friend that if the charges are dropped and stay dropped, he will start enjoying Aquila's friendship and its many benefits."

"What about his daughter?"

"Not my concern," Mr. Erwin replied.

Gavin's eyes glinted when he heard that, and a strange grin appeared on his face.

"Understood. I'll call him now," Mark replied.

"This is my last call to you," Mr. Erwin added. "You either get the job done this time, or there will be no further warning. You won't even see us coming, you and that loser partner of yours."

The call ended, leaving Mark and Gavin staring at each other with pupils dilated in fear. Then Gavin swallowed with visible difficulty, thrown by the threat as much as he wanted to play it cool. "Man, we got to get my money and split, while we still can. I'll keep the girl. I like her."

Mark's fist landed squarely on his jaw. "She's not yours to keep." Then he picked up the wastebasket from the floor, where Gavin had dropped it, and shoved it against his chest. "Ice!" Gavin nodded, rubbing his reddening jaw to soothe the pain.

"I'll call the DA. Let's hope he doesn't screw with us," Mark added, firing up his laptop and getting ready to use the text-to-speech app.

"How about my—"

"Then we'll talk about your money, and how we'll give the girl back."

38

MOTEL

"Gotcha!" Donovan exclaimed, rubbing his hands together, satisfied. He'd loosened his slim tie and had abandoned his jacket a while ago, throwing it on one of the dining room chairs. Two empty coffee mugs littered the table, and he'd been going through an entire box of donuts since that morning. The entire house smelled of Sunday breakfast, of powdered sugar and hazelnut and French vanilla, although it was only Wednesday.

Tess rushed to see what had got him so excited, and spilled some of the coffee she was hauling over from the Keurig in the Walshes' kitchen on her hand. Yelping quietly, she grabbed a tissue and tapped herself dry, then abandoned the offending mug filled to the brim with hot liquid on the table. She looked at the screen where two poor quality, black-and-white images of the stolen Chevy Tahoe taken from different angles were displayed. One showed the vehicle at the gas station, right when it was leaving, its Florida tag in direct view of the camera.

"That's the departure point," Donovan said, tapping with his finger on the image taken from the gas station. "And this is the arrival," he announced proudly, tapping on the second image that showed the same vehicle parked in front of a motel room. "It took me a while and some fancy data pulling, but I followed this sucker from camera to camera across town, and this is where it's at now."

Tess abandoned her coffee cup on the table and checked the magazine in her weapon. "It's still there?"

"Yup."

"And we know where this is," she stated more than asked.

Donovan grinned. "This five-star, worldwide famous hospitality dump is called the Crusty Crab Motel. It's off NW Twelfth, where the elite always stay," he quipped. He stood and tightened his belt, then grabbed his jacket. He was bursting with excitement after having spent the entire night tracking every move of that Chevy, from one place to another, one small diner to the next, and a series of various motels all over town. The unsubs were probably looking for that one receptionist who didn't ask questions and, by the looks of it, had found the right one at Crusty Crab.

Donovan pulled a handgun from his laptop bag and checked it.

"What do you think you're doing?" she asked. "You're an analyst, not a field agent. That's not a service weapon."

"So what? I'm coming with you, Winnett. Either that or you wait for HRT. Someone's got to have your back."

"Pearson is going to have my ass," she muttered, then beckoned him on. "Okay, let's go."

"What's going on?" Miriam asked from the bedroom doorway. She'd stayed in there for the past few hours, and Max had been with her the entire time, yet no arguments, no raised voices, and no sobs had disturbed the night. "Did you find her?" She clasped her hands at her chest in silent, unspoken prayer.

"Just following up on a lead for now, but soon we'll know more," Tess replied. "Please stay here by the phone, in case the kidnappers call again. If they do, call me right away. Remember, say yes to anything they want and get as many details as possible, but don't go anywhere by yourself." Tess frowned at the two large duffel bags Pearson's courier had dropped the night before. "Can I trust you to do that?"

Miriam nodded, looking at her intently, her green eyes filled with hope and yearning. "Please tell me how this lead will, um, pan out."

"I promise, as soon as I find out anything, you'll be the first to know."

She rushed outside, where Donovan had already climbed behind the wheel of his Suburban. Before she closed the door, she heard Miriam tell Max, "I think they found her, Max, I think they found our little girl."

There was no deceiving Mrs. Walsh; she was brilliant, uncanny. She would've made one heck of a profiler.

Donovan drove quickly to the motel, where Tess told him to slow down and enter the premises without drawing any attention to themselves. She wanted to verify the unsubs were there before calling hostage rescue.

"Pull over here," she said, staring at the cars parked by the doors of the occupied rooms. Most rooms seemed empty, with curtains open to let the light in. The red Chevy was right where Donovan had said it would be, and the curtains of that room's window were pulled shut.

"Keep your eyes on that Chevy, and be ready to—"

A man crossed the parking lot carrying a trash can filled with ice. He looked at the Suburban and froze, his eyes locked onto hers. It was the PE teacher, the man who'd stolen Michael Brennan's identity.

"Ah, shit," she said, her eyes fixed on the man. "Call HRT." Pulling out her gun, she climbed out of the Suburban, moving slowly. "Michael Brennan, we're with the FBI. We only want to speak with you."

After the initial shock, he threw the trash can to the ground, littering the parking lot with ice cubes, and bolted.

Instead of running into the busy street, like Tess would've done, he ran toward the room and went inside, not even closing the door behind him.

That was her opportunity. Before she had the chance to really think it through, she sprinted, narrowly avoiding the slippery ice cubes, and caught up with him by the door. Another man, taller, stared at her with a strange look in his eyes, not surprised she was there, yet sad and scared at the same time. He'd raised his hands but was retreating slowly toward the bathroom.

Her attention was focused on the little girl lying on the bed, a soiled scarf wrapped around her head. She was whimpering but seemed listless as if she didn't have the strength to move. Her right forearm was swollen and poorly wrapped in a dressing stained with blood and pus. A thermometer was set on the bedside table by the lamp. Her neck and armpits were covered in towel-wrapped ice cubes, melting into the bedsheets.

Brennan grabbed the girl's head, holding it by the knot in the scarf, and pulled his gun, shoving it against her temple. "I'll shoot her, I swear. I'm not going back to jail."

Paige cried weakly.

"All right," she said, raising her hands in the air, holding her gun by the trigger guard to make him comfortable. "Let's all be calm and figure out how we can all go home tonight in one piece."

Brennan shook the girl angrily, and she cried in pain. "Stop lying to me! Do you think I'm stupid?"

"No, I'm sorry," she said calmly. "Why don't you let the girl go and take me in her place. A fed as a hostage is much more valuable than a dying girl, right?" She gritted her teeth, seeing how erratically he was moving, his eyes darting all over the place, from the girl's temple to Tess's gun to the door. There was no telling what he would do. "She could kick the bucket

anytime, right? Then what would you have? Nothing but a
death sentence." She paused for a beat. "Let her be someone
else's problem."

A loud noise of shattered glass and a hard object clattering
on the floor came from the bathroom, but she didn't budge. *One
unsub at a time* was her unwritten rule, one of the many.

The man's eyes darted toward the bathroom. Something
shifted in his demeanor as if he'd lost something of value.
Probably his partner was making his escape through some back
window, but she couldn't help it.

"It's just you and me now," she said, taking advantage of
the opportunity. "Your partner fled and left you holding the
bag." She looked at the girl, her heart aching to see her like that.
"Well, the hostage. But I know this wasn't your idea. You were
just a good friend who wanted to help. I know that."

"You know?" He frowned, looking at her in disbelief.

"Yes, I do. I also know you struggled badly after you got out
of the joint, and had no other option but to take this poor
fellow's identity," she ventured, basing her entire strategy on a
prison gang tattoo she recognized, on the side of the man's
neck. "I'm talking about Michael Brennan."

He stared at her, unsure what to do.

"Let the girl go, and I'll drop my weapon. Then you can do
whatever you want. You can flee with your partner if you can
still catch up with him. If he cares enough to wait for you," she
added, not allowing him to think.

He looked at Paige, confused. The girl had slumped on her
side and wasn't moving. "I can't let her go," he said, his voice
riddled with confusion, not opposition. "She can't walk."

"Just let me set her outside on the ground, while you keep
your gun aimed at me. Once she's outside, I'll drop mine." She
continued to keep her hands in the air, holding her gun by the
trigger guard with her thumb and her index. "Then they will

call, and you can give them your demands because you have a federal agent for a hostage."

He tilted his head and scrunched his face as if wondering if he could believe her, seemingly angry with himself for not being able to figure out what to do. "You're lying to me. They'll come in here guns blazing and kill me. I ain't going anywhere but jail or six feet under." As he said the words, his reality must've hit him because his eyes turned a darker shade of steel, the color of desperation with nothing left to lose.

"Only if you want to," she replied calmly. "If I were you, I'd negotiate. A car or a plane, money, whatever, and they'll pay." He still wasn't convinced. "You know why? Because otherwise, they'll have to admit to the press and the public that a federal agent was taken hostage by a guy with a gun in some sleazy motel. Can you imagine how many FBI bosses would lose their jobs? The entire country would laugh over the evening news."

That argument hit home. Moving slowly, and careful not to lose Tess out of his sight, he picked up Paige and put her outside the room, on the ground, then quickly shifted his gun to point at her chest. Kicking the door shut with his boot, he reached for her gun. Reluctantly, she let it go.

"When will they call?"

"Soon," she replied, knowing that HRT's response time was only minutes.

Outside the door, footsteps rushed by and stopped. She saw Donovan's shadow through the curtain as he picked up Paige and ran away with her.

"How much are you planning to ask for?" she teased, watching for that one moment when he'd blink, he'd look at something else, or lose sight of her for the tiniest moment. "Can I sit?" she asked, gesturing at what had to be the hospitality world's dirtiest armchair.

He gestured with his gun, visibly annoyed. "I want the full ransom, what was supposed to be mine. The two million dollars, that's what I want."

She nodded, leaning forward casually as if captivated by the conversation, her forearms resting on the tacky armrests. "I believe they already have that money prepared in two duffel bags for the ransom drop." He frowned at her, doubting every word she said. He'd done time; he had experience with law enforcement and their infinite ability to lie. "People like the Joyces of the world have insurance for these kinds of things. They'd rather pay you off than risk you coming after their kid again, right?"

Distant sirens marked the approach of HRT and other backup units; HRT never traveled alone. As the sound drew closer, the man looked instinctively toward the door, taking his eyes off Tess. Quick as lightning, she pulled her backup weapon from her ankle holster and fired twice.

The man who'd posed as Michael Brennan fell to the ground with a loud thump, blood gushing from the double-tap into his chest.

Recovering her service weapon from his hand, she rushed to the bathroom. The window had been broken and the frame removed, to make room through the opening for a man with the unsub's build. Some fifty yards away, she could see him running toward the river, about to reach a parking lot and disappear into traffic.

Resting her elbows on the windowsill, she took aim carefully and inhaled. Then, slowly, she released about half of the air from her lungs and held her breath, steadying herself, then pulled the trigger. The man flailed and fell to the ground.

Never shoot a fleeing suspect in the back. That was the rule she'd just broken. It wasn't because he would pose a risk to other lives directly, but indirectly he would, through the work he'd continue to do for Allan Mitchell.

The world is a better place with him gone, she told herself, about to leave the room. But there was something gnawing at her gut, making her question the bullet she'd just fired.

Why had the unsub waited so long before running away?

39

In Court

Mornings in court were always chilly, overnight ventilation highly effective when the sun didn't heat up the walls and the people that usually took the seats were absent. Still, the temperature wasn't low enough to justify the slight tremble in DA Joyce's hands as he opened the briefcase he'd set on the prosecutor's table.

He clasped his hands together, squeezing hard, hoping he could steady them before anyone or everyone took notice. After an entire night spent tossing and turning, he'd abandoned the idea of sleep at about five in the morning and had started mainlining caffeine, willing his mind awake, alert, analytical.

But what was there to think about? His hands were tied. They demanded he throw the case, and he was about to do precisely that. He'd be able to file again when things settled, and Paige was back, safe and sound. He'd been telling himself that over and over, trying to make what he was about to do more palatable after he'd spent years trying to put Allan Mitchell behind bars and constantly failing. Now he'd walk again, albeit for a short time, until he'd file new charges and have his witness tucked somewhere safe where no one could reach him.

Who was he kidding? Not even the US Marshals could keep Ingram safe from Mitchell's reach; otherwise, he wouldn't've known when Ingram was being moved. No… given more time, Mitchell would find a way to reach Ingram and kill him before he could point his finger from the stand.

Still, he'd file new charges; that was the only hope he'd ever see Mitchell held accountable for a life of crime, for poisoning the streets of his district, of the entire southeastern United States. He could only hope Ingram would somehow survive long enough to testify, no matter how unlikely that was. He'd survived before, against all odds, and he'd pull it off again.

That was the plan swirling in his mind, plausible and reasonable and optimistic even. The reality was different though and he knew that well. He'd probably never dare file new charges against Mitchell. He'd never feel safe enough to do so and would slowly turn into a corrupt district attorney, doing his bidding, hunting down and charging his enemies but never touching him. He'd become the most despicable of dirty public servants, his sizeable power turned against the people who'd voted for him as their protector.

And still, as soon as Judge Pelaratti would take his seat on the bench, he'd have to say those few words that would forever end his tenure as an honest, decent human being and turn him into a mobster's errand boy.

During the call he'd received the day before, that insufferable robotic voice had told him about enjoying a life with the many perks of Mitchell's friendship. He wanted no part of that, the mere thought of it tainting his soul. How would he be able to live with himself after today? The very fabric of who he was as a human being would be destroyed, torn to shreds under the weight of what it took to save his daughter's life.

He'd do it, though, maybe hesitating somewhat, maybe with his hands trembling and his eyes lowered in shame, but his little girl's life was worth it. Then, after she'd been safely returned, he still had the option to escape the tentacles of Mitchell's organization. In his desk drawer, handy if ever needed, was a loaded nine-mil gun. No one, not Mitchell, not anyone else would stop him from pulling the trigger, choosing death over a life of servitude in the ranks of organized crime.

Once he reached that decision, his hands steadied, and he could breathe again, filling his chest with much-needed oxygen. He'd die free, an honest man, and that decision no one could take away from him.

When Mitchell took his seat at the defense table and their eyes locked, Joyce flashed a quick, crooked smile and a quick nod, as if reassuring him that everything was going to be okay. No one else noticed the exchange between him and the defendant. Mitchell breathed easily and leaned back into his chair, then whispered something to the defense attorney, who shot Joyce a surprised glance from underneath a furrowed brow. He veered his gaze elsewhere, pretending he wasn't paying any attention to either of them.

"All rise," the clerk called, surprising Joyce. Time had flown by, and the courtroom was almost full. He hadn't noticed any of that, having been absorbed in his own internal turmoil.

The clerk glared at a group of youngsters who continued to chat, seated and not paying any attention to their surroundings. Someone nudged one of them, and they immediately complied. He used to be just like them, in his first year of law school, when he still believed battles like today's could be won.

"The court is now in session, the Honorable Justice Pelaratti presiding," the clerk announced, then glanced one more time at the offending group.

Jurors started pouring in, forming a single file once they entered the courtroom and taking their seats quickly. This jury seemed more alert, more interested in the proceedings. Perhaps some jurors were even excited to be a part of a high-profile trial. It promised to be a dramatic break from the mundane.

Pelaratti walked into the courtroom quickly, and Joyce was the first person he looked at with a fierce, inquisitive glance as if to warn him to toe the line. That look sent shivers down Joyce's spine, but he held the judge's gaze firmly, reassuringly.

"Please be seated," Pelaratti said. It took a few moments of muted hubbub until everyone was seated, and silence overtook the courtroom. "Calling the case of the People of the State of Florida versus Allan Curtis Mitchell, trial part three."

Darrel's heart was thumping in his chest, dreading the judge's following words. He threw a glance over his shoulder, but the courtroom door was closed, and everyone was seated. He sat alone at the prosecutor's table, refusing the presence of the ADA who'd been helping him on the Mitchell case. He'd told the young woman there were issues with the witness, and she didn't want to be there for what was about to happen. She'd thanked him and sat trial part three out as instructed, probably thinking the DA had done her career a favor when, in fact, he was too embarrassed to let anyone on his own team witness his humiliation. His defeat.

"The prosecution may call their first witness for the day," Pelaratti announced.

Darrel stood and grabbed his notepad. It felt better to hold an object in his hands, steadying them as if the flimsy object was some kind of shield. "Thank you, Your Honor," he said, then choked. The silence in the courtroom was so thick, it seemed as if everyone was holding their breath. Pelaratti stared at him, waiting, anger building up in his eyes. "At this time, the People would like to—"

A thump, followed by rushed footfalls, interrupted him. He turned to look, but the woman who'd just entered took a seat by the aisle and crossed her hands in her lap.

"The court is waiting, Mr. District Attorney." Pelaratti's deep voice was scathing.

"My apologies, Your Honor." He cleared his throat; it felt parchment dry, and his voice didn't sound like his own. "At this time, the People are—must drop the—"

Loud clamoring drowned his hesitant words, and the gavel thundered in rapid sequence.

"Order," the judge called. "Order, or I'll have you removed." Pelaratti stared at him with an unspoken, dire warning in his eyes. He looked at him for a long moment, pleading without words.

A clerk touched his elbow, then quickly pasted a sticky note on his legal notepad. Only three words were scribbled on it, and the initials that confirmed the message was genuine.

We got her. TW.

A smile bloomed on his lips for a brief moment. Pelaratti stared at him in disbelief. He cleared his voice again and breathed. "The People call Jonas Ingram."

40

MARK

The bullet had ripped through Mark's shoulder and thrown him to the ground in excruciating pain. The forward momentum of his run caused his body to roll a couple of times before it stopped, leaving him gasping for air, staring at the blue sky as if he'd never seen it before, and wondering if he'd live to see it again another day.

Mark hadn't heard the bullet coming; he thought he was far enough from the motel to be safe but was he wrong... Lying on his back on the ground, in the tall grasses between the road and the mangroves, he started to pick up the metallic smell of blood and wet straw. He kept pressure on the wound with his right hand, but blood oozed between his fingers and trickled down his arm.

It was too much blood.

He had to keep on going, or that stretch of land overcome by weeds was going to be the place he died.

Grunting and gasping for air, he managed to get up on his feet and floundered toward the road. Twenty, maybe thirty yards away, he could cross underneath an overpass and reach the back end of a 7-Eleven parking lot, where the employees parked their cars. In his experience, low-wage workers didn't have fancy cars that required coded keys to run and could be tracked via GPS or LoJack or stuff like that. He could hope for a twenty-year-old Honda Accord or a Ford Taurus he could hotwire and be gone.

He didn't have much time; the sirens were drawing closer. He could see the red and blue flashers on a string of vehicles coming off the Dolphin Expressway ramp. Soon, cops would be swarming the area, looking for him. Each move driving stabs of fiery pain in his wounded shoulder, he struggled to close the remaining distance, one faltering step at a time.

By the time he reached the deserted parking lot, he could barely stand. Eyeing a beat-up, black Toyota Camry with a bent door, he tried the handle and found it unlocked. It smelled of cheap perfume and heated dust and burned engine oil and was littered with all sorts of objects, from lipstick and hairbrushes to empty water bottles and food wrappers. He slid behind the wheel and started pulling the wires from underneath the steering column when he noticed the key, dangling from the visor. A few moments later, he was peeling off, heading north on NW Twelfth. Less than a mile away, across the river, he'd seen a large hospital.

Holding the steering wheel with one hand, he could barely make it, feeling life draining out of him with every drop of blood he was losing. Not even the strong, freezing jet of air coming from the Camry's vents could keep him going much longer.

He turned into the hospital campus and missed the Emergency Room entrance. He didn't have it in him to drive around the building. He put it in reverse and stepped on the gas, ignoring the honks from other vehicles that had to veer out of his path.

He was almost at the entrance when everything went dark. He fell forward, his head hitting the steering wheel before the Camry rammed in reverse into a concrete post.

41

MOTHER AND
DAUGHTER

Tess drove Donovan's Suburban straight to the UHealth
Tower Emergency Room. He had left earlier with the
ambulance that had taken Paige while she stayed behind to
hand over the crime scene to the Miami-Dade deputies who'd
accompanied the HRT unit.

The first call she made was to Miriam; she dialed while
waiting for the light to turn green at Seventh and Twelfth.
When Miriam picked up, the woman's voice broke with fear.
"H—Hello?"

"Your daughter is safe," Tess said, realizing that was a kind
of phone call she rarely got to make. "She was taken to UHealth
for a cut on her forearm and dehydration. Can you meet me
there?" Her last words were drowned in Miriam's excited
squeals as she shared the news with Max. Their marriage
showed signs of resilience after all.

"Yes, we're on our way," Miriam sobbed, this time tears of
relief and gratitude.

Her next call was to Pearson and took less than a minute. Her boss ended it with, "Nice work, Winnett," then promptly hung up without another word.

When she pulled up at the entrance of the Tower, Donovan was waiting for her there, lying down in the sun on a wrought iron bench, his tie and shirt loosened, his dark shades on his face, his hands behind his head.

"Hey, Winnett," he said when she approached. He laughed and showed her his phone. "Crime scene just sent us the ID for the two men, based on fingerprints they found at the houseboat. This," he showed her a photo of the man she'd shot in the motel room, "is Gavin Martinez, forty-six, multiple priors for breaking and entering, assault, possession with intent. The other unlucky dude, the one cops are still trying to find out there, where you dropped him, was Mark Crane, forty-two. He served time for possession with intent and, since he got out, he'd been on the straight and narrow."

"I might've not killed him," she mumbled, still wondering if she hadn't made a mistake shooting him before he could answer some questions. She couldn't remember if he'd been close enough to the riverbank when she'd pulled the trigger or if there was a splash of water when he'd fallen. They might never find his body, and she'd be left wondering why he'd changed his behavior so abruptly, turning from an organized, strategic mastermind to a sloppy, reckless, and impulsive man who stole cars from parking lots under 24-7 video surveillance. "Never mind that," she said, willing the troubling thoughts out of her mind. "How's Paige?"

"She's in surgery," he said, his smile waning. "Why don't you go upstairs and deal with that while I swing by the Walshes and start collecting the equipment and everything. I need to get some shuteye."

"The Walshes are on their way here. How will you get in?"

He smiled and winked. "I have a key." Then he climbed behind the wheel of the Suburban and drove off. By the time Tess remembered she had something important to tell him, he'd already turned onto NW Twelfth, heading for the interstate.

She took out her phone and typed a text message.

Thanks for everything.

Before she reached the Emergency Room reception, a chime warned her she had a new message. It was from Donovan.

You bet.

She paced the room while they worked on Paige, counting the minutes. It wasn't long before they wheeled Paige out on a bed and placed her in one of the empty cubicle bays. They were still hooking up her monitors and IV when Miriam and Max rushed into the room and stopped by the bed, leaning forward and kissing her face hungrily.

"Mommy," Paige squealed happily, then wrapped her arms around Miriam's neck. Her right arm was bandaged, and her left arm had been hooked to an IV. "I missed you," the girl said, then placed a loud smooch on her mother's cheek.

"Oh, baby," she cried, then slid on the bed by her side, resting her head on Paige's pillow. "I missed you so much." She kissed the girl's forehead and caressed her hair. "You have no idea how much." Max squeezed the girl's hand gently on the other side of the bed, fighting back tears.

"They took my bracelet," Paige said, her smiling lips now pouting.

"We'll get it back," Tess said, reaching inside her pocket and retrieving the small objects she'd tucked in there. "We'll clean it, attach all the breadcrumbs you left for me to find, and give it back to you." She opened her hand, revealing the three silver charms. Paige squealed with joy. An unfamiliar feeling strangled her, making her wish she could walk outside, where the cold morning air would scatter the threat of tears.

"Baby, this is the agent who found you," Miriam introduced her.

Tess held out her hand, and the little girl gave it a weak shake. Her forearm must've still hurt. "Special Agent Tess Winnett with the FBI," she introduced herself seriously as if she spoke with the director of the Federal Bureau of Investigation himself. Then she smiled and winked. "But you can call me Tess."

"I heard about you many times," Paige said, smiling. "I knew you were coming to get me."

"Why? And where did you hear about me?"

Paige's cheeks flushed. "Um, from those men."

"What did they say, exactly?" Tess asked. Paige looked at her mother for a moment. "It's important you tell me exactly what you heard them say." She looked at Miriam apologetically. "It might be relevant."

"They said many times the, um, fed bitch was coming after them," she said, ashamed, avoiding Tess's look.

Tess laughed heartily, and Paige laughed with her. Max waved his finger mockingly and said, "Language, young lady." He pulled up a chair and settled by her bedside, her hand in his.

A doctor appeared, holding a chart on a clipboard. "Mrs. Joyce?" he asked, looking at Miriam.

She frowned at him. "Not in eight years, but I'm Paige's mother, Miriam Walsh. You can speak with me."

He checked the chart briefly. "Right. Your daughter came in with an eight-inch infected laceration of her right forearm, dehydration, and photophobia. We've cleaned and dressed the wound, and we're administering fluids and broad-spectrum antibiotics. It was a close call; a few more hours, and she would've lost the arm. The photophobia should resolve on its own." He was young, probably a resident. He tousled Paige's hair. "You have an incredibly brave little girl, Mrs. Walsh. She made our day here, at the ER." He shook her hand cautiously. "It was a pleasure meeting you, Miss Paige." He turned to leave as hurried as he'd approached.

"Doctor, just a second," Miriam called, "when can we take her home? What drugs will she need to take?"

"The nurse will be with you shortly to answer all that. I don't see why you couldn't take her home today. I apologize; I have to run. I've been called back into the OR."

Paige laid her head on her mother's shoulder, her eyes heavy; she was about to fall asleep. Tess had a few more questions for the little girl, but she couldn't bring herself to rob them of that moment. She leaned against the wall, watching them, wondering why the image of Miriam lying on the hospital bed with her daughter in her arms tore something inside her, shattering the inner walls she'd built over the years to protect herself from pain, from the world around her.

She felt a hand gently squeezing her shoulder.

"Aren't they beautiful?" Darrel Joyce asked quietly, looking at the bed.

She nodded, fighting back tears. "They surely are."

A loaded moment of silence, during which only a distant PA announcement and a bed being rolled out of the elevator were the only sounds between them.

"Thank you," Joyce whispered.

She turned toward him as two nurses wheeled a bed into the bay next to Paige's, then pulled a privacy curtain that hung from the ceiling-mounted tracks, the upper section made of white, metallic mesh to allow daylight to make it through from one bay to the next.

She didn't recognize Joyce. He was tired, but at the same time, his eyes were kinder, softer. "You're welcome," she said, then continued to look at Paige. "It's unbelievable what she went through, and still she's strong, good-spirited, undefeated." She paused for a beat. "Kind of like her father." She glanced over her shoulder to see Joyce's reaction. He was staring at his daughter, mesmerized.

"I know what I want to do with the rest of my life, Winnett. I'll prosecute Mitchell and won't stop until he's behind bars for life, then I'll go after each and every one of his acolytes until they're all gone, and we can sleep at night again. But I won't keep her at a distance anymore."

"There's always going to be someone to deal dope on the streets of your district, Mr. Joyce."

"Do you realize my little girl will soon be a teenager, a young woman, walking these streets?" He inhaled sharply. "I was thinking of going into private practice to make sure I don't put their lives in jeopardy again. But I don't think that's for me; I couldn't bear not going after the scum who did this to my family and who knows how many other families."

A moan came from the other bay, from behind the curtain. A nurse was still in there; Tess could see by the shadows moving on the curtain she was connecting that patient to monitors just as she'd done with Paige.

"Water," the man in the other bay whispered weakly.

"I'm sorry, but I can't," the nurse replied. Her voice was professional but stern. "I'll have to ask the doctor before I can give you anything."

"It's just water, for crying out loud. Please, I'm dying here."

Paige cringed. Tess listened to the exchange, wondering why it mattered to Paige. Her little body had stiffened while she grabbed a fistful of Miriam's blouse, listening intently.

"I'm sorry, but I can't," the nurse replied, a little harsher this time.

"Ahh, why do you have to be so difficult, woman. Just give me some bloody water, and I'll be super-duper fine."

Paige's eyes opened wide, terrified, and locked on Tess's. She approached the bed and asked quietly, "What's wrong, sweetie?"

Paige pointed at the curtain, shaking. "It's him."

Miriam stared at Tess with panic in her eyes while Tess's mind raced. Could it be possible? If she'd shot him and he didn't die, he could've brought himself to the hospital. If the deputies had found him on that field, they'd be right outside the bays, waiting, watching him.

She pulled open the curtain between the two cubicles and looked at the man. He was as pale as the sheets he lay on, but it was him, the man she'd seen retreating toward the bathroom in that motel room, the man she'd shot in the back while he was fleeing. "You're under arrest for the aggravated kidnapping of a minor," she said loudly. The nurse took a few faltering steps back until she ran into a cabinet.

Transfixed, Miriam got out of the bed and approached the man, her hands clasped tightly at her chest. "Mark?"

42

DEAL

Blood drained from Miriam's face as she stood by the man's bed. "Is that you, Mark?" she asked, her voice a coarse whisper,tears streaming down her face. The man turned his head away, avoiding her glance. "It can't be you, Mark. It can't be my brother, my own flesh and blood, who took my little girl."

"I'm going to kill him," Darrel Joyce muttered, lunging toward the cubicle. Tess's reaction was quick. She grabbed his sleeve, holding him back.

"Give them a moment," she urged him. "You might learn something."

"About what?" he pushed back, in a low but angry tone of voice. "About him? You think I don't know enough about my former brother-in-law?"

"I don't think you know nearly enough," she replied calmly. "I don't believe you know why he chose to kidnap your daughter." Joyce stared at her, slack-jawed. "I think I know why."

Tension vanished from the arm she'd clasped in her hand. She let him go and he stood by her, watching the siblings' interaction without interrupting.

Miriam still stood by Mark's bed, her knees visibly shaking. She seemed barely able to stand, and she reached for the bed's siderail and held on to it with white-knuckled fingers. Her tears ran silently down her streaked face as if she'd lost the power to sob.

"My daughter, Mark? How could you? You cut her arm? Tortured her? I never thought—"

"I didn't hurt Paige. I swear it on my life, I never laid a finger on her."

"But it was you who took her?"

"I was part of it, yes." He turned her way, and, for a brief moment, they seemed to connect. "I had no choice," he said. He raised his hand with difficulty and touched her fingers where they held on to the siderail. She didn't pull away.

"How could you not have a choice?"

He shook his head against the pillow wearily. "The people I met in jail, they didn't give me an option. The day I went inside was the day I stopped being who I was, and I became a slave, someone's tool. At least it was me who took her, not some—" his words trailed off as he grimaced in disgust. "If I'd said no, they would've killed me and sent someone else to take her."

"You could've called me."

"You?" he scoffed. "What would you have done, huh? I've seen what you did for me when I was charged, sis," he said bitterly. Miriam withdrew her fingers and took a small step back. "You married the man who put me in jail."

Her shoulders heaved once as if one shattered breath left her chest. "We were already engaged—"

"You knew I didn't deserve to go down the way I did." His voice was loaded with bitterness, yet unexplainably calm as if he were talking about another man's life, not his. "You knew I didn't deserve to get hooked on drugs. It was that damn accident. But nothing mattered, because my sister was dating the powerful district attorney for Broward County, and the world was at her feet." He pressed his lips together, staring at her with unspeakable sadness in his eyes.

"It wasn't like that," she said, reaching for his hand. This time, he pulled back. Her fingers clutched the siderail, seemingly looking for the strength that was leaving her, for the balance she'd lost. "I thought Darrel was going to help you."

"You know what your darling Darrel did?" He spat his name as if it burned him to speak it. "He used me to advance his career. He made an example out of me and charged me with possession with intent, so that he could show everyone he never cut anyone any slack, not even his own family. I was the poster child for his reelection." His eyes bore into hers. "I was never a drug dealer, sis; you know that. He made me into what I am today."

Miriam turned her head and looked at Joyce briefly with an unspoken accusation in her eyes. The DA lowered his head. Was that a trace of shame Tess saw washing over the man's face? Had he sacrificed his future wife's brother for his ambitions? Knowing Joyce the way she did, she wouldn't put it past him.

Watching Mark's hand slowly reaching to touch his sister's fingers again, then those hands clasping together, fingers intertwined like vines reaching for the sun, she understood everything she'd been missing about the case.

"All those times when we spoke, when I begged you to come back home—"

"I couldn't. Not after getting involved with the people I met in jail. Not while they paid my rent and asked very little in return. I thought by staying away myself, I'd keep them away from you."

"Were you ever in Texas?" she sniffled and wiped a tear from the corner of her eye.

"Never been there." He smiled sadly and he looked at her as if saying goodbye. "Come on, sis, take your baby girl home. Forget about me."

"What's going to happen now?" Miriam asked, turning a deeper shade of pale.

"They'll lock me up for life," he said bitterly. "It was always meant to happen, since the day that car rammed into me." He looked at her longingly. "It's fate, sis. You can't fight fate." Then he turned his head away from her and closed his eyes. A tear rolled over his temple and stained the pillowcase.

Tess approached the bed, Joyce one step behind her. "I'm Tess Winnett, the FBI agent—"

"Who shot me; yes, I know." He didn't open his eyes, but still held on to his sister's hand.

"I believe I understand now why you suddenly started making mistakes. Why you executed a perfect kidnapping with zero forensic exposure, only to start stealing cars under video surveillance two days later, or leaving a houseboat full of fingerprints for us to find, when you could've easily sunk it."

He opened his eyes and looked at her. "You don't know anything."

"I believe it was because you wanted me to catch you."

Miriam gasped and looked at her inquisitively.

"It was because Paige's wound had become infected, and you had no other way to get her the care she needed. Am I right?"

He pressed his lips firmly together, probably swallowing an oath. "Well, it sure enough took you a long time to track me down, didn't it?"

"And that's why you stayed behind the motel until you heard me shooting Gavin, didn't you? To make sure Paige would be taken to a hospital?"

Miriam's other hand squeezed Mark's arm. "Thank you," she whispered. "I don't know how I'm going to forgive you, but thank you."

He didn't pay attention to Miriam. "You seem to know it all, Agent Winnett."

"I don't know a lot of things, like why you were asking for a ransom too, when you didn't care about that, or what Randi the junkie was doing in this mix." She looked briefly at Joyce, then said, "But I do know there's a way out of this for you."

"Yeah, I thought of that too," he replied sarcastically. "You could learn to shoot better, and we could try again. I make a run for it again and this time you don't miss."

"I meant working with DA Joyce to bring down the Mitchell organization as a protected witness. He'll have your entire record expunged," she added, throwing a consternated Joyce a warning look. "In return, you can testify against everyone that made this kidnapping possible."

"Agent Winnett, it's the prosecutor's role to offer deals, not the investigator's." He seemed to think about it as Miriam looked at him with a plea in her eyes.

Tess shrugged. "The deal is good, and it's fair. It mitigates the errors of the past, at least in some measure." She looked at Mark. "I believe you can shed some light on how they found you, out of all convicts, Paige's uncle, the DA's brother-in-law."

Mark clenched his jaws. "I thought of that many times myself. I believe I was set up, many years ago, when I went to jail. That's when a Mr. Erwin, working for organized crime, went inside for under thirty days, just to get to me and rescue me from some conveniently threatening gangbangers." He shook his head. "Next thing I knew, I was wearing their brand on my skin." He touched his neck with a finger, where part of a tattoo was visible above his collar.

Winnett turned to Joyce, smiling. "Want to know what a fed like me would do with this trove of information? I'd find out how that man got inside at the right time, who helped him get in and get out. I'd set him up, then I'd turn him. I can make anyone talk, in case you were wondering. I'd also want to know if you're an Uber guy, Mr. Joyce, because they seemed to know that. Your own office might've sprung a leak."

Joyce shook his head, a trace of a smile touching his lips. "You still don't go by any rules, Special Agent Winnett. I wonder what it would take." His smile widened.

She grinned, turning to leave. "Not going to happen, Counselor."

~~ The End ~~

If *The Girl They Took* had you totally immersed and gasping at every twist and turn, then you have to read more unputdownable page-turners by Leslie Wolfe!

Read on for a preview from:

The Girl You Killed:
A shocking yet mysterious crime. A murder trial that polarizes a tightly knit suburban community. A web of secrets, lies, and deceit.

THANK YOU!

A big, heartfelt thank you for choosing to read my book. If you enjoyed it, please take a moment to leave me a four or five-star review; I would be very grateful. It doesn't need to be more than a couple of words, and it makes a huge difference.

Join my mailing list to receive special offers, exclusive bonus content, and news about upcoming new releases. Use the button below, visit www.LeslieWolfe.com to sign up, or email me at LW@WolfeNovels.com.

Did you enjoy Tess Winnett and her team? Would you like to see her return in another story? Your thoughts and feedback are very valuable to me. Please contact me directly through one of the channels listed below. Email works best: LW@WolfeNovels.com.

If you haven't already, check out *Dawn Girl*, a gripping, heart stopping crime thriller and the first book in the Tess Winnett series. If you enjoyed *Criminal Minds*, you'll enjoy *Dawn Girl*. Or, if you're in a mood for something lighter, try *Las Vegas Girl*; you'll love it!

CONNECT WITH ME!

Email: LW@WolfeNovels.com

Facebook: https://www.facebook.com/wolfenovels

Follow Leslie on Amazon: http://bit.ly/WolfeAuthor

Follow Leslie on BookBub: http://bit.ly/wolfebb

Website: www.LeslieWolfe.com

Visit Leslie's Amazon store: http://bit.ly/WolfeAll

THE
GIRL
YOU
KILLED

LESLIE WOLFE

1

A Letter

They'd taken everything from him.

In a matter of days, Craig Brafford's entire world had been torn apart, pulled inside out, shredded to unrecognizable bits in hues of nightmare.

About half a dozen cops had rummaged through his house looking for who knows what, sparing nothing and breaking stuff out of spite. Now the place was empty, front door unlocked, an invitation for local thugs to loot and occupy as soon as his arrest hit the evening news. He'd begged his lawyer, the widely successful Lamar Goodridge, to swing by and lock it, maybe turn on the alarm system.

"Not my job," the man had answered calmly, his voice low, frozen, loaded with contempt. "You can barely afford my services as it is," he'd added, glancing at the gold watch adorning his wrist. The man charged $900 per hour, and he would've gladly paid for his time, but Mr. Goodridge couldn't let himself be caught giving a crap about one of his clients, or running errands for them.

Humiliated, he'd lowered his head and never mentioned it again, cringing powerlessly at the thought of his beautiful home overtaken by hordes of street filth. Goodridge had taken his case on a retainer that had cleaned Craig's accounts. Regardless, Goodridge still frowned when he looked at him, as if the sight of the inmate clad in an orange jumpsuit was offensive somehow, as if he'd never seen inmates before.

Maybe Goodridge was wondering if Craig could pay his legal bills once the ordeal was over. Or perhaps he was trying to guess if his client had done it or not, although Goodridge himself had started their first meeting by saying, "I don't care if you're innocent. Either way, you deserve the best defense money can buy. Your money that is. Otherwise…" He let the word trail into silence, accompanied by a shrug and a hand gesture conveying his indifference for all the potentially innocent people who couldn't afford decent legal representation and would lose their freedom for that only reason: not being rich enough. Even if they were innocent.

He was smug, his lawyer. He rarely worked pro bono cases, and when he did, he only represented black defendants, "a tribute to his ancestry," in his own words. His inquisitive eyes drilled into the very fabric of whoever sat across from him, and there was little he didn't see. That was probably why he could charge that much or why he rarely lost a case.

His retainer had left no bail money to be posted; Craig was tapped out. The five-hundred-thousand-dollar bail could've just as well been five million. Too proud and too ashamed to ask for help from affluent people he knew, he braced himself for weeks of confinement. With a swift drop of the judge's gavel, he'd been remanded, his attorney shrugging off his concerns about the time he'd have to spend behind bars awaiting trial.

Then he was hauled over to the Houston Southeast Jail, where he was locked up with the general population.

He'd assumed innocent until proven guilty would somehow apply to his time in lockup. He'd been sorely wrong. With the expedience and efficiency of a conveyor belt, the system had stripped him of his remaining dignity, prodding and probing, inflicting physical pain whenever he didn't toe the line, and slapping a number on him without wasting a moment's consideration on his presumed innocence.

He was now prisoner number five-three-three-seven-one-nine.

The number resonated in his mind, the obsessive chorus of an unwritten song he couldn't rid his mind of, the epitome of his lost dignity, of his disappearing identity and his foreclosed freedom. Pale and feeling his insides tied up in a permanent knot of anguish and fear, he'd held his head down and had endured, day after day, waiting, hoping, reciting the unwilling mantra that had ensnared his rebellious brain.

Five-three-three-seven-one-nine.

That's who he was now. He'd unwillingly become five-three-three-seven-one-nine, quickly realizing it was far better than fighting back, than rejecting his new reality and its many insults and injuries, all in the name of a precept that only seemed to carry value in movies. There was no innocent until proven guilty. In prison, he was guilty. Nothing else. No one cared while he festered in that hell hole, forgotten by everyone, choking on his anger and shame.

Him, being there... it wasn't supposed to happen. Not to him. Not ever.

Yet three weeks had somehow passed, slowly, while he learned to respond when called "Seven-one-nine" or "inmate." He learned that some of the wardens were just ordinary people making a living, while others thrived on inflicting pain onto the prisoners under their control. Like E. Mellor, the six-foot-four, three-hundred-pound corrections officer with a sadistic glint in his eyes and a grin that stretched his lips over his grinding teeth like a predator's snarl. Mellor sometimes ran his hand over the tip of his rubber stick in an obscene gesture promising nothing good to the inmate who didn't keep his eyes lowered and didn't pay him off. Officer E. Mellor, who knows what the E stood for on his name tag, had taken the last few dollars Craig had on him the day he was remanded and had kept demanding more from the fountain that had already run dry.

That night, at least Mellor was out of sight, the guard pacing the hallways an older Latino, N. Chavez by nametag. His skin was darkened by years of smoking the cheapest stuff available, and his potbelly, stretching the buttons of his shirt to the point of snapping off like spat watermelon seeds, spoke of cirrhosis at some point in the man's near future. Dark circles under his eyes and a stained, grayed-out mustache completed the portrait of the only guard that had not laid a hand on him yet, since he'd been there. The others, Mellor more than any of them, had at least shoved him against the wall or took their rubber sticks to his kidneys in passing, just to show him how things worked. Just for the heck of it.

Garbled radio transmission came from Chavez's lapel, and he quickly responded with a numeric code, then headed straight to Craig's cell with a groan and an expression of frustration on his face.

Craig stood and approached the bars, clutching them with cold, sweaty, trembling fingers.

"Hands," Chavez said, waiting for him to turn around and put his hands through an opening in the bars. Then he slapped a pair of handcuffs on Craig's wrists, the touch of cold metal sending shivers down his spine. "Your lawyer's here to see you," Chavez added.

Craig's eyebrows shot up. "Now?" Goodridge had been there that morning, preparing him for tomorrow's day in court, the first in his trial.

Chavez shrugged. Grabbing his arm, he led him out of the cell and down the hallway toward one of the interview rooms. "What are you in for?"

"I didn't do anything, I swear," he replied, his voice sad, defeated.

A roar of laughter erupted from the cell they were just passing by. "Another innocent man thrown in jail," a guttural voice with a thick Guatemalan accent announced, and soon the entire section was hollering, shouting obscenities, and laughing at his expense.

"No one in here is guilty of anything," Chavez said, sarcasm layered heavy in his voice. "Not even the ones who take plea deals." He shot him a quick look, then shrugged as if deciding not to give a crap about him anymore.

"Murder," he said, lowering his voice. "They're saying I killed—"

"Okay, go in there," Chavez said, shoving him gently into the room.

A man in a tailored suit and expensive shoes stood when he entered.

Craig turned to Chavez. "This isn't my lawyer." Chavez balked at him, then grabbed his radio.

The attorney held his hand up. "Arthur Flanagan, estate attorney," he said, extracting a business card from a holder and handing it to him. Then he popped open the locks on his briefcase and opened it. "I have a letter for you." He took out a thick, bubble-lined envelope and handed it over to Craig.

Chavez took it instead, his gesture quick, determined. "I have to check this before you can see it. Procedure."

The attorney waited, standing, a fresh smell of pricey aftershave regaling his nostrils, reminding Craig of what he used to have and had lost. Estate attorney? What estate? Had one of his parents died?

Chavez pulled the tab and unsealed the envelope.

"Who's this from?" the inmate asked.

The lawyer's eyes darted toward his open briefcase. Maybe he kept a notepad in there. "It's from Andrea Wilmore Brafford," he replied calmly. "It was to be given to you in the event of her death."

His breath caught. He tried to speak, to ask when she had given him that letter, but his throat was parched dry, and only a strangled, raspy whimper came out. He took a step forward and reached for the attorney's arm, but the man stepped back. Chavez grabbed his elbow, and he stopped, frozen in place, feeling the blood draining from his face.

"Take it easy, all right?" Chavez let go of his arm and pulled out a few folded, neatly typed pages. He inspected them quickly, then handed the letter over to him. Before Craig could start reading, the guard looked inside the envelope. "There's something else in here," Chavez said, turning the envelope upside down above his hand and shaking it gently.

A pendant on a silver chain clinked quietly as it fell from the envelope and settled in the guard's hand. When he recognized the blue stones, a wave of nausea hit him hard in the pit of his stomach as the room started to spin with him. No. That wasn't happening, his thoughts raced. It couldn't happen. I still remember what I did. I know what I didn't do.

"Nice," the guard said, closing his fist around the pendant. "But you can't have this; you know the rules."

"No... no... please, let me touch it for a moment," he pleaded, stuttering, tears rolling down his cheeks. "Let me make sure it's—"

"Okay, for one moment, and that's it," Chavez said, reluctantly opening his palm and letting out a heavy sigh tainted with mustard and onion and cheap tobacco.

Transfixed, he touched the chain with trembling fingers, then ran his thumb over the center stone of the pendant like he'd done it so many times in the past. He swallowed hard, still staring at the small object curled in the guard's chubby palm. It was real. The nightmare was real.

Sweat broke at the roots of his hair and started trickling down his forehead. He raised his handcuffed hands to wipe his brow and noticed the letter he was still holding absentmindedly.

Breath caught inside his chest, he scanned the pages, looking for something that would make sense of it all, that would answer his questions. There was nothing, not until the last page, where the ending paragraph clarified everything for him with a few simple, paralyzing words.

The girl you killed is watching over you from paradise, lounged on cloud number nine with a Margarita in her hand, hoping you'll have everything you deserve in this life after she's gone. Goodbye, my love. You were the one.

Blood rushed to his head in a wave of rage, his heart pounding, his fists clenched so hard his knuckles cracked, the last page of the letter crumpled and stained in sweat as it fell to the ground. "No, Andi... no..." he whispered. Eyes staring into emptiness like a wounded, panicked animal, he rushed to the barred door and started pounding against the dirty, wired glass with both fists, the steel handcuffs cutting into his flesh.

"Let me out of here," he shouted. "I didn't kill her, I swear I didn't..." He repeated the phrase over and over, his voice breaking, threatened by tears of rage and powerlessness and despair. The only response he got was from other inmates, banging against steel bars in rhythmic, surreal resonance muffled by the closed door.

"Hey, cut it out," Chavez shouted, but Craig didn't hear him. He kept on pounding against the door, kicking at it, bloodying his knuckles against the scratched metal, pleading and calling for help. Unable to think clearly, he didn't notice the tears streaming down his stained face.

Chavez touched the radio button at his chest. "Need some help in here." Then he collected the pages of the letter scattered on the floor, slid them back into the envelope, and slid the pendant in there before folding the envelope and tucking it inside his chest pocket. "The DA will need to see this. It's evidence."

The guard's words hit him in the chest like a fist, but he kept on banging against the door with all his strength under Chavez's disappointed look and the attorney's disgusted glare until he fell to his knees, drained, sobbing so hard he couldn't breathe. "I didn't do it, I swear," he faltered, choked, gasping for air. "I didn't..."

Chavez walked over to him and grabbed his arm. "Get it together, already. You have court tomorrow."

He looked at the guard through the blur of tears. "You don't understand," he pleaded, grabbing at the man's sleeve. "The pendant, she—" He stopped in time, realizing what he was about to say.

The door opened, and Officer Mellor stepped inside with a glint of excited anticipation in his eyes. "Seven-one-nine, you're coming with me."

Like *The Girl You Killed?*

Buy It Now!

ABOUT THE AUTHOR

Leslie Wolfe is a bestselling author whose novels break the mold of traditional thrillers. She creates unforgettable, brilliant, strong women heroes who deliver fast-paced, satisfying suspense, backed up by extensive background research in technology and psychology.

Leslie released the first novel, *Executive*, in October 2011. Since then, she has written many more, continuing to break down barriers of traditional thrillers. Her style of fast-paced suspense, backed up by extensive background research in technology and psychology, has made Leslie one of the most read authors in the genre and she has created an array of unforgettable, brilliant and strong women heroes along the way.

A recently released standalone and an addictive, heart-stopping psychological thriller, **The Girl You Killed** will appeal to fans of *The Undoing*, *The Silent Patient*, or *Little Fires Everywhere*. Reminiscent of the television drama *Criminal Minds*, her series of books featuring the fierce and relentless FBI Agent **Tess Winnett** would be of great interest to readers of James Patterson, Melinda Leigh, and David Baldacci crime thrillers. Fans of Kendra Elliot and Robert Dugoni suspenseful mysteries would love the **Las Vegas Crime** series, featuring the tension-filled relationship between Baxter and Holt. Finally, her **Alex Hoffmann** series of political and espionage action adventure will enthrall readers of Tom Clancy, Brad Thor, and Lee Child.

Leslie has received much acclaim for her work, including inquiries from Hollywood, and her books offer something that is different and tangible, with readers becoming invested in not only the main characters and plot but also with the ruthless minds of the killers she creates.

A complete list of Leslie's titles is available at LeslieWolfe.com/books.

Leslie enjoys engaging with readers every day and would love to hear from you. Become an insider: gain early access to previews of Leslie's new novels.

- Email: LW@WolfeNovels.com
- Facebook: https://www.facebook.com/wolfenovels
- Follow Leslie on Amazon: http://bit.ly/WolfeAuthor
- Follow Leslie on BookBub: http://bit.ly/wolfebb
- Website: www.LeslieWolfe.com
- Visit Leslie's Amazon store: http://bit.ly/WolfeAll

Made in the USA
Coppell, TX
25 August 2021

61137145R00173